Sword Scroll Stone

Sword Scroll Stone

Scott Michael Decker

Published 2016 by Creativia
Book design by Creativia (www.creativia.org)
Typed by Joey Strainer
Cover art by http://www.thecovercollection.com/

Titles by the Author

If you like this novel, please post a review on the website where you purchased it, and consider other novels from among these titles by Scott Michael Decker:

Science Fiction:
Bawdy Double
Cube Rube
Doorport
Drink the Water
Edifice Abandoned
Glad You're Born
Half-Breed
Inoculated
Legends of Lemuria
Organo-Topia
The Gael Gates
War Child

Fantasy:
Bandit and Heir (Series)
Gemstone Wyverns
Sword Scroll Stone

Look for these titles at your favorite book retailer.

Scissors cut Paper
Paper covers Rock
Rock breaks Scissors

Chapter 1

The sword came out of nowhere, and Columba Riverford twisted to evade it, whipping his own sword from its sheath with barely time to block its second blow.

But the sword was just a sword—no warrior or sage wielded it.

The blade thrust itself at his face; he ducked and thrust his blade where his opponent should be. And cut through empty air.

He twisted and danced away, the courtyard just the size for a sword duel, the arena round, devoid of obstruction, the dirt packed. Columba ducked, parried, and blocked, grinning ruefully at the greeting he was receiving, his unseen opponent highly skilled.

The Hall of Swords, where the finest fighters from the four corners gathered, the magic in their steel propelling them to feats of legendary proportion, possessed an entrance of simple construction, a circular courtyard built of fitted stone twenty feet high all around, crowned with crenellations. The courtyard having only two doors, only one led into the Hall of Swords.

Did I expect them to applaud my request for membership? he wondered. They must have hundreds of supplicants every year whose eagerness far exceeds their skill. I should have expected a challenge! he thought, where he'd come seeking entrance.

And if they would have him, membership.

He twisted, parrying a blow to his side. Without a visible opponent, how could he win?

As in many prior duels, his sword knew where the other would thrust, his magic picking out subtleties that others missed. Think! he told himself. Magic's at work here, so I fight a sage afraid to fight me face to face.

"Coward!" he said, fending off a blow. "Show yourself to me and stop hiding behind your magic!"

The sword redoubled its efforts to kill him.

Columba fought off the fusillade of blows, picking out a pattern in the attack. He'd dreamt too long of fighting at the side of the High Sage Arcturyx Longblade, and the sword he bore had been obtained at too high a cost, to let a simple magic spell dissuade him, his village in northwest Swordshire having provisioned and equipped him to have the honor of one of their own inducted into the Hall of Swords.

Preferring to disarm in duel, rather than to kill, Columba wondered how to disarm a sword. "The safest place around a sword that you can be," an early teacher had told him, "is with your hand on the haft."

Letting his opponent gain advantage, he retreated, nearing the stout oaken door that he'd come through, and baited the trap. "Scurrilous charlatan, where's your spine?!" he snarled.

The sword attacked and Columba slid past it, grasped the hilt, swung himself around against the wielder's control and thrust the opponent's sword deep into the foot-wide door post.

The blade buried in wood, Columba leaned against it. "Yield, unseen Sage, or I'll surely break your weapon!"

"Enough!" Behind him, from atop the arena wall, came a soft laugh, where there appeared three garishly-garbed Sages, looking down upon the courtyard from behind the crenellated battlement. "Well fought, apprentice Columba, well fought," the middle one said, his face full of gentle amusement. "I am Arcturyx,

Lord High Sage." He turned to the burly, middle-aged man beside him. "Fairly and quickly done, wouldn't you say, Lord Betel?"

The black eyes smoldered at Columba.

I've made my first enemy, he thought, bowing to the High Sage and feeling the weight of the other man's gaze upon him.

"Stars above, desist and introduce yourself," Arcturyx bade his one companion.

"As you wish, Lord," the black-eyed man said, "though it's clear it was luck, nothing more." He waved his hand, and the sword extricated itself from wood and flew into his grasp. "My name is Betel, Apprentice Columba."

Nodding, Columba saw no relenting behind the eyes.

The third figure threw back a hood, and burnished auburn hair cascaded down the shoulders. "Forgive these rude curmudgeons," she said, "I am Pyxis, Sage of Auld." She floated down from the battlement to the arena floor. "They persist in depriving you of the pleasure of your victory. Congratulations, Lord Sage Columba, and welcome to the Hall of Swords. For the first two years as apprentice, of course."

Columba knelt at her feet, his heart aloft. "Praise the stars that guide me, Lady Sage Pyxis, I have dreamt of this day for years."

"Come, let not our standoffish greeting be a shadow upon your soul." She turned and gestured at the far door, which swung aside. "Many petitioners importune us with unworthy requests. Few demonstrate their worth as you have. Follow me, Apprentice, and see the domains where you shall stay."

Columba sheathed his sword and bowed to the High Sage on the battlement, feeling still the burn of Betel's stare. It was clear he'd made no friends this day, for to them he was upstart, his family humble serfs who farmed the wheat that fed these fat-belly Lords.

He followed her into the castle beyond, traversing a long, ill-lighted corridor. Glints caught his eye, the walls difficult to see.

Ahead the corridor widened and grew lighter, and he realized the glints were metal—the hafts, blades, and sheathes of swords. From the foot of one wall up its side across the ceiling to the foot of the opposite wall were swords, each one carefully mounted to take advantage of every inch of space.

"Our legacy," Pyxis said, her hair the copper of many a haft.

Columba could not imagine how many swords he beheld. In the thousands, he thought, his eyes traveling the length and breadth. "Whose are they, Lady Pyxis?"

"Sages of Swordshire who have long since passed, their swords now extinguished of their magic. Only one sword retains its power, the original sword, the One Sword. Genesyx, we call her, but none knows her real name, a thing long lost in the fog of time. Only our Lord High Sage Arcturyx may wield her, and only then in time of dire need."

The hall opened into a vestibule, its walls covered just as thick with blade after blade. On the other side, the hall continued. And the swords.

"The Hall of Swords," Columba said to himself.

"Just so, Apprentice." She led him across the vestibule. "Down this way of course is Genesyx herself, the one—"

Shouting ahead of them interrupted her. A guard rushed toward them. "It's gone! Sound the alarm! It's gone—Genesyx has been stolen! The One Sword has been stolen!"

Pyxis gasped, her hand going to the hilt of her waist.

More shouting, and the High Lord Arcturyx strode swiftly toward them, Lord Betel right behind him. "Did you sense anything, Lady Pyxis?"

"Nothing, High Lord! Who would dare?"

"Him!" Betel leveled a finger at Columba.

"What?" he said, taken aback.

"Evince your innocence all you want, upstart, but we know your scheme. Distract us at the arena whilst your accomplice absconds with the one sword Genesyx. Deny it!"

"I do, Lord Betel. You allege without evidence. What proof have you of your foul words?"

"There! I knew he would, High Lord. The criminal always denies, the alacrity of his denial proof of its preparation. Never fear, Lord High Sage, for this fiend shall plague us no more!" Betel drew his sword.

Arcturyx held up a hand. "Be not hasteful, Lord Betel." The High Sage turned to Columba. "The ease of your tongue dismays me, Apprentice Columba Riverford. Your proximity to the theft implicates you, and it was far too sly how swiftly you neutralized the challenge."

"I swear by the stars that guide me, Lord High Sage, that I wasn't involved in the theft of the one sword. I swear!" Columba knelt and bowed.

"Look at me, Boy!"

Columba snapped his head back, the compulsion irresistible.

The gray eyes bore into his, the gaze many times more wrathful than Betel's burning black eyes. "You desire membership in the Hall of Swords, eh? I sense in you that great ambition. Aye, but I sense a cloud as well, one which masks a foul intent. So be it! You are banished from the Hall of Swords on pain of death and your face is forbidden within these domains lest you have your redemption in hand, for only one thing can repair this rent in the heart of the Hall—the return of the One Sword, Genesyx." Arcturyx thrust an arm toward the door. "Go, and do not return without it!"

* * *

Aridisia Myric stood twelfth in a line that went out the door, a small scroll protruding from the pocket of her cape, silently wishing that the trollish Magus who was spell-scribe today would hurry. Even from this distance, she knew his thoughts jumbled and disorganized.

I could write them faster than that, Aridisia thought, begrudging her fellow supplicants ahead of her their every moment with the scrollscribe.

This her third day in line, her last day, she paid no mind to the flurry of activity behind the Magus, save to wish that she were there. Snatches of thought floated to her.

A low railing separated the supplicants from the Maguses in the Crypt of Scrolls, the oval floor cluttered with podiums covered with parchment where scribes dashed off runes, each couplet an invocation of magic.

Twenty scribes crowded a space fit for fifteen, shelves climbed to the ceiling, scrolls crammed in their cubbies, and in their midst, toward the rear, the High Magux, her beetle-brow furrowed in concentration, one finger phalangitating a quill to set forth on a scroll the spell she inscribed.

Not just any scroll.

The Ancient Scroll, Canodex, the oldest scroll known to the Crypt of Scrolls. The legend told that the Crypt had been built to enshrine the Ancient Scroll.

And there, the Ancient Scroll, Canodex, suspended above the chaos, a shimmer of gossamer holding aloft their prize possession, the High Magux sitting hunched over below it, directing the quill across the parchment with but the motion of a finger, there was where Aridisia longed to be.

Having practiced since she'd learned to write, she had no other ambition than to become a Magux, adept at conjuring through the written word the magic that had seemed from the moment of birth all around her. Her parents, siblings, aunts, uncles, cousins, and fellow villagers all had encouraged her from the time she could toddle, the magic seeming to slough off her, leaving the word aglow wherever she went.

Their poor village sat at the edge of the Barony, abutting the forest preserve, the villagers forbidden to reap from the forest's bounty. There were no schools nearby, and in their poverty, they had not the wealth to send her. Further, they lacked a Baron nearby to importune to sponsor her, not a single local noble of even modest means.

Unbeknownst to Aridisia, they had begun a cache years before with the little wealth they earned, and upon her twentieth birthday, had given her this bounty and bade her to come to the Crypt of Scrolls to petition for membership.

Standing in line twice before with folk as poor as she, Aridisia had spent nearly all the village bounty, the fee to place a simple request more than the village earned in an entire year. On the first occasion, two days ago, the gnomish Magus had scrawled her request.

Then he'd looked up at her, had grinned, and had burst out laughing. He'd laughed so hard he'd fallen off his stool, spilling ink across the scroll, spilling tears down his cheeks, spilling hilarity across the floor, all the Maguses laughing at her.

Her cheeks a flame with humiliation, Aridisia had fled.

The next day, her caped hood pulled far forward to cowl her features, she'd returned.

This Magus tall and dignified, he'd etched her request in the words she'd uttered, and then had frowned, his brows drawing together. "Oh, it's you." He swung his nose in her direction.

She could just see his eyes beyond the cannons of his nostrils.

"Ludicrous request. No wonder Shorty laughed so hard." The tall Magus giggled. "Become one of us? Request denied."

Today, the money in her hand too little to cover the fee, her determination as strong as ever, and a well of anger percolating inside her from two days of humiliation, Aridisia saw she was but one petitioner away from placing her own request. Whatever will I do if I get turned away? she wondered with burgeoning despair. How will I face my family and village, all those good loving people who bade me well and gave freely from their hearts and pockets? Oh Almighty Scribe, help me!

She brought out the humble scroll in her pocket, its parchment stained with use and travel, its pins crudely carved and dingy from frequent handling, and she pulled the quill from her hair, her golden locks cascading down her shoulders, for it was all she might afford to keep her hair pinned up, and found the last little patch of parchment yet blank of scrawl.

As the trollish scribe turned to look at her, he who had wept with laughter at her request two days ago, she penned a phrase: "Ye who laughs to denigrate shall succumb to suasion insensate and do my bidding hastilate."

His gaze became unfocused. "What is thy request, child Aridisia?"

She picked his name from his mind. "Magus Quercus, do hear me, invite me to take your seat, and avert the attention of your brethren Mage. Give me scroll and quill, and weave for me the illusion that you sit there still."

"Tis a modest request, my child, and one easily granted." Magus Quercus dashed out a quartet of lines with a flourish.

From her perch on his stool, Aridisia accepted the next petitioner's fee and adjusted the position of the quill in her hand, a basket of blank scrolls beside the lectern, what seemed acres of blank parchment within reach, the world looking bright as though a glow surrounded her.

"Magux Aridisia," a frail old woman said, "my son is ill with a wasting disease, and the butcher is wont to let more blood. Can you help?"

Aridisia picked a fresh scroll from the basket and plucked her son's name and face from the old woman's mind. "Cedric Ironsmith," she scrawled, "be not afraid, for this illness shall dissipate soon. Be the iron that you smith so well, and find your temper in the forge of ill."

The words glowed as they settled upon the paper, the circles perfect, the lines true.

"Here, take this to him, Dam Ironsmith, and go with light of heart." Aridisia rolled up the scroll and handed it to her.

The old woman clutched the scroll to her breast and scampered to the door, eyes glistening.

The next supplicant handed her the fee.

Aridisia saw instantly it was not enough. She probed the man's face.

Middle-aged, his gaze sharp above proud cheeks, his hands gnarled and cross-hatched with scars, in them a large double-bladed axe, he met her gaze with a challenge: You can't help me, his face told her.

"I can and will," and she handed him back his coin. "What is your request, Samshad Woodwright?"

"Magux Aridisia, I would no more give you parchment without payment than you should give me a spell for the same. I would not have it."

"You fear your wife of many years seeks attention elsewhere. Your fear keeps you from your work, and you sit in your mill, day in day out, your wright machines idle, fretting what to do. Your fear softens your desire at night and leaves you both unsated, where before you were always a virile man. Your fear puts hesitation to your word and touch and keeps from her the attention she has heretofore enjoyed." She smiled and patted his hand. "I won't be giving you a spell, so no payment is needed. Go to her and say your love in fulsome praise, beg her to stay with you all the day even at your mill, tell her all the years with her have brought you closer, that she brings you deep fulfillment and happiness beyond belief. Tell her you have struggled to find the words to tell her, that your desire to tell her so has pressed upon you so much that the tongue has lain thick and still in your mouth at this weight upon your soul. You are blessed to have each other."

And Samshad Woodwright blessed her and set off.

Her spirit brightening at the bounce that had now returned to his step, Aridisia turned to the person next in line.

A young girl stood before her, just a year or two shy of her own age. "My father lies captured yon west of Scrollhaven, kidnapped by outland raiders yesterday, probably to be sold into slavery today. Please I beg you, Magux Aridisia, please help bring him back." She handed over a stack of coin.

Her heart went out to the girl—Chiona Anthus—and she laid out a scroll, the vellum soft and smelling fresh. Upon it she wrote: "For she who bears this spell of mine, give to her a gift divine, shield her from these eyes of mine and any other who might stop her."

The ink moved into place, and Aridisia rolled the scroll and gave it over. "I wish you well, Chiona, in bringing your father back safely."

"You cannot bring him back?"

"The magic wouldn't work at this distance, child, and alas, I can only wish I might go there. You would be prudent when you do to—"

"What gimmickry is this?" a raspy old voice interrupted.

Aridisia whirled.

Behind her stood the High Magux Ravenna Cithara, her brow beetled by consternation, her forehead a palimpsest of wisdom. "Magus Quercus, explain this creature in your place!" She shoved a finger at Aridisia. Three rings glittered on each finger, two on thumb.

"Forgive me, Lady High Magus, Mother of us all, I didn't see her. She surely stole into my place when I looked the other way."

"Absconded with your stool, quill, and scroll, she did?"

"She did, the thief! Next you'll see she'll steal the Ancient Scroll itself," Quercus protested. "Give me that, you thieving witch!"

She snatched the quill out of reach. "My spells are better than any this illusionist might cast, Lady High Magus. My apologies for borrowing these implements, for my only wish was to be among you and mayhap become so learned as yourselves, Lady. I lay myself at your mercy and beg your forgiveness."

The eyes darted back then forth, and Magux Cithara frowned. "By what means did you snatch that quill?" Her finger flared and in them appeared Aridisia's quill.

"By more sophistication than that simple phalangitator, Lady High Magux. Twas a spell I cast upon my scroll."

"Twas not!" Quercus protested. "Preposterous that this provincial child might beguile the likes as me."

"Better to bewitch the dislikes of you," Aridisia riposted.

A chuckle spread through the room, the hint of a smile reaching the High Magux's furrowed brow. "A spirited one you are, Aridisia Myric. The crypt itself to start is my thought." She turned upon Quercus. "Take this waif and show her—"

"The Scroll!"

A shout, many gasps, and all eyes turned.

The gossamer veil ashimmer, where heretofore had hung the Ancient Scroll, Canodex, now hung empty.

"Thief!" cried Quercus "Said I not this witch would!"

"What've you done with it, foul beast!?" Magux Cithara curled a gnarled, ringed finger, pointing its yellowed, crusty nail at her.

"I did no such thing, I swear!"

"Protest her innocence she will," Quercus averred, "More's the guilt, the louder she'll wail!"

"Where it be?!" Ravenna roared, her face thrust into Aridisia's, spittle spattering her.

"What need have I of your Ancient Scroll? Twas not me, I say!" She realized as despair sank deep inside her that no amount of assertion would unscape her goat. Their eyes turned upon her, their minds turned from her.

"Say what you will, siren," Ravenna said, her voice low, her breathing hot, "Your actions speak your mind. For this desecration, ye shall never return. Never!"

Her face flush, Aridisia shook her head. "Ah, but I shall, and bring the One Scroll Canodex when I do!"

* * *

Baron Marl Gneiss started at the minion, disbelieving. "What do you mean, the Lord High Adept won't see me? Don't you know who I am?"

"Your raised voice tells me precisely, upstart. Be gone, or I'll have you removed."

Marl stopped himself from strangling the impertinent clerk. He tapped the plum-sized ruby in his pocket and muttered, "Be gone yourself, self-important peon, away with you to another eon."

Sparkling dust replaced the bureaucrat.

Careful not let any touch his immaculate shoes, Marl kept his smile to himself.

The other denizens in the anteroom appeared too absorbed to have noticed. Despite the purported wealth ensconced inside the Vault of Stones, the outer accommodations looked penurious indeed—plush carpets thick with embroidered design, gilded-back chairs with satin seats so slick that a person had to concentrate to stay seated, tapestries of florid artistry, their tassels glittering with gold thread.

Penurious indeed! Marl thought. I should decorate my new manor house in a similar style. He looked among the remaining clerks for the eye he might catch.

Three months ago, when his uncle, the Baron Gossan Breccia Jaspil Gneiss, had died tragically in a landslide en route back from Swordshire to Stonevale, perishing with his two sons and their families, Marl Gneiss had found himself the sole heir to the

Gneiss estates, he of the disowned profligate side of the family, his father having disported himself until his purse was empty and his sack was dry. And the vast fortune contained therein became his alone.

His only ambition to attain membership in the Vault of Stones—and having enough cupidity to think he might eventually become the Lord High Adept—Marl had donned his finest couture and packed a satchel with a few baubles, then had selected the finest gemstone from among his deceased uncle's collection. For it was said amongst the serfs and guilds that a man with wealth and talent might find his way to a seat within the Vault, where the appetites of even the most avaricious might be sated.

His talent not inconsiderable, but his appetites voracious, Marl had practiced all his life with the paltry materials available to him—a tiny quartz monzonite, a thin sheet of marble whose translucence lent itself to the sight, a sand-grain diamond to light the darkest night.

The plum-sized ruby, when he'd lain eyes upon it, had whispered to his dreams of inexhaustible wealth and power beyond his ken.

The power in Stonevale of course belonged to the Lord High Adept, Gabbro Scoria Hornfels, who ruled the land with the One Stone, a fist-sized diamond called Luxullian.

High Adept Hornfels rarely emerged from the Vault, the last occasion having been the funeral rites of Marl's uncle, the Baron Breccia Jaspil Gossan Gneiss.

For a moment, during the ceremony, Marl had come face to face with Adept Hornfels, and he had seen the old man recoil.

Not with the obvious hands-to-the-face, I-can't-believe-the-evil-I-see, I'm-so-revolted,-I-feel-defiled kind of recoil, but more the mental withdrawal, the deep retreat, the what's-happening-to-my-domains? type of recoil. Marl in his so recent vault into high society felt as though the rejection carried all the qualities of the former and was sensed by the assembled Stonevale nobility, their wagging tongues spreading the whispers among them with the virulence of a plague.

And here, at the entrance to the Vault of Stones, some scornful minion would have the audacity to deny him audience with the one person who might grant him his only wish.

Unable to get another clerk's attention with just the baleful gaze, Marl cleared his throat.

Another clerk deigned to notice him. "I'm sorry, Lord Baron, but it appears you've been dismissed already. The Lord High Adept isn't avail—"

"Betwixt and between, I will be seen," Marl whispered.

"—able at the moment, but if you'll begrudge his Highness a few minutes to freshen up, he'll be pleased to have your company."

"The pleasure is all mine," Marl said, removing himself to one of the tricky chairs.

Probably made these chairs this way deliberately, he thought, having to use both legs to keep from sliding off the slick satin.

Discomfort in the guise of luxury, how ironic, how clever, Marl thought, the idea appealing to his finer degradations. Might as well cut the leg off a stool before inviting a disliked underling to sit.

While waiting, he examined the portal into the Vault of Stones. From his vantage he could see three stout doors, the first a thick, oaken slab strapped with shiny steel bands, the second a pewter-colored slab of metal, and just visible the edge of a third, a multi-layered multi-locked plug of a copper-tinged alloy.

Likely there's a fourth and fifth door, Marl thought, the Vault itself the most secure place in all the three realms.

On approach that morning, passing through increasingly tall battlements, portcullis beyond gate beyond drawbridge, helmeted guards thicker than thieves throughout, Marl had felt humbled by both the size and the extravagance, and he'd realized quickly that the High Adept Hornfels, his Adept Council, and the Vault of Stones, had no need of the Gneiss estate, nor of the new Baron.

Thankfully I have other talents, he thought.

Belatedly, Marl realized he'd been waiting far longer than it pleased him. They couch their insults within grace, he thought, fuming.

Pulling out the ruby, its facets winking at him, he looked across the gilded railing toward the clerks. "Delay me not or ye shall rot, snooty minions in tiny dominions, be as doors and open mores."

Once clerk nose, his gaze unfocused. "Lord Baron Gneiss, please come with me." And he opened the low gate between them.

Marl followed into the multi-doored passageway, the corridor claustrophobic, the ceiling too low for his height. It wouldn't surprise me to discover that even this little humiliation was deliberately designed for my benefit, he thought.

Beyond the third door, the multi-layered, multi-locked, off-tint plug, the clerk stopped.

"What is it, Felsite?" muttered a raspy voice.

"A visitor, Lord High Adept, the Lord Baron Marl Gneiss."

"Incompetent fool, I told you to be rid of him!"

"Be as lice, say it nice," Marl murmured.

"Forgive me, Lord, but his charms were so suffuse with grace and aplomb that I could not resist his gentle persuasion."

"Unbelievable! What mockery is this?" roared the unseen voice. A chair scrapped on floor.

"No, Lord, I'll attend to this parvenu," said another, gentler voice. A woman in gossamer gowns stepped into view. "Return to your duties, Felsite."

The clerk slid past Marl, who'd not removed his gaze from the apparition before him.

He swore her skin glowed with translucence, and the sequin dress that fell to the floor lent luminance to her already refulgent beauty.

"Lord Baron Gneiss," she said, as mellifluous as morning doves, "I'm Minette Hornfels, my father's daughter. My pardon for my absence at your uncle's rites. This is an inopportune time for the Lord High Adept. Come with me, and leave him in peace."

Marl followed her past the Adept, who sat hunched over parchment thick with scrawl, his shoulders stooped, worry furrowing his brow, oblivious to the guest.

For a moment, seeing the depth of the Adept's concern, Marl felt a twinge of guilt. What could possibly be of greater concern than a visit from me? he wondered, the twinge quickly gone.

The corridor glittered with embedded gems, many rivaling the ruby in his hand.

She led him to an anteroom similarly adorned, its furniture likewise aglisten with fine stone and gem.

"The council chambers," she said, gesturing toward one end of the long mahogany table, stones under resin winking beneath the elaborate chandelier. "Please be seated, Lord Baron."

A servant pulled a chair away for him; he'd not seen the servant appear. "A pleasure, Lady Hornfels."

Midway along the chamber wall stood a portcullis of solid gold, the soft metal seeming a poor guard for what Marl guessed lay beyond. A shimmering glow fell through the bars onto stone slab flooring, the light like the dapple of sun through leaves. Two soldiers stood on either side. Marl hadn't initially noticed either guards or gold portcullis. Obscured by some spell, he was sure.

"Yes, Lord Baron, beyond lies Luxullian, the One Stone, the embodiment of all that makes Stonevale great. Again, Lord Gneiss, my apologies for my father's indisposition. How may I be of assistance?"

Marl had not expected any such forthrightness, a prolonged exchange of pleasantries the usual prelude to the business at hand. Perhaps her brevity presages a swift refusal, he thought, secretly relieved to forgo the platitudes.

"Forgive my importuning myself at a time of inconvenience, Lady Hornfels. My business is simple, my request uncomplex. The council of Adepts, the Lord High Adapt Hornfels, and the Vault of Stones have need of my talents."

She blinked at him.

Twice, the silence prolonging.

In his mind, he heard her laughter, a mocking guffaw that echoed off the walls, as so many of his boyhood companions had laughed at his previous penury. No self-respecting noble would entertain such a request. Her utter silence betrayed her. How utterly brazen his petition!

"It would be an honor to place your request before the Lord Adept and the Adept Council, Lord Baron. Further, as evidence of how impressed I am that your talents have achieved you ingress even unto Luxullian's Vault itself, I myself will place your proposal to my father, the Lord High Adept. Your ambition is clear, Baron, but let it not cloud your mind, nor let the grandeur of your desire distort your view. Your road is long and beset with foul hazards. You would be wise to tread it carefully. Your parlor tricks today are no substitute for the arduous task at hand." Her face impassive, she looked toward the gold portcullis.

"The Gneiss Manor sits astride the road to Swordshire and abuts the dark forest that serves as bulwark to the outlands. A cloud of threat thickens toward storm, and all the nobles of Stonevale will be summoned to battle soon. Our enemy has not made itself manifest but lurks as yet beyond our borders. Trust that you will be among those summoned. As for your request, I bid you to return to your manor and gird yourself for the fight ahead. You will hear word soon from both the Council and the Lord High Adept." The Lady Minette stood and gestured toward the door.

Marl stood, a bewildered feeling beginning to nettle him. Somewhere in the murky thoughts beneath his gnawing avarice, it occurred to him a single word might summarize the response he got: "No."

Her gaze left his face and went to the gold portcullis. She gasped.

He followed her gaze, seeing that the shimmering glow filtering through the bars but moments ago was gone.

"Guards!" she yelled, pointing at the portcullis.

One peered between the bars. "It's gone, Lady!"

"What thievery is this, Gneiss?" Minette hissed at him.

"I, Lady? But, but—"

"What ill tiding is this?" thundered the Lord High Adept Gabbro Scoria Hornfels.

Marl whirled.

He stood just inside the door. "Gone? The One Stone is gone?!"

"And this illusionist stole it," Minette said, leveling a finger at him. "Conjured some spell to hold us all enthralled, he did."

The High Adept thrust his face into Marl's. "The heart of Stonevale, how could you, fiend?"

"But I didn't, Lord, I swear!"

"This churlish brute protests too much," Lady Minette said, "and we know his heart by his denials."

"For this foul deed—"

"I beg you, Lord, I've done no such deed!"

"For this foul feed, you're stripped of title and banished forever, Marl Gneiss, who is no longer Baron, and all your lands and assets are forfeit."

His head aswirl, Marl shook it. "No, no! You can't do that! I didn't take anything! I'm innocent!"

"I can and have and you'll leave forthwith. Guards!"

The two soldiers, deprived of a stone to guard, converged on him.

Marl struggled until one showed him his knife.

"Take him away!"

They hauled him toward the door.

"But what if I bring it back?"

His entreaty was met with silence and they took him away.

Chapter 2

Dorad Fallentree caught sight of the lone traveler far down the path and grinned. "My pretty does hunger for fresh blood," he whispered to the blade, which called itself Serpens.

Its haft looked pewter but was light, and set at its base where blade met haft a single sapphire was mounted, embedded in metal. At the pommel was a screw-on cap, and beneath the cap was a tiny scroll, the spell upon it written so long ago that the ink had faded and the vellum flaked.

But Dorad had no learning to read and would not have cared if he had. All he cared was that it worked, for Dorad was a brigand, preying upon the lone traveler such as he who approached, prowling roads that twisted through forest or up steep hillsides, where terrain made ambush more facile, where help was hard to come by, and where Dorad might pit his paltry wit but considerable strength against another's without fear of interference by a passerby.

The hooded traveler who approached wore a sword at side, Dorad saw.

Serpens whispered warning, the blade cooling its ardor for blood. "Follow but delay attack."

Never much for thinking deeply, he'd never wondered at its whispers, not had he linked the glow of blade, the sparkle of sapphire, the warmth of haft with the times Serpens spoke to him. Had he pieced together these phenomena, he might have noted that the blade just spoke, or that the haft whispered when he considered relieving a scribe of her quill, that the sapphire glowed when he sighted a Stonevale native.

His wit dulled by the misfortune befallen him when young, Dorad rarely saw beyond his outstretched hand, and even that was blurry to him. At an early age, a fallen tree had caught his head a glancing blow, and though the skin had stayed intact, his skull had swelled like a mother's belly. When the ache began to fade, so too had his depth of thought, and the village Magus had declared him idiot.

And what might have been a normal life reaping wheat alongside his family in the southern fields of Scrollhaven had turn instead into a nomadic life absent home or family, as he was wont to go where his eyes were pointed, without a thought for food, clothing, or shelter. And many the time he'd been found wandering the forest without a stitch, gaunt from lack of food, hungry without a plan to feed himself, cold without a thought to warm himself.

As Dorad clambered over rock and deadfall, his fleet of foot startling against his sludge of brain, tracking the lone traveler from a distance, he did not think how short his life might have been had fate not handed him the blade he held and launched him on his foul career.

Serpens had lain dormant in the bosom of an old dam who lived in southwest Scrollhaven, her modest ranch beside the road to Swordshire. A guesthouse beside her own, she housed the weary traveler too tired to get to the next village, but she charged a fee so steep that most avoided her unless they had no choice. How this old dam had been spared the brigand such as Dorad was of course Serpens doing.

Dorad wandered through one eve, sans a single thread, his baser impulses protruding in front of him, making a handle he could not keep his hand from. Thus the old dam regarded him with a mixture of dismay and delight. The old maid's tale deceives, that virility fades with age.

Serpens too exerted its hungers and persuaded the lady to behave in not so ladylike ways.

Suffice to say that Dorad in his excited state was more tractable, his hands near her neck as the pressure built within him. As he exploded, his hands contracted, and in the morning when he saw what he had done, he stumbled into the road, the knife in hand, naught else on his person.

The hue and cry of rape and murder caused him to flee, and the whispers of Serpens fed his fear and but for its guidance he could not have escaped.

Thus began a symbiosis of evil, man and blade doing the other's bidding. Thus Dorad tracked the lone traveler deeper into the darkening outlands, as he had many such others, all of them tracked with a vision supplied by the blade itself.

"Wait until the eyelids close," Serpens whispered to him. Dorad followed a game trail across stony escarpments, the narrow path far below glimpsed at intervals, winding its way up the mountainside.

Winded and tired, his path more treacherous than the road below, Dorad wanted just to rest, but each time he stopped, the lurking whisper prodded him onward.

In the gloom of dusk the traveler below stopped for a time, and Dorad circled around and down, hoping to find a place for ambush. He knew a cleft beside the trail he'd used before. Secreted for about an hour, he grew weary.

"What ill intends thee me?"

Dorad started awake, the sting of cold steel upon his neck. Even in the dim evening glow, the sword was plain as day. "Ill? I intend thee? Forgive the retort, my good Lord." Dorad said, wondering where such speech came. "Tis not *my* steel at *your* neck."

"Tis not I followed you from below til the day grows long. What is thy name, bandit?"

"Dor—" the knife whispered—"ando Hillwalk, kind Lord. Forgive me my caution, that I didn't show myself sooner. There are brigands and thieves between these realms. A man about alone should always be approached with caution, especially one with so fine a sword." Dorad was sure it glowed, its appearance deceiving. Little expert in fine arms, he felt a fascination quite beyond his dull diurnal wit. He almost felt he should covet the other man's sword. "What of you, traveler, what is thy name?"

"Columba Riverford," the other man said, withdrawing the point an inch or two. "Hillwalk, eh? Know these parts well?"

"In a fair way, Sir," he said, still not quite believing he spoke so well. "Courier, and available for hire if you've a missive needing to get hither and yon. Between the principalities too. Just delivered one across this very same road from Scrollhaven." Dorad grinned widely at the warrior. "I'd be a bit more comfortable without a blade at my throat."

"Uh, well, I suppose." The sword point dropped. "I've got a fire a hundred paces back. Join me, Dorando?" The sword went into the sheath, its glow peeking between threads.

"Certainly, Columba, certainly, and thank you for it. I've a bit of cured rabbit to throw into a stew, if you'll have it?"

The man's eyes brightened, and the pair walked back along the trail.

His face to the warmth, his back to the cold, he settled himself, digging the leaf-wrapped bundle from pack, and unsheathing the knife. Its haft seemed overly warm, and the sapphire seemed to sparkle overmuch. Dorad paused, little understanding such things, but knowing they preceded trouble.

Columba leapt abruptly to his feet. "Great stars above, what's that?" He pointed over Dorad's head.

He craned his neck to look.

The eastern sky was clotted with cloud. Their undersides flickered with orange light. "Ah, appears to be the Warlock's Mount, looking unsettled this eve. Rare to see it flare so bright."

"Warlock's... the volcano?" Columba blinked at him.

"The very same," Dorad said, returning his attention to the rabbit. "Not a concern for us, this far away. If'n you stand on the shores of the southern sea, you can feel the earth tremble under your feet. Sends an occasional wave inland as well, tidal waves they call 'em."

The man across from him sat again, looking perturbed, his eyes going to the skies behind Dorad intermittently.

"What about you, Sir? Mayhaps you're a Sage? Not that you'd tell a stranger. Wouldn't put me off for a moment if you didn't."

The man shook his head, his gaze dropping to the fire. "I wanted to join them ..." He blinked rapidly.

Tear in his eyes, perhaps? Dorad wondered, the thought coming to him as though from elsewhere. "Didn't mean to intrude, Sir." He turned his attention to the rabbit.

The stew took most the gaminess from the meat, and the fire lent its weight to their eyelids too.

"Wake up!" Serpens told him. "Kill him now whilst he sleeps!"

Dorad found the knife in hand, hot in his palm, and he gathered his legs beneath him and leapt.

A hand caught the knife arm and the sword point caught his sternum, and as he died in bewilderment, Dorad's last thought was, *Why did Serpens order me to throw myself onto Columba's sword?*

* * *

Perched on a branch fifteen feet above the glowing remains her campfire, Chiona Anthus watched the cowled figure below approach her empty bedding.

When her senses had alerted her to the approach of magic, Chiona had silently scrambled into the tree and out onto the limb that hung above her campsite.

If I'd only been awake when the outland raiders captured my father, she thought, biting back her despair at ever finding him again. Sometimes for ransom and sometimes for slave trade and sometimes just to be cruel, outland brigands would launch raids across the border and into Scrollhaven and capture the country folk before the local sheriff could stop them, knowing no deputy fool enough to chase them into the wilderness and risk their own capture, or worse. Scrollspells might be obtained to warn of the trespassers, but only the wealthy might afford those, Chiona having filched her father's life savings to obtain the one she now carried, which obscured her from the interloper below.

She'd managed, in the confusion caused by the trickster, Aridisia, to abscond from the Crypt of Scrolls with both the scroll she'd requested and those same life savings, and so perhaps was feeling overly adroit in trying to intercept this interloper now.

Her sense of magic, a passing soothsayer had once told her, was like an eye that glimpsed the spirit world, or allowed her to peer over the shoulder of the Almighty Scribe to see what He scrawled on the Scroll of Life for her. The location and intensity of magic around her were clear to Chiona, clear as villages on a map, clear as trees on a plain when surveyed from a nearby hilltop.

The intruder below glowed with a brilliance that almost hurt.

Chiona hadn't seen such intense magic since her trip to the Crypt of Scrolls two days...

It's her! she thought, startled. "Aridisia!"

The woman looked up.

Chiona's foot slipped, and she yelped and fell.

"Bright one, fall none!" Quill scratched on parchment.

Chiona hung a foot above the pit, the glow of coals hot on her face.

"Fastest spell I've ever done," the woman said.

"Thank the Almighty!" Chiona tried to figure out how to extricate herself, looking around at the ground on either side of the fire pit, but puzzled as to how to get there.

"Here," and Aridisia pulled her to one side and righted her.

It was a curious feeling, to have no weight.

"Avaunt!"

And she dropped to her behind, giggling. "Sorry, I don't mean to be so silly."

"Silly is being here in the outlands, at night, with a beacon like this." Aridisia gestured at the fire pit.

China brushed herself off. "I was cold, and beside, no one can see me anyway."

Aridisia looked at her.

"Unless I intend it, right?"

"True, but what I wasn't able to warn you about was others' being able to cast aside or subvert the magic from a simple scroll."

Chiona frowned. "Then how am I supposed to rescue my father?"

"I don't know, child."

She felt her despair rising again and struggled to keep it suppressed.

"You look overwhelmed."

China burst into tears, and the woman pulled her close, the embrace reminding her of her long-dead mother, her imprisoned brother, and her kidnapped father. Everyone she'd ever loved had been taken, one at a time.

Their farm on the outskirts of the Phorbi estates at the west end of Scrollhaven, the Anthus family herded sheep for livelihood, their few acres barely able to sustain a dozen head, the wool and milk and occasional meat bringing in enough to keep them only in abject penury. Their land mown bare by grazing sheep, the lush forest preserve adjacent to their homestead looked horribly inviting, and as sheep were wont, they tried

their best to reach through fence to nibble the hardy grasses beyond, their nature to find the weakness and break on through to
greener grasses. A year before through one such break, the herd
had plunged, their absence not noted until the evening when her
brother Notho had gone to bring them into for the night.

He did not return.

A Phorbi patrol—a trio no better than hired thugs—had
caught Notho on their grounds, and claimed he'd been poaching,
the squirrel he'd bagged earlier still in his pouch, the scrawny
rodent not worth the meat they might have picked off his bones,
and no amount of plea or bargain would sway Baron Phorbi to
clemency. Notho was sentenced to a year in the mines of the
High Magus Ravenna Cithara, and when the expense of trial,
room, board, and cloth were added, it was likely he'd not be
seen again.

Chiona wept as she told her woes, disliking her own weakness, wishing she were stronger.

"Ah, but you are strong," the woman said to her, "Look at
what you've been through, and how you're still trying. By the
Almighty Scribe, that's strength, real strength."

As they talked into the deepest night, Chiona wondered at
this wise exotic woman who looked but a year or two older, but
who exuded wisdom and power of someone twice her age.

"You're very bright in my sight, you know," she said.

Aridisia looked at her oddly.

Chiona explained her sight, and how she had seen Aridisia's
intensely bright magic even at the Crypt of Scrolls.

"Weren't you in line behind me with the other supplicants?"

"Behind you? I don't think so, else I'd have seen you. I don't
miss people who shine as bright as you."

"When did you first notice how bright I am?"

"When you helped that old woman, Dam Ironsmith, with her
son's illness." Chiona saw Aridisia's withdrawn gaze.

"But not before?"

"No, Lady Magux." Seeing how deep in thought she was, Chiona dared not interrupt. After several minutes silence, she burst, "What's it mean?"

"I don't know, Chiona, but you mustn't address me thus, for I'm no Magux."

"But weren't they about to offer you—"

"Mayhap, Child, but whatever they offered, it was swiftly withdrawn. My returning with the Ancient Script might change that, but they might as like to bind me in perpetual suspension as not for its theft."

Chiona lay her head back to Aridisia's shoulder, the comfort long absent, long before her father was abducted. He'd been wrapped deeply inside his own losses before he himself was lost to the outland raiders. "Your magic is stronger than you know, Mistress."

"Eh?"

"You said after scrawling your spell for me that you could only wish you might go rescue my father."

A soft chuckle and a sigh. "I did so say, yes, indeed."

"I wish I had an older sister like you."

This time just the sigh. "And I, a younger like you."

Chiona blinked back tears, warm to her heart. Then she stirred uncomfortably. "I'll need to step behind the tree." She rose and was struck by the cold, making the urge the more severe.

Behind the tree, trousers at her ankles, tunic stuck up under her arms, Chiona sighed, the bulge of the scroll digging into her ribcage.

"What ill intends thee me?"

Her stream stopped, panic seizing her. Chiona peeked around the tree.

Aridisia was surrounded, two of them with swords, two others with arrows nocked, a fifth man grinning at her past a knife.

"No ill at all," said the grinning man, grinning wider. "Bind her hand and foot!"

* * *

Skarn Arkose tracked the traveler carefully as the stranger crested a hill and descended into the ravine. The encroaching dusk deepened in the canyon, and she signaled to her lieutenants to close off the traveler's escape, this stretch of the road to Scrollhaven her favorite.

Her magical cloak in hand, Skarn put her fingers to her lips to tweet a call, the morning dove as mournful as the tragedy about to befall this solitary soul.

The news that day from Stonevale disturbed her little, the avaricious Adepts cowering in their precious Vault of even less concern without their sacred stone, Luxullian.

With it, they might be formidable inside their own domains, Skarn thought, but without it they're whimpering weaklings. She rubbed the burnished belt buckle at her waist, a small ruby adorning its center.

She slipped from her cleft and stood in the path.

The traveler stopped twenty paces away.

She liked his fine dress and elaborate coif. "Give up your geld or find yourself gelded, traveler."

His hand leaped to his pouch but the blow from behind laid him out on the path with a crash.

"The way he's dressed, we'll get a fine ransom, eh boys?" Skarn stepped to his side and tore the satchel from his belt. The ruby inside was larger than any she'd ever seen, and it illuminated the ravine. Quickly, she shoved it back in its satchel and bound it firmly inside her sash. "A prize seen but once in a brigand's lifetime, both the Adept and the stone he carries." She gestured to one man. "Trocto, you recognize him?"

From Stonevale, Trocto Sovite had been accused of theft at his former post and had fled to the outlands to evade the law, the sheriff as like to inflict the sentence as to bring him to justice. He owned no more to Skarn than the vengeance he'd sworn upon the injudicious accusers. "Aye, my lady, I do. Tis no adept we have here, but him who they say stole the big stone itself, the spendthrift wastrel, Marl Gneiss."

Skarn threw her head back and laughed. "Well then it's for sure we'll spare his life and ransom him to the Stonevale Adepts, for with deeds like those under his belt, he's far and above our richest catch."

The figure on the ground began to stir.

"Bind him hand to foot and get a pole."

Trocto bound him while two others plunged into the forest to do her bidding.

Skarn saw an eye flick open. "You'll want to keep still or get more of the club that hit you."

The eye blinked at her once and closed.

Two men returned with a smoothened pole. Hoisting the bound man between them, they set off for the bandit camp.

Skarn hadn't always lived on the fringes. A guildmaster she'd been, a leader of one of the skilled trades, the Woodwrights in Scrollhaven. Second only to the Scrollscribes in power, the Woodwrights supplies the Scrollscribes their sacred parchment and of course the pins on which the scrolls were wound.

Then her name had been Glabra Vyburn, and her renown in working wood seeped even into the two far kingdoms, the couplets that tripped from her lips shaping the wood like satin, her parchment the most desired among the Scrollscribes.

But her magic worked only the wood.

Like her counterparts in the metals, farming, and clothing trades, Glabra could not exert her skills on their materials, nor they on hers. The one scroll, the Ancient Scroll, Canodex, proscribed the use of magic beyond the confines of each guild save one: the Scrollscribes. Theirs was the freedom to practice their craft on the entire world around them, a freedom envied by all the guilds. Though they practiced their craft upon the world around them, they did so only through the power of the scrolls.

Woodwright Glabra chafed against the confines of her craft. When she might have filled her mind and time with mastering all the subspecialties of woodwrighting, shipbuilding, house building, furnifacturing, fence building, etc., instead she schemed and slaved on how to shed the force that restrained her, how to cut the harness that kept her from running free.

As Guild mistress and the arbiter of all things Woodwright, Glabra oversaw the conduit through which the Crypt of Scrolls obtained its craft tools, and in her mind she concocted the thought that small encouragements might persuade the Lady High Magux to broaden the constraints confining her trade. And so she set about finding the geis that might inhibit the range of the Scrollscribes' power. At first it was subtle—a shipment of parchment disliking of ink, a case of quills allergic to parchment, an ink obstreperous to staying in line, scroll pins without the friction to hold onto parchment.

The Lady High Magux was not amused.

Guild mistress Glabra, when called before the nettled Cithara, calmly proposed that the Crypt of Scrolls might consider relinquishing or at least softening its iron control over the flow of magic.

The Ancient Scroll then unfurled, the High Magux unleashed Canodex upon her, and when the storm subsided, Glabra was a shell of the once proud Woodwright she'd been, her parchment withering into smoke the moment she made it, the wood chips off her scroll pins turning to termites which ate the pins that she'd just made, and even the trees she went near groaning as though with revulsion as they bent themselves away from her.

"For unto thy geis be true, unto you your geis will do."

In despair, Glabra had fled Scrollhaven and wandered, the contrageis a contagion infecting all she tried to do. Even brigands preying upon the likes of her shunned her, as though they too might catch the spell laid upon her.

Then one day, her name now Skarn, she'd come upon a traveler, a tall man easily seven feet. She thought at first he was some great beast for all he wore was hair.

Cascading hair from head to foot, only the belt around his middle his one adornment, the hair a mix of black and grey, the eyes behind a veil of the same, his nose and mouth visible under a down speckled like a bird's egg.

Fishing from an outcrop, Skarn saw the figure emerge across the stream, his eyes already upon her, compelling even from a distance.

The silence was eerie, for even the birds and squirrels had ceased their calls, and the air was still as though the wind itself was afeared to blow.

He made no gesture from across the stream but she felt the pull and set aside her rod, climbed down and forded the stream to stand beside him on the other side, his gaze so compelling she could not look away.

His eyes drew her in and she felt she was falling, falling, falling. And in his hands now was the belt. She'd not seen him remove it, but there it was. Its burnished buckle was plate steel, the kind used in swords, a steel much too strong to waste on baubles. At the buckle center sat a ruby, as red as blood from a fresh cut. He tripped a latch on one side, and the buckle opened. Underneath was a slip of parchment, the runes so small she could barely read them. He closed it up and shoved it at her, his wordless stare compelling her to silence.

Skarn startled at the tug on her line, and she pulled to set the hook. While the fish struggled, she glanced around, wondering if she'd dreamt.

Later as she packed her pole and line, she cinched her catch to her belt, a belt she didn't remember having before.

And couldn't remember where she'd got it.

After that, misfortune went away, and Skarn had found first one brigand who seemed not repelled. Soon, as even the lawless were wont to accrete to those alacritous in tongue and deed, she did find a following, by then her name had changed to Skarn.

The company arriving at camp, a river-ripped canyon beach whose waters rose each springtime, Skarn made sure their captive was comfortable and fed him herself, her spirit forever the Woodwright as she sought to chisel him to the shape she needed. She kept her magical cloak in hand.

"Aye, the suddenly wealthy heir, the benefactor abruptly deceased, the ne'er-do-well father with the profligate tastes." Skarn look at him fully. "An easy life it hasn't been, for to lose so quickly in so foul a way a bounty one would never expect. As it happens, this High Adept Hornfels so quick to accuse, his daughter breathtaking to behold, but ugly in her asseverations, both astung with the Luxullian's loss, must grope for cause and impugn the obvious, neither wanting to face the betrayal inherent in one of their own being perhaps the culprit." Skarn watched his face in the light of the fire, saw as though scrawled upon scroll the thoughts in his mind, and even as she condemned his transparent face, she felt relieved he seemed so simple.

"You're saying one or the other of them as stole it?" Marl said.

Not the brightest crystal in the chandelier, Skarn thought. "What a time, eh? A stranger finds egress, as best a time as any. Tis clever of her, wouldn't you say, Sir Marl, to assert that your denial is proof of your culp? My thought is her implication of you is simply ploy to divert from her any suspicion at all. For who within the Vault of Stones will likely benefit from a house bereft its most revered treasure?"

"Minette herself, you say?"

He's so tractable, she thought. "In her cupidity she obscures from herself with her blind ambition to become the Lady High Adeptryx. How the scales balance in the end!" She saw the twitch in his gaze and knew she'd scored the place where his soul itself yearned for power. So that was your design? she thought, knowing now the role of the ruby, a plum-size chunk so aglow with magic that many might envy the beauty alone.

In the right hands it was power.

"So they took your land and cast you out? Mayhap a ploy to rid themselves of unwanted fruit from a shriveled tree."

Marl snorted. "The apple may not fall far away, but birds and squires and people themselves might carry the seeds for miles. And who knows what fertile fields the seeds might find?"

Platitudes, she thought, hearing the ring of the off-recited, the glib assertion evidence of its repetition. "More's the pity they fail to discern the talent they would so readily reject, the brighter the flame, the larger their buckets to douse it with." She glanced toward the fire. "But enough banter while the night grows late. We retire, for we rise with the moon. What need have ye before we slumber?"

Marl looked away and squirmed.

"Ah, forgive me, captive though you be." She turned to the troop. "You, you, and you, take him downstream for a little relief. Do I have your word, kind Sir, that you'll heed their command? Very well, then, and to you a good night."

Chapter 3

First, a bear feasted on his still-warm corpse, each bite sending shrieks of pain lancing up his spine into his brain. Then the bear bit down on his calf, reared back on its hind legs, and flapped his body back and forth until the leg separated at the knee, flinging his body into an embankment, where his head struck a rock and split open like a cantaloupe. Gnashing through the small bones of his lower leg, the bear ambled over his body and found a thigh, where the prognathous teeth sank. Foot long spikes of iron pain perforated him, and with a wrenching pop, the bear tore the thigh right out of the hip. As the jaws chomped through the thick meat on his well-muscled thigh, he wondered that he still felt pain in a limb no longer attached to his body, and yet with each chomping bite, a surge of excruciation ripped through him. He watched in utter helplessness as the bear consumed his other leg, and then started on his arms. With just his torso remaining, head still attached, Columba prayed to the stars above for relief as the mighty jaws closed over his face and ground his head into tiny bits.

Then his body dropped as though from a cloud and plummeted toward the earth, the wind rushing by him so fast that it sucked all the air from his lungs, dried out his eyes instantly, screaming so loudly in his ears that he couldn't hear his own scream, tossed heels over head so violently that he no longer knew which way was up, and all he knew was that he continued falling and falling and falling. Trying to see where he was falling, he discovered that by extending his arms he could stop his tumbling, and his terror subsided if oh so incrementally, and he looked down to see where he was falling. Below a roiling black cloud bulged ominously toward him, and into it he plunged, the hot sulfur gasses searing his lungs and scorching his skin, hot ash pellets pummeling him and scoring his flesh with branding-iron hot burns, his clothes burning off his body in a short few minutes, exposing his every part to the hot ashen plasma. The fall through the billowy volcano exhaust went on and on, and a tiny thought occurred to him, If this is the ash plume, then the vent is right below me.

And into the lava he plunged, the ends of his fingers crisping instantly and sloughing off along with his toes, the liquid burn scorching into his wrists and ankles, and like an underground fire following a seam of coal, the fire ate its way up his legs and along his arms, peeled back his scalp and consumed his brain, charred chunks flaking off his body until the heat had boiled his very heart.

He leaped from a tree onto the schoolgrounds, his sword swinging, the slight young bodies of children coming apart cleanly under the sharp edge of his blade, their screams echoing off the schoolhouse a hundred feet away, and he swung the sword back around, catching two more, the head coming crisply of the neck of a pretty young girl staring in disbelief at him, a silent plea in her eyes, a plea that faded as he cleaved through the spinal cord.

And he dropped into the chambers of a maiden just stepping from a bath without a thread upon her, and he too lacked a stitch, but what he wore was thrice its usual size, and he saw her eyes drop to his encumbrance and go wide, and he leaped onto her, his desire like a solid rod of molten fire, grasping an ankle in each hand—

"Sleep," said a distant voice. "Banish nightmares and end all cares, be gone the scares of ill-done snares."

A cool hand brushed the sweat from his forehead, and Columbia could not get his eyes to focus.

"Peace, boy, be at peace and sleep."

He slept, and in his dreams, he walked the meadows, his soul at peace, whilst at the edge of the forest around him terrors lurked, bears drooling with desire to gnash his bones, volcanoes rumbling under pressure, ready to spew their hot ash and lava, swords that itched for his palm to swing their eager blades through innocent unarmed victims, tumescences ready to burst from his loins to rape and pillage in wanton destruction. But all these menaces distant, threatening to encroach but held at bay, no longer able to touch him.

Columba woke and sat up, disoriented.

The soft susurrus of surf nearby carried to him on a brine-laden breeze brought him instant comfort. He lay in a canopied bed, the marble-floored pavilion reflecting the cloud-wisped sky, the gentle cry of seabirds mixing with the slosh of surf.

Out to sea, a dark plume pumped black smoke into a pristine sky.

From the remote memory of a horrific nightmare, a volcano seared and crisped him into ash.

Shuddering, Columba pushed away his dream and pushed away the blankets. For a moment he was mystified that his body was intact, and not protruding in bits and chunks from some bear's scat, or roasted to cinders in some pyroclastic flow.

The urge to relieve came upon him, and he found a chamber pot beside the bed, and in using it, he saw his member wasn't outsized. His bladder empty, he found his sword beside the bed, its blade unbloodied.

Columba began to breathe easier, wondering what had ailed him. Picking up his sword, he saw it had sat atop a knife, its pewter handle and blade looking too soft to do real damage, a single nut-sized sapphire set in pommel. The wastrel Dorando's knife.

The wastrel who'd stalked him, and when confronted had convinced him otherwise, then had tried to kill him in his sleep.

Tis a prize of combat, Columba told himself, picking it up.

The world lurched then righted.

Standing feet away between him and the beach where he'd somehow failed to notice was a Queen.

She stood seven feet and was proportioned to match and wore a waterfall for a dress, which fountained down her and splashed at her feet but left nothing wet, her form as clear as if clung by night, upon her head a modest tiara, her majesty evanescent from both stature and posture, her eyes boring through him like spears.

Columba bowed slowly at the waist. "Your Majesty."

"Lord Sage." Her voice was sultry with surf, in tune with time, melodious with measure.

"Forgive me, your Majesty, but no, I am no Sage."

Her brows narrowed. "You carry such a sword, and the knife bespeaks otherworldly power. Forgive me, Lord, but why are you not among the initiate?"

Columba rose, realized but for mishap not of his doing that he would be Sage, or at least apprenticed. "I stand accused, Ocean Queen, of theft. Accused by Lord High Sage Arcturyx of stealing Genesyx herself, the One Sword, the Original Sword."

The woman's soft laughter carried annealing, as though a salve were rubbed into wound. "Then Arcturyx is a fool, for your magic is plainly inadequate to such a task. Be not nettled at such assertion, as only magic of inestimable caliber may disturb or disrupt the Order. Come, Sage Columba, walk with me, and see the cosmos for a time from my view. I am Octans Tala Chert, Queen of Southern Seas. As you might have noted, I'm clothed in sea, an affectation reserved for my land-based travels."

He stepped to her side, and she gestured toward the beach. "What is that, by the way?" He pointed out to sea, to the dark plume that blemished the impeccable vista.

"The Warlock's Mount," she said, turning toward the sand.

He realized as he stepped off the marble-floored pavilion that the structure reached deeply into the jungle, the curving palms, lush ferns, and spidery boas all exotic and indigenous to this warmer, wetter clime and obscuring the temple from visibility.

Somewhere overnight, he'd crossed into another land and climate without knowing he had done so. "How, your majesty, did I arrive here?"

"Twas a frightful night you had, it seems. Your screaming woke us all, and you would have plunged blindly into the waves had my servants not intercepted you. Magic brought you here from yon, and magic stopped the vision that possessed you. No, you need not feel ashamed of the illusion, for neither were you doing what you dreamt, nor did you will it to become."

"But—"

"What is magic but an expansion of desire innate to the human condition? A force tapped into aversion and the urges at work deep in your soul, inflated them beyond proportion, and fed them to your mind as fantasies." She chuckled and soothed him. "Worry not about the content, for no one was raped and no one was murdered."

Columba sighed, his guilt and shame subsiding. "You know what I dreamt?"

"Certain indications arose, but no matter, as a maidservant of mine was willing to assist. Now, as to—"

"You didn't—"

"Lord Sage, avail thyself to sagacity, please. We all see every day truths we never say because they just are. Things of little consequence must be allowed to remain that way."

Columba considered her, a gentle soul whose soft rebuke was likely the sharpest word she'd spoke in many seasons, whose only protection from the elements was an element itself, whose very flow of thought circulated throughout the mundane matters, and whose capacity for forgiveness was as vast as the ocean itself.

"I didn't see you until I picked up the knife." He saw the crease that furrowed her brow. "What is it?"

"An evil boils deep beneath our realm of magic," Queen Tala said. "All that is good and whole amidst and betwixt the three realms is laid bare under the evil, and none shall escape its taint." She turned to look at him. "You who aspired beyond your humble beginnings knows in some ways the pernicious cancer ambition sometimes brings. You yourself stand accused in Swordshire of heinous deeds beyond the ken of your circumscribed imagination. Be not miffed, for limits serve a noble purpose."

She resumed walking, the jungle on their left, the slosh of sea to the right, soft sand underfoot. "You have scruples, Lord Sage. This evil does not. Beware its insidious influence for it would pry you loose from your moorings with desire you can only dream about."

Columba looked up into her face, a foot above his, and suddenly the water that clothed her dried up.

She was magnificent.

Then the water turned back on, and the glimpse left him breathless.

"It was you, not I, who rendered me clothe-less."

* * *

"Why shouldn't I send you back to those fat quill cushions?" Drupa Juni said, running his eyes up and down the body of his captive. He and his band of miscreants prowled the woods outside of Scrollhaven for just such tidbits as she, this pretty young maiden whose poise bespoke an age beyond her years.

"They who recently cast me out?" Her laugh was dainty and delicate and all the more disconcerting for its defiance.

He fumed like the blaze beside him, two of his trusted henchmen between the woman and him, her hands and feet still bound but his instinct telling him to place no faith in rope. But it was more than instinct.

Around his neck, he wore a piece he'd had for as long as he could remember. His existence simple, he had little need to remember much, but it bothered him some that he had no life before his twentieth year. Rather, didn't remember one.

The piece was time—a timepiece. The face was round and nocked at regular intervals around the edge, and the center turned with the sun and moon, its single arrow pointing straight up at noon, straight down at midnight, disconcerting how it knew. Sparkling like a noonday sun, a diamond twinkled in the middle. Twice a day at noon and midnight it flashed like fire, just the once. The metal casing was stainless steel, the color of blade metal manufactured in the great smithies of Swordshire, and Drupa had once been told by an itinerant swordsmith that the timepiece had certainly been forged from a sword. And on the back although smooth, a concave spot invited a fingertip. When pressed, the backing did open, showing inside a myriad of gears and springs, and to one side a rolled-up scroll. Without the learning to decipher such script, Drupa had never gazed upon it, for his instinct was that the timepiece would cease to function were the scroll removed.

But it was more than instinct.

Drupa would swear it talked to him.

Not in words he could hear, but only in urges.

Like the urge to empty his bladder, which came upon him then. "Watch her like you would yer thievin' grandma, boys." And Drupa stepped from the firelight behind a tree, the timepiece dangling from a chain inside his tunic. He raised his tunic and lowered his breeches and sighed in relief, aiming with one hand and caressing the timepiece with the other.

A rustle to the left.

His hand to sword, he peered into darkness. Pulling his clothes back into place, his eyes probing the forest around him, he retreated toward the campsite, stopping at the perimeter. "Runi," he asked the sentry, "anything suspicious?"

"No, Sir, all's quiet."

His eyes still probing, Drupa nodded. "Keep your vigilance. Mine instinct hints at trouble."

"Yes, Sir!" Runi called over his shoulder. "Virgal, do a walk-about. Fifty feet out, all the way around. See if you can do it quiet, too."

"Whatever for?" Virgal called, not moving from his perch beside the fire.

Drupa leaped, sword in hand, and slugged him with the pommel. The others scattered, except the two guarding the woman. "Perhaps you didn't hear me, Virgal."

The younger man picked himself up, rubbing his reddened cheek. "Wasn't listening, Sir. Right away, Sir." He fled into the darkness.

Drupa returned to his seat and contemplated his captive. The others slowly recoalesced. "Evil walks the night," he muttered, glancing at the dark perimeter.

He turned his attention to his prisoner. "You sneer, but why? Pretty thing like you don't need to fill your head with spells or quills to fill your purse, now, do you? Why'd they give the boot to you? Some dumb scroll? Hardly seems the half of it." He saw her eyes and knew she followed his every word and breath. She wants to get away but also wants to stay, it occurred to him.

Now where'd that thought come from? he wondered.

Wants something from you, she does.

Drupa looked at the woman sharply, wondering if she was working subtle magic on him. Not all the spirit shifters had to voice their incantations, he knew. He felt the urge to ask her.

"The other half is you want something, isn't it?" He saw by the light in her eyes it was. "From rogues and thieves? What could you possibly have of interest?" He leaned toward her, the firelight warm, almost enough to singe. "You can tell me."

Resting on her elbow, hands tied, she leaned toward him. "I was wanting … to empty my bladder."

He threw his head back and laughed at her impertinence. "Untie the whore and let her use that bush. She won't run, you'll see. Won't get far if she does, besides."

The guards did as he bade them and she came right back, as he knew she would.

"May I sit here?" And she did anyway, not two feet away, as though one of the band.

"You, tie her ankles. Yes, mysterious witch, as I thought. They won't call you Magux but there's depths to you that merit such."

"The same might be said of you," she said.

He heard no hint of irony or insult. "That they follow me is honor enough." He gestured at his troop.

"Honor? Even among thieves?"

"Dishonor among men may to thievery lead," he replied in rejoinder, a chuckle escaping him. He'd not had cause for mirth in awhile.

"Rogue and poet, how quaint."

"Quaint hasn't ever been described of me. Out with it, what you're wanting, eh? I capture you when instead it appears you're capturing me—or trying." He felt her eyes probe his face. How odd these Maguses, their furtive motives and subtle ways. Far be it for me to understand them.

"A few nights ago, a man named Zibeth Anthus was captured near here, and I desire to learn his fate."

Drupa regarded her, nettled by how direct she could be, mystified that she would concern herself with someone else when she herself had lost so much. Not that he cared in any way for either. "A simple Woodwright, of the guild but no more than a member. I sold him to a slave train bound for Swordshire. Crafty, over there, forged some papers for me, under sentence for some thievery or other." He gestured to a rogue sitting back from the fire.

"A girl yearns for her father, and you sold him into slavery."

"You want me to cry?" He snorted. "She had a father, be glad of it. If he was yours, sorry he's lost to you." He felt annoyed at her sentimentality, a feeling he'd long since dismissed as interfering with his feeding himself and his band.

"So what will you do with me?"

For the second time in as many minutes, he felt disconcerted by her directness. "Better that you don't know."

"Something analogous, I presume?"

"What?"

"Similar, you'll do something similar, won't you?"

"Maybe you didn't hear me. I told you not to ask. Now, I'm tired, and I'm going to roll up and go to sleep." He turned to her guards. "Take her over there." He pointed to a spot near his own bedroll. "We rise at first light and travel to reach the Swordshire border by the next day dusk." He looked at the woman. "You'll keep up with us or you'll be carried."

Drupa saw to all the watches, glancing uncomfortably at the dark forest night around them, his skin crawling for reasons he couldn't name.

Returning to his bedroll, he checked the prisoner one last time, hearing her soft sounds of sleep, the sentry on the rock above her watching.

Beside his bedroll stood a weather-bleached trunk, twelve feet tall and bare of branches, its top shorn off as if by some giant hand, the burnt edges hinting at a lightning strike. One chest-high branch poked out from it, broken off a foot out from the trunk, sheared off as though by blade, its end a wicked point.

Drupa slipped out of his tunic and hung it on the chest-high branch, then did the same with breeches. He stood naked under a fingernail moon, wearing only the timepiece on a chain.

As though possessed, it rose, filling him with overwhelming desire, and his member filled and rose with his desire.

The guard turned away as Drupa approached the woman, the timepiece pulling him along, his mind engorged with urges and appetites long dormant.

He stood over her, his flagpole quivering with desire, the timepiece heavy and pulling him down toward her.

"What?" Her sleepy voice evinced no alarm, then her hand shot up and grasped the timepiece. "Reprobate, you've met your fate." Her other hand motioned, and an invisible net yanked him backward, the chain breaking, leaving the timepiece in her hand.

Drupa slammed into the twelve-foot trunk, and the fire through his back and into his chest burned so terribly he wondered what it was.

The sharp end of the sheared-off branch, he saw.

And he died.

* * *

Marl awoke before anyone else, and even the sentry they'd set upon him snored in happy oblivion.

But no matter how he struggled, he couldn't squirm from his restraints.

So instead he took stock of his surroundings.

The wastrel's camp lay at the bottom of a ravine, a river-cut embankment over their heads, its underside caked with moss, the sandy shelf where he lay a good twenty feet wide and thirty feet long. The far wall too was water-worn rock, erosion marking the canyon side fully thirty feet above. The river this late in season was now a trickling stream gurgling pleasantly nearby.

Ten brigands were visible from where he lay, only the leader slept apart, her slight figure just visible in the dark, innermost reaches of their cutaway.

How am I going to get away? he wondered, knowing his paucity of brain cells no match for the wily leader Skarn. Marl felt helpless and hopeless, seeing no way out of his predicament. Either she'd hawk him to the Stonevale sheriff or pitch him to a passing slaver, perhaps even auction him off to a lumberjack crew.

Marl wasn't sure which he feared more, the debasement of ignominy in being remanded unto the High Adept Hornfels, or the grueling labor he'd face in servitude to a slavemaster. For Marl hadn't worked a lick in the last three months, and the thought of returning to arduous work terrified him. And for little or no pay!

One small mystery nettled him.

Her belt.

The instant he'd seen her, he'd felt something odd tugging at his mind. The tinkle of the sun off her shiny steel belt buckle, the ruby red glimmer at its center, had sent him back to the day he'd found in his deceased uncle's treasury the plum-sized ruby mounted like a prize in a wall sconce.

The treasury vault was windowless, buried five level deep under the Gneiss mansion, barricaded behind five doors, each locked with five different keys, the number and complexity nearly overwhelming his feeble mind. On display at intervals in the vault, a long room ten by forty, were precious relics of past majesty, the Gneiss family ancient and once revered. On pedestals stood gem-encrusted tiaras, glittering necklace, gold chalices, silver dining ware, diamond monocles. Embedded in sconces between the pedestals sat other valuables—filigreed books, gold-threaded bustiers and corsets, diaphanous veils interwoven with diamonds.

At the far end, mounted on a silver stem itself encrusted with gold glitter, sat the ruby, cut to an oval but thick through as a plum, elongated like the point end of an egg, its facets winking under the lantern-light, its darker faces so deep red in color that it almost looked liquid.

And Marl felt when he laid eyes upon it that it drew him into its liquidity as though he'd fallen into a deep vat of blood.

The tiny specks of precious stone he'd practiced with endlessly and hoarded for years were suddenly useless. With this ruby he might achieve his only dream, the one wish he'd secretly harbored all his life from the time he'd realized as he watched his profligate father squander his fortune and seed, that Marl's one route to the wealth and influence denied him by his wastrel forebear was membership in the Vault of Stones.

Instead he lay, bound hand to foot among captors who'd taken the last vestige of a life redeemed, and all Marl could think about, bizarre as it was to his shallow mind, was the ruby.

Not the large, plum-size ruby that Skarn had liberated from his possession, but the grain-size ruby embedded in the face of her steel belt buckle. The thought of it occluded all else, and he could not have said why.

Hands and feet bound, all he could do was scooch on his side, using shoulder and hip, across the gravelly ground. The grind and clatter of his passage was sure to wake someone, but did not somehow, and Marl was convinced they were bewitched. Pulled by the winking of the tiny ruby, lacking any thought of what he'd do then, Marl scooted to Skarn's side. Wrapped tightly in her fingers, he saw, were the thongs of the satchel holding his plum-size ruby.

The flames of pain at hip and shoulder told him he'd likely lacerated both, and he stopped to rest, his breathing rough. A big man, and like his father prone to fat, Marl winded easily, and no amount of exercise or restraint in consumption kept him from accumulating pounds.

Marl looked into Skarn's face. For all his noise, the brigand slept peacefully. His hands tied at wrist still left his fingers unrestricted. Just able to grasp the buckle, he undid it slowly, watching for the first sign of her waking.

The clasp fell away.

I'll never thread the belt from around her waist, he thought, and slipped her knife from its sheath. His sawing through the thick leather strap did not wake her. The buckle in hand, he used the knife to cut his bindings, wrists and ankles both.

Then he cut open the satchel and extracted his ruby.

Marl fled, quickly finding the steep incline out of the ravine.

Chapter 4

As soon as Columba passed the crest, he felt the distinct change in climate.

The colder lands to the north, where Scrollhaven sat, were legendary for their stately conifers and evergreens, while the more temperate regions, which included Swordshire and Stonevale, included primarily deciduous forests. Only in the bowl that he'd just left, the vast crescent of the Halfmoon Sea, bordered on three sides by outlands, were the lush jungles dense with fern, boab, and palm.

Columba glanced back once, and in the evening light he saw just a blot due south, the volcano called Warlock's Mount.

Octans Tala Chert, Queen of the Southern Seas, had gestured only once toward the ominous black splotch on the horizon, shortly before provisioning him for his journey. "The ancient talismans of Sword, Scroll, and Stone have held their dynasties stable these many thousand years, wisdom preserved and institutions maintained across hundreds of generations, and it's my hope that this stability continues. But there is one who conspires otherwise—" And she glanced out to sea toward the viscous oily plume "—whose influence will be felt all too soon."

She'd not said more, but had bade him, the Accused Sage of Swordshire, to travel north and find allies for his cause. "For the one sword Arcturyx has not passed from this world, but you won't find ally in Swordshire in your quest to return it to its home."

"But whom shall I seek?" Columba had asked, knowing no one beyond his natal village in the South of Swordshire.

"You'll know when you see, just as you knew Dorando Hill-walk bade you ill."

And Columba had left her beside the shore, traveled quarter way round the Halfmoon Sea as she'd instructed, and thus had found the dirt-covered track that seemed to shoot straight north into the jungle, at whose junction he slept. The next morning he took the road.

The long miles of arrow-straight road had alerted Columba to what he'd find long before he found it: a road, paved with stones of equal size, at first buried in silt and verdure, but eventually emerging from underneath at higher elevations, until he'd reached the saddle, where mountains towered to each side, their upper reaches obscured in cloud, and behind him, a single straight strip of road pointing directly at the distant blot, the volcano called Warlock's Mount, which he surmised must be a torrid inferno, just to be visible from this distance.

The cold enshrouded him as he began the descent, the valleys below covered in fog, and only the mountains marching away to east and west visible from this vista.

"A day to reach the jungle breach, a day to top the summit," Queen Chert had told him.

Wondering whether to push onward, Columba measured the amount of light left. He'd seen not a soul in his travels, and for that he was grateful. Absent now the hot southerly breeze that had blown at his back all that day, he decided to stop at the first likely place.

A stream crossed the road, the bridge railing long since rotted away but the masonry looking in good repair. Below the bridge a sandy beach beside the meager trickle.

In the bridge's shadow the dusk was deeper, and he soon had a small blaze glowing, casting a small rock-burning spell. Last night on the beach he'd not dared to light a fire, for the light was surely visible from far across the sea: Here under the bridge he had nothing to fear but passersby, of whom he expected none.

"Care for company, traveler?"

On his feet and sword out before she finished speaking, Columba looked her over.

"Perhaps not, it appears," she said, her hands deceptively still at her sides.

The stance of a fighter and the stealth of a woodswoman, Columba thought, having neither heard not felt the least sign of her approach. "I wasn't expecting any, but I'm not averse to some. Startled me is all. What's the name, traveler?"

"Skarn, it is. Skarn Arkose. And you?"

It was disconcerting that she hadn't moved. "Columba Riverford." Her dress, he noted, was clean if patched, the breaches and tunic appearing loose in a way that a belt might remedy. So she wasn't wealthy and didn't live nearby. Brigands roamed these hills, he knew, and far to the north, he might find safety inside the borders of Scrollhaven, but that was at least a day's travel.

"So you won't be dismayed if I stay a spell?"

Dorando came to mind, and he'd known by the thief's following him for long hours that he'd try to harm him. Wary of the lone traveler, knowing himself to be one, Columba demurred. "Where are you headed?"

"I pursue a thief who stole my belt and stone. Mayhap you've seen him? A fatling with a plum-size ruby."

"I've seen no one here today, but I came from yon and headed hither." He gestured vaguely south and vaguely north. "Whence came you? And if you're alone it bespeaks magic or perhaps a quick blade."

"Or maybe both."

And she isn't saying, he thought with a wry smile.

"East I came and west I'm headed." she said.

"Well, come on then and share my fare, and I pray to the stars my luck is better than a few days ago." He settled himself beside the fire, his sword across his knee, his newly acquired knife in his boot top, his back to the bridge abutment.

"You sound like a Shiree," she said, settling across from him on a rock. "Had a mishap yourself, eh? What's the free world turning into, these days?"

"Invited a fiend to share my campsite, and he tried to skewer me as I slept. Just promise you won't try the same, eh?"

"About what happened to me," she replied. "Just want my property back is all. Thief put me under spell and absconded with my worldly possessions, all I owned but the clothes on my back. Of course I should have known." She looked at him. "Had you heard the news? The One Stone Luxullian stolen by this same spend-thrift rouge who stole my belt, this Marl Gneiss."

"No!" Columba said. "Tell me more!"

"How could you not have heard? Where've you been? All three are gone, or didn't you know?"

"Just Genesyx, the One Sword. Stole the day after I left the shire. And the Ancient Scroll, Canodex too? Tis no wonder you pursue this rouge. His hide'll fetch a fair price in Stonevale."

A furrow crossed her brow. "Took you three days to get here from Swordshire?"

He shrugged. "Wandered a bit, got attacked by a bandit—last time he'll attack someone." Columba didn't like the way her eyes weren't focused—and then her weight shifted. "Astray away," he blurted, and deflected the knife an inch from his nose. "Bind and wind," he said, drawing his sword.

Invisible ropes bound Skarn, and she felt to one side with a thump. "Attack!" she shouted.

"Rhyme for time," he said, moving to a crouch.

Deftly with his free hand, he deflected arrow, knife, hatchet, and spear. "Flame flush game!" And pointed his sword.

A gout of flame seared the brush, and four bandits fled, their clothes aflame.

Columba put his sword to Skarn's neck. "All right, thief, tell me the name of the other one, the one who supposedly stole Canodex, the One Scroll, or I'll flay you alive and use your hide for my scroll."

"Aridisia, but that's all I know, I swear!"

* * *

Aridisia put her quill to the slaver's neck. "All right, Trader, tell me who you sold him to, or I'll scrawl you into slavery myself."

Sweat broke on his brow, his lips aquiver, his eyes pasted wide, but they weren't on her face.

Between her beasts dangled the timepiece.

She was sure it wasn't her breasts he was looking at. "Out with it, Slaver!"

"Betel!" he blurted. "Betel Edgeword, the Sage, Hall of Swords, in the Shire."

"What name did you sell him under?" Aridisia threw a quick glance at Chiona.

"Shribeth Canthus," the slave trader whimpered, his glance going to the group of chained people cowering around a tree nearby.

On their way to Swordshire, Aridisia and Chiona had intercepted the same slaver who'd bought Chiona's father from Drupa, now returning toward Scrollhaven to the northeast with a new cache of prisoners, most of them condemned criminals in Swordshire. She and Chiona had set up an ambush, traders rarely traveling without armed guards to protect their goods, and with a few spells, Aridisia had separated the armed warriors from the trader.

"All right, Slaver," Aridisia said, withdrawing her quill, Chiona ready to intervene if he attacked. "Now, why shouldn't I free this batch, eh? How do I know they weren't captured under false pretense like Zibeth Anthus?"

"Lady Magux, please, please," the trader said, his glance straying again to her breasts, "Take them if you insist, even though I obtained them legally from a certified broker, it doesn't matter, just take them and let me go. Please." He winced again at the timepiece.

Aridisia frowned and raised it on its chain.

The trader held both hands in front of his face and whimpered.

She glanced at Chiona, who shrugged. "Seems you fear this more than me. What of it, Trader?"

He peeked from behind his hands, looking pathetic on the ground. "Please, Lady, don't make me say it."

Aridisia sighed, hating having to force things from people. "Node explode," she scrawled in the air.

A pebble beside his arm exploded; he screamed and rolled away, begging her to spare him.

"Just tell me what you know, for Scribe's sake!" Aridisia was fed up. After killing Drupa by throwing him against the tree, she and Chiona had scattered the remaining members of his band, capturing Crafty, the forgery expert. She'd had to torture from him the name and description of the slaver to whom Drupa had sold Chiona's father. Aridisia had had enough of torture.

Through tears and pleas, the trader told her what he knew.

* * *

I heard tell of a piece like that, so powerful it ruled time itself, its gears and levers more mighty than movement of the stars themselves. Tis not a trifle, this story I hear, for in the Guild of

Trade they tell the tale for the stake of coin it sold for, a stack so high, it sank a castle!

I swears upon my purse, it's true!

Hundreds, maybe a thousand years ago, a king sought to conquer all—

Beg pardon, Lady, but your interruption won't let the tale get told. Twas before the Sword, Scroll, Stone it's told, now let me get about the story.

This king did seek to conquer all and thought by selling fantastical gadgets, he might fill his coffers to pay his soldiers. How he knew to harness the celestials, 'twere never told, but he did and gathered unto his domains in the sweltering south all the wise ones, gathered them from all the four corners, did he.

Splendiferous, it's said, the show he staged, the skies a-streak and trees growing backward and water flowing uphill! Raindrops leaped from leaves into the sky, and the clouds evaporated whence they came, and babies grew smaller, to dive back into their mother's wombs.

Such wondrous magic this was, but neither Sage, nor Magus, nor Adept could pay his price. Twas not like today, where lies ensconced in the Vault of Stones the largest ever hoard of wealth. No, then it was chaos, with twelve to twenty little kingdoms rising, falling, fighting, losing, winning, surrendering, aligning, capitulating, all their fortunes so in flux a man might live in five different principalities throughout his life and occupy the same house too.

So the magicians formed an alliance to gather together this one king's price, and on the day of trade, the weight of gold all in one place caused the very bedrock under the castle to give and into the sea, this kingdom plunged, leaving a pit so deep and wide that the liquid rock all fiery and hot burst from beneath and hurled into the sky a plume of smoke and ash so tall it were seen from all four corners.

What happened to it?

Why, Lady, it were destroyed, of course.

Oh, the timepiece? Thought it was the castle you asked. Nay, Lady, no one knows what happened to it, except that the stories grew too tall for tellin' perhaps.

* * *

"Why'd you let him keep his slaves?" Chiona asked.

"Well, I'm not sure." She looked at the younger woman. The girl who'd come to her but four days ago to beg her help after finding her father was gone, and in the girl's place stood a woman who'd seen adversity and wrestled it under control. "In his view, he'd acquired them fairly, purchased with money he'd earned through honest sweat. But I should have extracted from him the price he got when he sold your father."

Chiona frowned. "What will we do when we get there? How will we free him?" She waved away the dust kicked up by their passage, the steep hills here funneling the winds up canyon.

Taking a swig from her canteen, Aridisia shook her head, peering toward the setting sun, a glimpse of the valley below just visible. They'd traveled south from the Scrollhaven border, where Drupa had captured her, then when they'd nearly reached the crest—the continental divide that separated the northern half from the southern—they'd turned west, Aridisia reasoning that traveling further south would only take them into the geographical bowl known as the Halfmoon Sea.

Two nights ago, nearing the crest, Chiona had remarked how straight the trail was, most tracks through the forest taking the path of least resistance—i.e., around trees, across fords, up gullies—but not that one.

Aridisia had thought it odd that the path appeared to stretch straight north to Scrollhaven.

"Why is that, do you suppose?" Chiona had asked.

Due south of them in the evening sky flickered an eerie, orange light. Aridisia had shuddered and abruptly turned them west, a heavy heart settling upon her, as though somewhere deep in her soul, she felt they'd gone the wrong way.

All the next day she'd slogged through wood and dale, inexplicably yearning for the comforting warmth of the Halfmoon Sea, a nebulous sense of doom descending upon her. Pushing onward, barely speaking, Aridisia had seen Chiona's looks, the something-bothers-you-deeply looks, accompanied by a wistful silent plea to talk.

But she had not asked, for which Aridisia had been grateful.

I still can't explain the way I felt, she thought, glad the feeling had dissipated.

"What'd you think of the slaver's tale?"

I like the way she asks first before postulating her own response, Aridisia thought. "He certainly believes the legend. Seems preposterous that a gadget might move stars and sun. There doesn't seem a magic potent enough, eh?"

"No, Ari, there doesn't. Tis clear he feared the timepiece, though. At first I thought he were guessing the price your bosom might fetch at open auction." Chiona grinned at her.

Aridisia snorted and shook her head. "In the depths of the Crypt lies a scroll that is whispered to consume the unwary scribe who attempts to decipher its meaning, written in a script no longer understood even by the most learned of scholars." She swigged from her canteen and offered it.

Chiona took it, her face flushed. "Which do you think it is—a veil to ward off the novice, or a truth whose lash has flayed the most daring?"

Shaking her head, Ari gestured at the valley before them. "Tis said they have their legends as well, their enigmas and chimeras. When was the last time you heard a tale as fantastical as the slaver's?"

"Perhaps not that fantastical, but …" She gestured in question.

"Certainly, I'd love to hear the tale."

* * *

In a meadow rich with juicy grasses lived a keen old woman who'd devoted her life to breeding sheep with wool so fine and strong that its threads once spun would glow in the night but deflect the sharpest of blades and withstand the hottest of fires. For decades, she crossed one strain with another, some sheep the white of snow and others the black of night.

Her wool was fine and strong, it's sure, and widely known to fetch a handsome price, travelers coming from the four corners to sample a swatch or buy a bolt. As many tailor who left with product to sell or cloth to work, the same number or greater left empty-handed, the bidding high and hot, despite only certified guilders able to bid.

And as too the shepherds brought their finest sheep to the keen old woman, who culled all but the finest to breed with her stock. And if they were to sell her but one measly lambling, they might then claim the worth of their stock to their subsequent buyers, her eyes and feel for the sheep unerring, and her pay for the finest unequaled.

One day there approached what appeared to be a man whose skin looked as calloused as rock, and with him he brought a sheep so sparse of hair it was sure to suffer alopecia, and at his waist, he wore a knife whose blade looked pewter, and set at its base where blade met pommel was mounted a single sapphire. Now in the mockery leveled at him for his spindly, spare-haired sheep, few took notice of the knife, until the keen old woman herself nearly keened over the pitiable sheep he'd brought.

This strange man with thickened skin evinced no response at her mournful calling, itself so sad it sounded mocking, but naught did he but unsheathe that knife and brandish toward her its single small sapphire, did she look off as though mesmerized and purchase that ewe and then for a far higher price than any had heretofore. Of course, he stood accused of witchery and blandishment, and the Guild of Herders fined him heavily and banned him from their membership.

But the sale was done and the ewe engendered pity from all who saw her. The old woman couldn't bear to send it to slaughter. And in the spring, the ewe grew fat with lamb, for as ewes do, she bred with ram.

The litter of three were born on the first day of summer, the sun so high in the sky, it looked it might not descend again. Their down once dry shone just as bright—'tis said, mind you, so I can't rightly say they were bewondered—as bright as that very same sun.

And the wool shorn two years hence from the same three lamb was too bright to see, the thread it made too tough to break, and the cloth it made too strong to tear.

The strange man with skin like rock returned anon and claimed these lambs, proclaiming as proof of his honest sale the quality of wool that they produced.

And when she balked, this keen old woman, the rock-skinned man pulled out his knife and brandished at her that single small sapphire, and avaunt he went with lambs *and* ewe, never to be seen again.

Tis said at the Herder Guildhall, late at night over pints of brew, that somewhere still there dwells a man with herds so white they can't be seen, their wool so fine and strong there's none better, and it is this chimera, fanciful as it seems, that holds the herder enthralled today.

* * *

The belt buckle in a pocket, his plum-size ruby in hand, Marl Gneiss glanced up at the encroaching night and swore he wouldn't freeze again under the cold black sky.

He couldn't remember ever lacking a roof over his head. Even in the years of destitute penury right before his father died—his belly bloated like a blowfish, his skin so yellow it looked like curry, the whole time swilling his drink nonstop while his wife and son went hungry—even then Marl had had a roof to sleep beneath.

He'd escaped the brigand Skarn with only the buckle, the knife he'd cut it loose with, his ruby, and the clothes on his back. Now, three days on the run, sure he was somewhere near entering Swordshire, his clothes had seen better years, tattered down his left side, splotched and stained everywhere else, dried sweat and unwashed body saturating them with stench, he looked now like the fugitive he was.

Glancing back again, his head spun from how many times he'd glanced over his shoulder, expecting Skarn to leap from the bushes, finally overtaking him, knife in hand, scream on lips, death in eyes. Oh, he'd used aversion spells and invisibility spells, and he'd even laid down spells of subterfuge, enticing signs to lead surveillers astray.

But these were all distractions, and Marl was no woodsman, convinced he left a thousand signs of his passage for even a novice to follow.

He stood at a fork in the road, the inviting glow of light from a structure on the hillside above. "Odor stanch and cloths repair, show me to be debonair." He waved the ruby above his head.

Hoping it enough, he trudged up the road, his body complaining. A big man given to fat, Marl now tightened his belt to the inner-most notch, and his tunic sloughed off him like some tent. His stomach growled from lack of food, and his belly hurt in constant ache.

Above the compound entrance was a sign.

"Mines of East Shire," it said.

"Halt there, traveler." A guard stepped from the shadows. "What be your business?"

Marl just now saw the twelve-foot fence that enclosed the perimeter, the reinforced gate, the guards both inside and out, the towers each a hundred yards both east and west. "Forgive me, Sir. I'm Earl Ford Knox. I mistook the lights within for the inn. Might you tell me how far it lies?"

"There be no inns this near the border, Lord. Five miles further along is the hamlet Waterford, but no inns there."

"Well, whatever shall I do? Misled it seems I've been. Might I impinge upon your master for a bite to eat and a pallet to lay my weary bones?" Marl didn't need to feign fatigue or hunger.

The guard's eyes narrowed. "What would a gentleman of your refinement be about these domains at this hour? Where are your guards? Forgive me, Lord, but most unwise to be this close to the border without escort."

"I'd sent them ahead to the inn to prepare the way, and I fear I've missed them somehow. Pardon my imposition."

The guard waved it aside. "No imposition at all, Lord, but you'll find our lodgings humble and our portions meager. Tis the High Lord Sage's mines you've found, a far journey from any inn."

"A blessing I've found something, eh?"

"Stars above, it is. If you'll wait here, Lord Knox, whilst I check?"

Marl smiled, watching him go.

The soldier soon returned. "Captain Volans welcomes you, Lord, this way." And the soldier led him not to the main building but to a small side building standing alone near the forward corner of the compound. "Our guesthouse, Lord. Oft used by the Lord Sage Edgeword, who was here just two days ago to buy a dozen slaves for the mines. I've sent for the servant to assist you with bath and clothing, Lord, and Captain Volans bids you when you've finished to join our fare."

Simple clapboard on the outside, the guesthouse was modestly appointed inside. The down mattress five fingers deep, the curtains filigreed with gold strand, the carpets plush and silent under foot.

He found the bath and started to shed his rags.

"Lord, no, unthinkable you should do that yourself." The young woman pulled his hands aside and swiftly undressed him. Once off his body, they looked and smelled as they really were. "A prudent spell, Lord." Undismayed, she warmed the water, hustled him into the bath, dunked him, then made him stand while she lathered him thoroughly.

"Cost a few coin for more than a wash, Lord," she said, grinning at him. Sitting him in the water, she started on his hair.

Rinsing him off with a bucket, she stood him up and began to dry him.

His hand full with her breast, she sighed, her gaze unfocused. "Perhaps less than I usually charge."

It occurred to him that as a servant she rarely earned anything extra.

She picked out an outfit for him, smirking at the rags he'd shed. Choosing pieces he thought large, she put them on him then wiggled her finger.

The clothes drew taut then loosened a might.

"Reach up, reach out, crouch down, lean to the side."

He did as she bade him, and she made a few adjustments, her prestidigitation swift.

"Handsome, Lord. Now, you go have dinner with the Captain, and I'll have dessert ready when you return. Oh, and don't forget your possessions."

His ruby, the belt buckle, the knife, and a coinpurse.

Captain Volans welcomed him like a long lost friend.

Dissembling his discomfort, he tried not to drool as the plate was slid in front of him.

"You look like you haven't eaten in days, Lord Knox."

Marl mumbled something around his food, his usual glutinous appetites amplified by hunger.

He almost didn't see her come in.

A second plate slid to a stop under his fork as the first one was whisked away, and Marl would have plunged right in if Captain Volans beside him hadn't stood.

"A seat for the two fine young ladies," he said.

Marl looked that direction.

A tall raven-haired woman with piercing blue eyes raked them across the assembled company, the shorter blond-haired understudy just behind her probing everyone with equal scrutiny, both of them brandishing quills. A Magux and her apprentice, he thought.

"My peace destroyed, their looks avoid," Marl murmured.

Their scrutiny managed to miss him.

"I'll forgo a seat for a favor, Captain Volans," the tall one said.

"Our custom is to conduct business when our appetites are sated, Lady Magux. Please, won't you join our fare?"

"My appetites are for a different fare, Captain. Among slaves purchased two days hence is a man miss-sold by brigands into slavery, his name Shribeth Canthus by your reckoning, but his real name Zibeth Anthus."

Captain Volans nodded and sat. "The defiant one whose head's all gray. Forgive me while I dine if you'll not join me. What of him?" The Captain settled next to Marl.

"I've come to claim him, and take him back home."

Marl saw on a chain around her neck, dangling between her breasts an object that looked to be a timepiece. He could not take his eyes from it, its draw as irresistible as the belt had been at the brigand camp.

A silence fell, he noted belatedly, the eyes all along the table now focused upon the Captain.

"You'll have to see the Lord Sage Betel Edgeword, I'm afraid," Captain Volans said. "I don't own him and have no say."

"But you know how much was paid?"

"I do, but what of it?"

"How much was it, please?"

"Two hundred shirecoin, but—"

The younger, smaller woman stepped around her proctor and laid a coinsack on the table. "Now, give me back my father!"

Volans stared at her, consternation clear on his face. "Forgive me, child, but I cannot. You'll have to go through channels."

The tall woman muttered something and they both disappeared, coinsack and all.

"Surround the slave quarters!" Volans ordered, "Secure the Anthus man! Don't let them abscond with him." And the room emptied of soldier, Captain Volans following his men outside.

Forgotten at table, Marl finished his meal, then grabbed the half-eaten plate of food beside him. That finished, he contemplated the one beside it, belching satedly.

"And who might you be?" Before him stood the raven-haired woman, the timepiece hanging between her breasts.

He didn't know which to admire more. "Marl Knox," he said, grinning and extending his hand. "Pleased."

She sat. "Aridisia Myric." And helped herself to a plate.

"So now that you and your companion have recovered her father, what now?"

"Disturbing times these be, the Sword, Scroll, Stone now missing." She looked him over carefully. "You're a long way from Stonevale, Gneiss."

"Knew I couldn't fool a Magux long," he drawled, liking her, watching her eat slowly, seeing how her eyes never left his face. "You've come a ways from Scrollhaven. Tragic, this thievery going on."

"And the accusations that follow."

He saw the hollow look in her eyes. "You've lost everything."

"So have you."

He didn't want to think about it, but he wondered if he might find ally in her. "Where to from here?"

"I seek a thing elusive. Tis not a scroll at all I quest for, not a material thing like a sword held sacred or a diamond revered. Tis my reputation I want back, a chimera that tantalizes just beyond my reach, around the next bend in the road, the faster I give chase the farther out of grasp it goes."

Marl smiled, caring not for his good name but only for the membership in the Vault of Stones that he'd desired since a young lad. And if in obtaining that, his name were smirched and besmirched, he cared not. For the wealth he once possessed and maybe a full plate, a warm bed, a dry roof, a clean cloth, yes, helpful to have those, but in the last three days of flight, Marl had lacked them all, and had not found his life wanting significantly.

The value of the ruby in his pocket lay not in the coin he might obtain in its exchange but the focus it gave to his magic. Adept he was determined to be, if poverty were required and grueling work in the pit of mine or logging tree.

Finding the diamond was the key. The restoration of Luxullian to the Vault of Stones was Marl's price of readmission. But he cared not what he had to do to achieve that, and would sully body, name, and soul, without regard for cost.

Marl looked at Aridisia. "I would propose an alliance, but I fear our methods ..."

"Would diverge and bifurcate," she said. "Yes, I sense in you the rapacious spirit," she gestured at the three empty plates before him, "and the gluttony of will."

"You who would bring back together father and daughter even while your fate teeters on the edge." Marl shook his head. "Tis a nobility I admire but scorn. Fare thee well, Aridisia, and beware the bandit, Skarn Arkose, who has the keen like you but the name like me."

"By which you mean none at all."

Marl nodded. "None whatsoever."

"Fare thee well, Marl," she said and stood.

He stood too, his belly bumping table.

Her eyes alighted on his buckle. Her glance danced up and down and settled on his face. "Too small a stone for the magic you wield. An odd bit of ostentation it would seem."

"Pleasing to the senses, as are your own ostentations," he rejoined, glancing down.

"Which of the three do you refer to, Sir?" She held her hands under her breasts.

"All three, of course. Well met, Lady Myric."

"Well met, Lord Gneiss." And she was gone.

He stood at the open door, the night brisk upon his face, and looked toward the guesthouse, where his other appetite awaited sating.

The servant would serve a poor substitute, he knew, glancing after the raven-haired Magux.

Chapter 5

The road north thick with traveler, Columba coughed the dust away and peered over the top of those in front. The road no narrower, the number had thickened suddenly.

"Benighted soldiers!" Spat one man beside him, big load of wool bending him half over. "I can't carry my load forever!" he called out over those in front.

"Fear?" asked the shepherd beside him. "The One Scroll stolen and you wonder what they fear? By the feathers of the Great Scribe's quill, are you daft?"

Since descending along the arrow-straight road, Columba had seen signs that not all was well in Scrollhaven.

The landscape had gone from thick, old growth deciduous forest clotted with moss and fern and the musk of decay, and had gradually thinned as the elevation lowered. Here on either side, the trees were thirty to forty feet apart, their canopy gapped here and there, and in between a low cut grass, almost manicured from herds of sheep grazed across the gently rolling hills.

The villages too had struck Columba odd, as they had started as sparse as forest had been thick, but when espied he'd seen no soul as though deserted. As the day wore on, more traveler joined him, most going his direction, and the villages larger as the forest grew sparse, he'd not thought it odd how busy the road. Then he'd noticed that the villages now held a dearth of occupant, their windows and doors standing empty-eyed, their pens emptied of livestock, their rooms emptied of possession.

The travelers who'd thickened the road appeared to bear a proliferation of item, some with cages of domestic fowl, wearing multiple layers despite balmy weather, carrying myriad household implements, wheeling barrows bulky with belongings, carrying packs stuffed with gewgaws.

Indeed I must be deaf, Columba thought, the signs of turmoil all around him. The soldiers ahead must fear incursion, as must all these peasants, he thought.

With Canodex now missing, the canon of the land on codex now absconded with by persons unknown to parts far afield, the preservation of law that it had promulgated was now repealed.

A thousand years was not too long for people to forget the tumult they'd endured before the advent of Sword, Scroll, and Stone, and though the Lord High Magux Ravenna Cithara might extend her reach with her innate power, she held far less sway without Canodex, the breadth of her reach diminutive in comparison.

Which all the villagers knew, hence their flocking deeper into Scrollhaven, seeking protection in numbers.

"But why slow us down with inspections?" the old man grumbled beside Columba.

"How about I shoulder your load for a time?" he asked.

"Mighty kind of you, stranger. Cedric, Cedric Ironsmith." They shook.

"Columba Riverford." He hoisted the load onto the shoulders, his broad strong frame easily balancing so unwieldy a load from long practice with sheaves of wheat and bales of straw. Sunup to sunset in the wheat fields of Swordshire had given him endurance to match the perseverance of mind.

"Bit of relief makes it all tolerable," Cedric said. "I was just in Haven four days ago when this all started."

"Blacksmith, eh? What need would a hearty man like yourself have of quillpushers?"

"Ah, a little distance with the wife. The scribe didn't even charge me, just told me to tell my wife how I feel and to keep her close. Of course, almost forgot what she told me, as just minutes after I left, the One Scroll Canodex disappeared, stolen by that very same scribe. Aridisia, she called herself, raven-black hair, as tall as many men, a wise face. Wise words too, worked better than any charm." Cedric told him the rumors.

Columba was intrigued. An amateur seeking membership, just as he'd been, and had dissembled her way into scrawling spells for supplicants, or so it was said. A trickster saboteur, so sly as to escape detection in a scriptorium full of Maguses, able to abscond with Canodex, the One Scroll.

"What brings a Shiree to these parts?" Cedric asked.

"We too suffered something similar."

"Tis what I'd heard. Scoundrels all, how dare they!"

Columba shook his head. "A thousand years of peace." He gestured at the fellow refugees on either side. "It's said a man seeking membership foiled the challenge put to upstarts and was being shown through the Hall of Swords itself when Genesyx the One Sword disappeared from its sheath."

"Wouldn't suppose making another would do much good. I've always wondered why just one. Aye, but there's the simpleton in me. Just forge a sword to take its place."

Columba saw they were nearing the blockade, nearly everyone let through. I wonder what they're looking for.

"Or substitute another, like the one at your side."

Columba grinned at the older man.

"That all your belongings?" The soldier asked his eyes traveling up the bundle strapped to Columba's back.

"Actually mine," Cedric said. "Kind enough to help me carry it."

Columba and Cedric endured a battery of questions.

"Sir Ironsmith, I'll have to ask you to carry your own from here. Sir Riverford, step this way, please."

Cedric threw him a glance of concern.

Columba shrugged and did as the soldier bade him, setting down the heavy pack.

"You need me to vouch for you? Haven't known you long but you're a kind soul and we need more of you, we do."

"Thank you, Cedric, and well met."

"Likewise, son." Cedric threw a dismayed glance at the soldier. "He comes to harm, you'll hear from me." And Cedric hefted his pack and headed north.

The Sergeant approached. "What's your name, Sir?"

"Columba Riverford."

"But the order of the Lady High Magux Cithara, I ask that you come with me. She's been expecting you."

* * *

"What now, Lady Myric?"

Aridisia looked at father and daughter, little expecting such formal address. She'd come to like Chiona, even to think of her as younger sister. The thought of parting saddened her.

In the confrontation with Captain Volans, their disappearing had prompted the Captain to order the newly-acquired slave secured, and as planned, the soldiers had led them right to him.

While China had escorted her father out of the compound under an invisibility spell, Aridisia had created a small diversion, then had gone to speak with the well-dressed traveler whose aversion spell had very nearly blinded her to him.

But like the vision blindspot, he had drawn attention by his absence, he place she could not see. A small counterspell had shown him to her, and a small conversation had exposed her to enough of his character that she felt sullied, as though his soul were sick. She sensed in him proclivities that would make her shudder, and she knew she'd said too much to him.

After first the soldiers and then the scoundrel Knox had leered at the timepiece between her breasts, as though the locket gave them leave to undress her bosom with their eyes, she'd resolved not to wear it so. She didn't mind the admiring glance but felt revolted by the visual fondling she'd received since dangling the timepiece on a chain between them.

"The women envy you as much as the men admire you," Chiona had said in a moment of candor.

Aridisia had laughed it off. But now she wore her tunic higher, buttoned to her collarbone, the timepiece buried under blouse. She looked at Zibeth Anthus, his arm around his daughter's shoulder, Chiona beaming up at him, and she opened her mouth to answer his question: "What now?"

Nothing came out.

Her thought had been after freeing Zibeth that she might approach Arcturyx, the Lord High Sage of Swordshire, and request his assistance, but now that they'd liberated one of his slaves, she was sure she'd at least face a hostile welcome or worse, perhaps even be shackled and chained and sent to take the place of that freed slave.

"Not *that* difficult a question, was it?" Chiona asked.

"No, it wasn't," Ari said, extending a hand, "but I'll miss you terribly, I will." And she pulled the younger, smaller woman to her. "I've always wanted a sister, and it's been a joy to have you near."

Aridisia watch them go, sad and yet uplifted.

She set out along the road that wound down toward the lush, temperate valleys below, the dawn just purpling the skies behind her.

She thought she'd be alone on the road but soon passed first one then two families caring their worldly possessions. She thought it odd, then passed a campsite, the family packing up as she came abreast.

"Going?" They replied to her question, "As close to the Lord High Sage Arcturyx as we can get. Without Genesyx, he can't protect us here."

And as the sun splashed across the valleys below, the road became packed and plumes of dust clogged the air. Aridisia considered the slope, wondering whether to set off cross country rather than follow the winding road, its switchbacks taking it gradually down the steep mountain side.

Ribbons of road visible below, she realized how many hundreds of people were now bound for the Hall of Swords, seeking shelter from the coming storm. Perhaps thousands, she thought, guessing that roads up and down the Swordshire border looked the same.

The robust woman beside her carried a pack piled high with picks. When asked, she said, "I could a' buried myself in my own mine, or built myself a door and nailed myself shut inside, but that's no life for the family. And when I get to the Hall of Swords? Stars above, I wish I knew, but me and the husband, we'll find something. How I'll feed the six of us, I just don't know."

"Ever have anything happen like this?" Ari Asked.

The woman looked her up and down.

Gauging where I'm from and why I might be asking, Aridisia thought, knowing she'd have done the same. What would I see if my eyes were hers?

A tall, slender, long-legged woman with a quill sprouting from a busty breast pocket, raven-haired to her waist though bound in braid, cheekbones high and gray eyes wide, their gaze on distant horizons and inner thoughts, clothing adequate and in good repair, without ostentation except a chain that fell inside the tightly-buttoned tunic.

"That scroll sticking from your pack might tell a tale or two," she said. "All I know is the legends of the time before the Sword, when kingdoms rose and fell with the sun and moon. If ye be Magux from Scrollhaven, then you've a story or two to tell yourself."

"Aridisia Myric, of Scrollhaven, yes, but Magux, I'm not. I practice toward that day but in the chaos to come, it may never be."

"Chaos indeed. Vela Tunnelbore, I am, member of the Miner's Guild. Chaos and pray to the stars in Heaven it never reaches the turpitude that once ravaged the land to all four corners.

"Ah I see by the rise in your eyebrows, you'd not expect such speech from the likes of me. But there do appearances deceive, and it's safer to dissemble the sharp wit when out among the hills. You'll be a learned one to decrypt my abstrusity, I can tell. Tis a comfort to speak with the breadth of language availed to me with the gift of tongue, were I not to brandish too refulgent."

Aridisia threw her head back and laughed at the sly look on the miner's face. "Only a miner might peer into the labyrinth of your speech."

Vela grinned at her companionably. "Well, if it's a story you're wanting, I've heard a few, the Miner's Guildhall rife with 'em."

* * *

Twas south from here in the southeast mountains where in places there be outcrops of aphanite spread throughout the range, but just upon the surface, as though thrown there in a child's tantrum, the mountains mostly granite.

In the mines of Baron Cetus Footsore, a great Lord long deceased, a story began to float, a rockman living in the mines, his countenance a terror to behold. At first the stories were discounted as it be known when gasses seep from seams of certain rock, a person mayhap see or hear thing which aren't there.

Soon the sightings coincided with cave-ins, and miners who nearly lost their lives began to swear the Rockman had just fled the scene before the tunnel collapse.

Rumor was mine deaths were up and Lord Baron Cetus tried to refute the fact, but his tables and numbers did little to disabuse the notion. Miners took their picks elsewhere and all but the older and hardier among them stayed. One of them named Cygno Surepick told Baron Cetus he'd find Rockman and break his hold on the Footsore mines.

Now Cygno Surepick couldn't be dissuaded even by his brother and sister miners, and he set himself a camp inside, picking the place as close to where the Rockman had been seen most often. For months he dwelt underground, joining the crew each day as they worked this seam or bore that tunnel and returning each eve all worn and tired. Wouldn't you know at the outset of his ensconce that the sightings stopped as though his vigil warned away the Rockman. Nearly a year had passed since Cygno Surepick took up sentinel, and his eyes grew white from lack of sun and skin grew ghostly, beard and hair bleached, his being wan and pale.

Begged by friends and family to give up the guard, Cygno demurred, seeing that production had returned to its prior levels, the miners losing their fear of Rockman. Twas odd and little noted that not a single ceiling collapsed nor wall gave in—which if you think deeply is quite the oddity, for the earth and rock are not as solid as one might conclude, nay it moves and flows as water in the sea, its currents much more slow but always in motion.

For nearly a year no cave-ins, and even a dolt might see Cygno was near a ghost himself.

Hearing these accounts, the Lord Cetus Footsore took upon himself a descent to the campsite of his loyal miner Cygno Surepick, mayhap to suade him to relinquish his vigil.

This was at the end of the shift, and the mine had cleared, the miners at home with husbands, wives, and families, and all we know is Cetus climbed down alone, the great lord fearing little, and soon after the mountain shook with a rumble that lasted hours.

When it had ceased, the peak was shrouded in dust and the aphanites and pocked its face had disappeared, and in the mine which had collapsed they found three hands protruding from rubble.

Two hands held an amulet—a circular metal locket, its edges nocked evenly, whose center it was seen turned with the sun, a single arrow on its face that pointed straight up at noon and straight down at midnight. In the center was embedded a small diamond whose—

Hush for now while I tell the tale.

—whose brilliance flashed at noon and midnight.

Those two hands protruding from rock—eerily, solid rock at that—both grasped this amulet, as though they struggled for its possession.

Stranger than that was the other hand, an old hand, presumed to be the other hand of the old miner Cygno Surepick, who was known to be an old hand at it. And in that hand there was a scroll, its parchment filled with the cramped irregular scrawl of someone old, infirm or poor of sight.

Alas no one knows where the scroll be, now, shush.

Upon the scroll was Cygno's tale, and what it said has come to me in bits and pieces, and there is no telling how much is true or fancied up or bellished.

Living for months below the earth, Cygno found hints of Rockman's passage, deduced where Rockman lived and confronted the strange creature. When told of Rockman's avocation, Cygno agreed to keep still and assist. Tis true the cave-ins had stopped and not a single miner died since Cygno had encamped inside, and this was due to Rockman's work, who when the mine was emptied at night would secretly shore up walls and ceilings nearing collapse.

When asked why, Rockman told of debt he owed for deeds anon of deep regret, and how in his nefarity, he'd brought upon his name and people a tale that only he deserved, hurled thousands of miles through the air and splashed against the side of peak, only to be awakened hundreds of years later by the vibrations coming through granite, that of miners boring through the mountain. A talisman of his former life all that was left to him, the amulet served to remind him every passing day of the terrible fate he'd brought upon an entire kingdom.

And when he felt the cave-ins from below and realized how often people died, Rockman set about trying to protect them, often holding up collapsing ceilings long enough for miners to escape. It meant little that he was often blamed for the cave-ins, for the condemnation he felt was deserved, his opprobrious acts of heretofore still requiring his penance.

When Cygno came to set up camp, Rockman protected him too, the older passages more prone to collapse as the mountain settled ever downward.

All that was left to be told on the scroll that Cygno had set down was what had happened when the Lord Baron Cetus Footsore entered the mine to retrieve Cygno Surepick.

A catharsis that remains untold.

* * *

In disgust, Marl turned south the first chance that he could. The traveler- and dust-choked road offered him neither anonymity nor comfort. And if I arrive at the Hall of Swords with all these hordes of other supplicants, it'll only prolong my quest for allies and avail me no relief from pursuit, Marl thought, if indeed Skarn Arkose still pursues me.

The evening at the soldier's table and the night at the servant's pleasure had reinvigorated him. Over his fancy tunic, he wore the new belt with its ruby-adorned buckle, holding up his fine silk breeches. It wasn't exactly traveling attire, and the clothes identified him as aristocracy, and instead of obtaining him an ease of passage along the traveler-choked road, his clothing appeared to earn him the opposite: multiple disparaging remarks, a few hostile invitations for him to remove his large buttocks from the path, and a shove from a luggage-laden man into a pyracantha bush.

Marking the man for later retribution, Marl carefully extracted himself from the thorns without damaging the fabric, and continued along without complaint, hostile looks from other pedestrians warning what side they'd take if he were to challenge the culprit.

Eager to put such pedestrian behavior behind him, he turned south at the first opportunity, the fork virtually empty of traveler in comparison. The fork he took quickly descended into a defile and then out again, the other branch now out of sight. Relieved to have the path to himself, Marl strode for awhile with renewed energy, the occasional oak breaking up the monotony of grass- and rock-strewn hill, to his left the mountains and to the right glimpses of valleys.

The problem with following the mountain southward, he soon discovered, was the rolling path, the downhills followed by uphills, each descent followed by ascent, each gully slightly different but eminently the same as the last, and every view of mountain east and valley west also of such sameness that he wondered whether he made any progress whatsoever.

After one particularly long ascent, he found a tree atop the crest and stopped in its shadow, the sun high enough that he realized he was sweating. The base of the tree sprouted an inviting couch convenient for resting, and so he settled himself, the valley below checker-boarded behind a slight haze.

"A finely dressed noble awaits us!" woke him up.

The swordpoint at his neck set him sweating again.

"By the stars, where be your guards? If ostentation is truly the measure of a man, you should have whole armies at your command!" Beyond the young warrior stood an old man, his back bent as though under great weight, the ends of his moustache nearly touching the ground.

What Marl had first thought warrior now looked to be a late adolescent.

"Stop poking, him, boy, and ask him his name," the old man croaked, as though he couldn't speak to Marl directly.

"What's your name, Noble?"

Marl pushed the swordpoint aside. "Marl Gneiss, Baron of Breccia, Stonevale, at your service, sir." He grinned. "And what fellow nobility have I the honor of making the acquaintance?"

"Huh?" the boy said.

The old man chuckled and shook his head. "Tis no noble you've come upon, just a guild woodwright too gnarled to wright the wood without page Pavo. Me, I'm Sagit Smoothgrain, and pleased."

Marl shook the outstretched hand, which had the texture and rigidity of a claw. "Tis a pity you no longer work the wood, as I sense your talent. Does the boy Pavo aspire to follow you or join the Hall of Swords?" He stood, easily outweighing both together.

"I can do both, Baron, you watch!" he said, sheathing the sword and standing at attention.

Marl and Sagit both laughed. "I'm bettin' you will," Sagit said. "Traveling this way, Lord Baron?" he asked Marl, gesturing south.

"That I am. Care for company? Not knowing the roads I had to send a contingent ahead, leaving me just one guard, and then he left his pack at the Betel Minesite, and so returned. Where do thou go?"

"Tis Itinerant work we do, Pavo and I. Enough work to keep a travel-boned man in employ, but not enough were my tree to grow roots, as they say. Let's not tarry in the shade nor let the dust settle into our joints. Ah, yes, much better for the arthritis to have these bones moving."

Marl found the old man's pace vigorous, and secretly he'd have fallen asleep on his feet, the scenery bored him so.

"Long way from home, you are, Lord," Sagit said, throwing a glance in his direction, his gaze mostly on the road.

"Aye, agreed I am. On the outskirts of Stonevale be my barony. The rumors of the theft disturb me greatly, as the Lord High Adept has not so great a reach now."

Bent over, Sagit had a view of things other couldn't see under the bulge of Marl's belly.

He could tell from the silence and the glances that he wanted to say something. "Have I stained my breaches or tunic?"

Sagit met his gaze. Then turned to look ahead. "No, no, it's the buckle, metal clearly of Swordshire origin, the small ruby in the center from Stonevale. In my travels, I've heard of similar that retains the magic of the sword from which it was made. Magic from Shire and Vale, and I'm willing to wage, somewhere aside a small scrap of parchment from the Haven."

Startled, Marl unbuckled it to look closely. He felt the nock at the lower edge and slid his nail along it.

Click! And the backing popped open, cradled inside a scrap of parchment, the scrawl so small he couldn't read it.

Quickly, Marl closed it and looked sharply at Sagit. "How did you know?"

"Sagacious Sagit, they call him," the boy said, mocking over his shoulder.

The old man chuckled. "Mind your business, boy!" he said with clear affection. "Well, Lord Baron, tis a twisty tale, if you care to hear?"

* * *

A tale to pass the trail then. The meander may be discursive, but what is a destination without the journey?

Ere anon in north Swordshire lived in woods so deep and dank that trees grew beards of moss and lichen, and tales abounded of seven-foot peoples hirsute as trees, ancestral man, vestiges of ages long past, clinging like the moss itself to trees about to tumble with age.

Among these ancients so thick with hair but one affectation delighted them—belts with buckles of elaborate design, the more intricate their fashioning, the more intrigued they were with its owner.

Why did they need such belts and nothing else?

To tell where their waistlines were, of course! How does a person mate if he or she doesn't know where the lower half starts?

Forgive me, I forgot that part. These ancient beings were harrier than any you've ever seen. Instead of the tuft atop the head and over the crotch, these creatures were hairy all over!

All over! Everywhere there might be skin there was hair. Oh such thin spots around the mouth and eyes but otherwise as thick as any animal you've seen. And hence the belts to help denote where the upper body ended and the lower began.

As it is with any group with human peccadilloes and foibles, influence was desired, status among the group a higher aim, the recognition of one's fellow being a deep-seated desire, so deep it sometimes goes awry.

As these buckles of elaborate design drew respect and praise among their peers, so these beings sought to embellish their buckles with ever more fanciful fashioning.

Ere but wouldn't there come along the one heterodox whose apostacy rejected these affectations. Spinos Musca was his name, and he sought and found a belt whose buckle was impudent for its simplicity, but as he deigned to secure such praise and respect from his own that he sought far and wide between four corners what might win over his peoples.

Now at the time their descendants known to you and me as human beings had formed some understanding of magical forces that rule the world but not so sophisticated to have yet derived the Sword, Scroll, and Stone of the Shire, Haven, and Vale, but even so the rudimentary magics were forming, and so Spinos sought among his human cousins those devices that might secure for him the praise he so deeply desired, and in his journeys all he dreamt was the day he returned to receive his glory.

Stumbled he did first upon the swordsmiths in the town where today resides the Hall of Swords, and he persuaded a smith to fashion a buckle from a sword imbued with magic. From there he traveled to the burgeoning colony that would one day become the Crypt of Scrolls and there he suaded a scribe to scrawl in letters small a spell to capture minds. From there he ambled to the village already renowned for its gift with jewels whose future was the Vault of Stones and begged a jeweler to spare him an ever so fine chip of ruby.

With these adornments affirmly fixed—er, firmly affixed to the buckle made of magical swordblade, Spinos Mosca practiced endlessly to strengthen his spell. The unity of Sword, Scroll, and Stone welded together the best of the burgeoning power of man, and in that tripartite assembly, the magic therein resided, each spell he cast building the sway he so desired, until the buckle seemed to glow of its own accord.

In his travels Spinos took the circuitous route and circumambulated south into jungle basins great, the canopy stretching farther than the eye could see, where if one spent too long a time the clothes would rot right off you, so damp and wet and humid was it.

And so to the fourth corner Spinos went, practicing his spells and infusing the buckle with his influence.

Here anon he reached the southernmost shore and at the point of the isthmus stood a smoking mountain belching fire, its sides slathered with the brimstone of many eruption.

Eh? No isthmus! The Halfmoon Sea was yet to be, now quit interrupting.

And there upon its desiccate slopes lived a peoples as vain as he, and its leader was a man so hard that he could not let this stranger pass without a reattribute, for his was a fire refusing to be outshone, yet here was a stranger, a hair-covered being seven feet tall who drew admiration from all, even what the leader desired for himself. As he was wont to remain the leader even after this admirable stranger had gone, he fashioned a spell so subtle that none noticed, and at a banquet in Spinos' honor, where the wine flowed thick, the food exquisite, and Spinos fell into a drunken slumber.

Satisfied at the efficacy of his buckle, Spinos bid goodbye to his sycophants, the leader sending him off with lauds grandiloquent.

Upon arrival back at home, the forest itself alight in his refulgence, and his people gathered to his brilliance like fireflies to flame, and in spite the modesty of his buckle, the smallest among those worn by his fellows, they sang his praises and elevated him to their highest esteems.

But in the spell insinuated into the buckle by the leader of the volcano people was a pernicious twist. As people are, they may say other than they think, and sometimes do other than they wish, and even as they admire so they envy, for what is behind us when we lionize another but the secret wish that we ourselves were the recipient of that praise? This spell as said perniciously emphasized the envy, enlarged the guilt, provoked them to more effusive accolades, until the yawning chasm between their words and their desires could no longer sustain their collegial unity nor their fragile psyches.

Not only did they turn on him, but tragically they turned on each other, and after the slaughter, so few remained that the race is said to have died out, their fate unknown, as the northern forest in its ancient wisdom keeps to itself its own counsel and does not divulge from its silent depths what befell the hirsute people.

* * *

Marl looked up at the boy's shout, but it was already too late. Spears bristled from either side of the path, and he didn't need to look to know their points glinted behind him.

The livery that the soldiers wore said it all: Dark green tunics with picks at left breast and shovels at the right kidney, and at right breast the monogram CF emblazoned in gold thread embroidered into cloth.

"Pray tell what in the stars would cause Lord Footsore to apprehend such minor travelers as us, Lord Captain?" Sagit Smoothgrain did declare, his voice booming with command, his bent-over aspect ludicrous in contrast.

A woman in thigh-high leggings stepped out from behind a tree. "Woodwright Smoothgrain in the flesh. Well, My Lord, perhaps it escaped your notice but the High Sage Arcturyx governs no more, his precious blade Genesyx stolen by the rogue Columba." She stepped to the fore and stopped in front of him, her sword loose in the scabbard. "All trespassers are suspect, Woodwright."

"Captain Lacerta, you speak as though his loss is your boon." Sagit shook his head. "All Swordshire loses with the purloined sword, as you well know, much as it might please your Lord the Baron Footsore that it's gone."

"Might or might not, as it pleases him, Woodwright. What's this lard you bring us hence? Clad in fine cloth but lard even so."

Marl's hackles rose and he felt tempted to squelch her tongue with a spurt of magic.

"A civil tongue might serve all better," Sagit said. "'Tis Lord Baron Gneiss, Lady Captain. Did you not see his advance guard come this way?"

"Advanced guard, Woodwright? There've been no travelers this direction."

"They, uh, must have stopped or detoured," Marl said, throwing a look at Sagit.

"Gneiss, you say?" Captain Lacerta glanced at a lieutenant. "Grussus," she said.

They pounced upon him before he knew it and hurled him to the ground, gagged him, tied him and rolled him on his back.

Her swordpoint at his throat, Lacerta grinned at him, her face so close the breath was hot on his cheek.

"What are you meaning by this, Captain?"

"Silence, Old Man. Well, Thief Extraordinaire, purloiner of Luxullian, you'll find no refuge here."

Chapter 6

High Magux Ravenna Cithara ran her gaze up and down the thief as a herder might a sheep at market, her left hand wrapped around a quill.

Not just any quill.

The feather was from eagle tail, the long arching withers as dark as the blanket of night until the end, where white as snow sprouted. Ribbons of gold lace wrapped the handle, for human touch, yes even hers, would spoil the quill itself, and if one looked closely at the stem, a glitter might be seen, the shimmer of a spell to keep the quill full of ink.

Her left hand had lain so long in perch around its quill that a palsy now kept it that way, the muscles and tendons calcified into position.

Underneath the quill on a pedestal at her side was the finest vellum scroll to be found, its upper half filled with writing, an attendant close by and ready to turn the scroll when more was needed.

Beside her throne sat a basket, in it scrolls of highest quality manufacture, smooth silky vellum wound round pins of deep rich mahogany.

Around her the lecterns and rostrums of other scribes were arranged, at each her ministers and sycophants, their quills poised above blank scroll, ready to spell her least command, prepared for any trickery this miscreant might attempt here at the Crypt of Scrolls, although their most valuable item had already been taken by the interloper Aridisia, the One Scroll gone, Canodex stolen.

The column of light where Canodex had hung stood suspended still and glistened as though rays of sun shone through the roof, but where Canodex for a thousand years had held sway over Scrollhaven now stood empty.

Also stood empty were many of the rostrums surrounding Ravenna, the Maguses who had previously stood at each sent to search far and wide for Canodex, with orders to kill if necessary to bring it back. Among those sent had been the magus Quercus, the dolt who'd allowed himself to be guiled by the imposter Aridisia.

Ravenna had thought deeply how to make another Canodex for if it were now destroyed or otherwise unrecoverable, Scrollhaven could not survive long without the codex that had governed them for a thousand years. Unlike Swordshire and Stonevale, Scrollhaven was a sophisticated society whose laws were set forth in minute detail, and Ravenna rarely decided matters without exhaustive consultation with the scrolls within the Crypt.

She'd devoted much of her time since the theft of Canodex to poring over the most ancient of scrolls to find some clue as to how the One Scroll had been made in the first place. And although she'd found texts almost as old, describing the wondrous changes brought about by Canodex, nowhere did she find a hint as to its manufacture.

The content of Canodex had been copied and recopied a hundred thousand times, of course, and its contents analyzed and expanded upon ad infinitum, for around and under Ravenna in the scriptorium were those texts, the three walls around them stacked to the ceiling with cubbies stuffed to bulging with scroll, and then of course the multi-tiered crypt beneath the scriptorium contained many thousands more, which despite her having a contingent of scribes to organize and catalogue, likely hid secrets long forgotten and tales long untold, for in the deepest darkest depths of the crypt, the scrolls were piled haphazardly, and even among the most learned of scribes circulated a rumor of a scroll bewitched, one whose contents would kill the person who attempted to decipher the ancient runes.

Even Ravenna had shied away.

In the daily life at the Crypt, she had longed to explore the deepest depths but of course the Haven required attention, and the scribes her guidance. And then Canodex was gone and the Haven in an uproar, with herders, woodwrights, farmers, coppersmiths, cobblers, tailors, blacksmiths, shopkeepers, lumberjacks, and all converging on the crypt as though Ravenna herself might protect them.

It had been five long unsettling days.

And then they'd intercepted this thief—no, not the one who'd filched Canodex itself—but the one who'd snatched the sacred Sword Genesyx from the Shire, this Columba Riverford.

For this audience, she'd asked him to set aside his weapons. His reluctance evident, Ravenna had extracted a compromise: He leave his weapons by the door on a rostrum set there for that purpose, in full view of both parties, while they conducted their business. "There is precedent," Ravenna had told him. "A hundred twenty years ago, the High Lord Sage Adelyx visited Scrollhaven and stood there in your shoes. His sword remained near the door. His magic Sword."

What she hadn't told Columba was that under the sway of Canodex, the great sword Genesyx was neutralized, for only Canodex ruled Scrollhaven, and the farther Genesyx was taken from the heart of Swordshire, the weaker it became, the same being true for the One Scroll Canodex and the One Stone Luxullian.

Her inspection of the thief complete, Ravenna frowned at him. "You dare enter lands where thieves are unwelcome, seeking to steal a scroll already taken perhaps? What foul intent brings you here?" From her position twenty feet from the railing that separated her rostrum from the supplicant, she could see in her periphery the sword and knife that lay near the door.

"I seek, Lady High Magux Cithara, only to clear my name." The man rose from his obeisance but not all the way, his upper body leaning slightly forward, the position of a supplicant. "It appears the smirch to name precedes me, and your opinion is already dirtied with the accusations leveled against me in Swordshire."

"You have yet to prove them otherwise, swordsman."

"I was accused not because I am guilty of theft, but guilty of ambition. It was Betel Edgeword who laid down accusation against me, and he because I foiled his guard to upstarts seeking entry into the Hall of Swords."

Her eyebrow rose quite of its own accord. Intrigued, she frowned. "You gained entrance?"

"Yes, Lady, I did."

"By the honest sweat of your own sword arm?"

"Indeed, Lady."

"The tale of theft neglects to mention this laudable feat. An inferior vehicle, word of mouth. Much better to set it forth on scroll, lest the tale be lost in the telling."

She saw his glance go to the scroll-stacked walls. "Indeed, Lady. Would you have my tale so inscribed?"

"No reason you could not. Have you practice with a quill? Or is your sword your only instrument?" She saw him blush and realized he might have been accosted for his instrument of love, not war. As handsome and strong and comely as he, Ravenna in her youth had taken many lovers like him, and were she younger would have considered him. "Ah yes, I forgot you have a knife too." She glanced toward the weapons near the door.

"I believe I could set out the tale with fair legibility."

Ravenna considered, her gaze on his face. The sword and knife in the periphery of her vision flickered. She turned her gaze there.

There they sat, placidly awaiting their master, the sword of standard make without embellishment, but the knife stood out, the ruby in its pommel giving off a rosy glow.

Why does a man professed to the sword carry a knife with a stone set in its pommel? she wondered. Surely he isn't able to use its magic. It would nullify his own unless he's found a way to circumvent the ancient proscriptions, she thought. This stranger introduces anomalies requiring deeper consideration and consult.

"Gymin," she barked.

A scribe detached himself from a rostrum, his aspect tall and spare. He stopped beside her and bent in supplication. "Yes, Lady Magux?"

She spoke quietly. "Arrange for a guest cottage, but choose the farthest from the crypt: there is more to the Shire thief than meets the eye. And when you personally return his weapons to him, look over them carefully—very carefully."

"Yes, Lady Magux." And just as calmly, he returned to his rostrum.

"Lord Adept, I would like to invite you to stay long enough to set down upon scroll the sequence of events that day."

"Forgive me, Lady, but I've not been awarded that title—"

"Out of spite, it appears."

"—but, yes, I would be happy to do as you request."

Ravenna glanced again at the sword and knife near the door. Again she saw a flicker of something else. "Gymin will escort you, Lord Adept."

She suffered through the protracted obeisance, smiling broadly as the Shiree took his leave.

Rising, she retreated into the Crypt, the scriptorium itself only a workspace. Behind and below it, the Crypt was a catacomb of corridor and stairwell, its every shelf and cubby packed with scroll. Prior Maguses had tried to bring order to a chaos of documents whose very contents invited multiple categorizing schemas but whose diversity resisted any single system.

Cithara stepped into the crypt, the uppermost floor the smallest. Like the four floors below it, the top floor held shelves fifteen feet high, their diamond-shaped slots bulging with scroll rods, some scrolls having two such rods indicating their frequency of use, but most were wound around just one.

The oil from the human hand the worst enemy of the scroll, it was blasphemy to handle a scroll except by the rod. Some scrolls showed the deleterious effects of such handling anyway, few scribes so careful they never touched the parchment, their edges flanking away, in some places eating into the script.

Under each diamond-shaped cubby was an inscription describing that cubby's contents. Her eyes flickered across the inscriptions, but she knew where to look already.

She headed to the stairs, and the open staircase allowed her to see many of the inscriptions here, and she knew what she sought was not here on the second level. Twice as large as the upper level, the second through fifth levels reached under the scriptorium itself which took up about half the above-ground portion of the Crypt.

She dropped to the third level, feeling now the spells that kept at bay the water that always sought to seep into the underground labyrinth, the water as deadly to a scroll as the oil from a human touch.

When she reached the fourth, she slowed her eyes, taking in more of the inscriptions, the scroll here tending to be older, more arcane, more abstruse. Some scrolls were held closed by protective spells to keep their contents shielded from the novice, others from the delicate at heart, their content judged horrific.

Some on this level hinted at the treasure waiting on the fifth and deepest level, the prohibitions wrapping some such scrolls so powerful that apprentices and Maguses with fewer than twenty years' experience were prohibited from descending to that innermost crypt.

Cithara located a codex in the very back row of shelves in the uppermost cubby to the very rear of the fourth floor. Inscribed under the cubby was the label "Obscuritus Catagoricum."

Holding up the scroll by its rod, she waved her quill hand at it, and the scroll unrolled. In the dim light cast by her glowspell, Ravenna Cithara perused a text that had not seen the light of eye in hundreds of years.

* * *

For in times of trial, when Canodex is insufficient to provide guidance, or its annotated concordances shed no light on the matter at hand, there does lie in deepest sleep a scroll passed down from so ancient a time that the script is a scrawl resistive to decipherment, for under the writing lies the trap ready to enslave the mind and trap the soul forever in the intricacies of its tale.

For it does tell of a time of ill when magics were blended and cataclysms struck, the natural balances thrown askew when powers gathered in interactive synthesis whose exponential multipliers overwhelmed even the most masterful of sorcerers.

The Sword, Scroll, and Stone of modern time serve to channel the magics to their elemental streams and obviates the inadvertent synthesis that wreaked such havoc in ages of distant past.

Let this codex of ancient scrolls be seen by eyes wise to their own cupidity, for the texts described here do play in pernicious way upon the flaws and foibles of human character, and only they who have mastered themselves will find they can master the content of these ancient scrolls.

Forewarned, forearmed, tis said, but ye who venture into these murky depths do so not only at risk to self but also to humanity itself, for the most recent attempt to master this content did result in widespread destruction and chaos.

We speak still of the Four Corners but of those four only three remain. The fourth has now reduced to a pinprick in the crust of Earth, a pinprick reaching down to mantle, in a place now known only as Warlock's Mount, surrounded by the Halfmoon Sea.

Whence had come the tragedy that sank a land as lush as any? From these scrolls, my learned friend.

From these scrolls.

* * *

Ravenna snapped back into the present, waving her quill in the direction of the parchment. The scroll rewound itself.

She looked around to insure she'd gone unseen then carefully reinserted the scroll into its cubby, insuring that it lay not on top but under scrolls of lesser import.

Her destination fixed in her mind, Ravenna climbed down the ladder and made her way to the fifth and deepest floor of the Crypt.

Here, cobwebs festooned many of the cubbies, the spiders carefully trained to intercept any intruders but the Maguses, for as many spells as might protect a scroll, little would prevent its theft.

Unfortunately, we had no cipher to protect Canodex, she thought wryly, running her eyes across inscriptions. The scroll she hunted was a palimpsest of arcane esoterica even to the initiate, abstruse to the sagacious. Further, it evaded the human eye as a jackrabbit might evade a hawk. Its evasion did of course reveal to her exactly where it lay, the place in her vision she could not see, the absence giving away its presence.

Three quarters of the way to the rear wall, she stopped and lifted her left hand, her eyes upon the floor.

Above her, a web-shellacked cubby strained against its skein of webbing. A bundle of scrolls extracted itself, then one by one the scrolls returned to their places, all the while Ravenna's eyes upon the floor. Were she to look at it, it would disappear. Scroll by scroll replaced itself until the one remained. The thick layer of web reattached itself, and the remaining scroll descended slowly into her outstretched hand.

She brought her right hand up to grasp the other end of the pin, the wood light and seasoned by the centuries.

Bringing her hands slowly down, she lowered the scroll into the range of her vision. Now a snake, it reared to bite. Suddenly a spider, it snapped its pincers. Writhing into a scorpion, it lashed with tail. Back to scroll, it remained in her hands.

These artifices meant to trick her into dropping it, she smiled. What other surprises have you got for me? Ravenna wondered. Holding it horizontal before her, she nodded at it and turned her head. The scroll unrolled and pitched a poison at her.

The stench of burning hair filled the air.

"Sly little scroll," she said, convinced that a less suspicious scribe would now be blinded. She neutralized the acid and deigned to glance at the parchment now revealed.

Matrices of time twisted across the page, the dance of ink mesmerizing.

She quickly averted her gaze, but found she had to wrench it away, the patterns at a glance already grabbing her mind. "Obscuration dismiss, so we're not remiss."

A peek at parchment showed harmless scrawl. The letters glittered, the ink a gold flake, the vellum looking soft even now, easily twelve or thirteen hundred years after its authorship, the scroll long predating the crypt that housed it. The finest materials and inks, she knew.

As she read a line, the ink faded from the page.

Startled, she stopped. Only one reading each time opened, she thought. Preparing herself, Ravenna took a deep breath and plunged into the apocryphal text.

* * *

Arcturyx Longblade frowned at the woman in front of him. The Hall of Swords seemed so empty recently, he mused, so devoid of its usual evanescence.

Once so vibrant with competition, the innuendos fueled by pretty rivalries, the intrigues and machinations powered by shifting alliances, the Hall of Swords now lay limp and deflated, a pensive sense of doom weighing on everyone, as though apocalypse approached like a hurricane out of nowhere, a major earthquake without a pretemblor, an inferno without that warning wisp of smoke.

He'd never felt so helpless in his life.

He, the Lord High Sage, Arcturyx, Ruler of Swordshire for twenty years, wielder of the One Sword Genesyx, his magic able to reach halfway to the southern sea and all the way to the eastern mountains, more than a million souls under his care and guidance, and he felt powerless.

Emasculated! he thought disgusted. Eviscerated! Edentulous! Excoriated! Lobotomized! Eunuchificated!

Fuming and frustrated, he looked toward the supplicant, the foreign woman with a quill strapped to her right hand.

Her raven hair cascaded to her waist. Her thick gossamer robes of robin's egg blue could not obscure the full proud breast. She stood taller than most women, and in her gaze Arcturyx saw how she looked not down but through, as though she followed not the outer workings of the face but the inner workings of the mind.

An emissary of the High Magux Ravenna Cithara? he wondered. Surly she knows her magic is weakened here? For although Genesyx had been stolen and Swordshire bereft of its founding talisman, the Hall of Swords remained the locus of blade-edge magic, the ancients who'd laid down the quadpole structure having coalesced and bound each stream to its respective place, and thereby taming for mankind's betterment an energy that had nearly caused a cataclysmic destruction of the entire planet.

But a raven-haired parvenu stole the One Scroll Canodex, he reminded himself, a village provincial who'd somehow insinuated herself into the Crypt of Scrolls and had absconded with the One Scroll from under the very quills of thirty-odd scribes, including the High Magux herself.

Formidable was his first thought.

But isn't that what the upstart Columba did to us? Arcturyx thought, suddenly furious.

"What brazen gall to come here, witch! Put her to death this instant!"

Guards converged but she was gone.

"Lord, surely that's a rash decision?" said a gentle female voice in his ear.

For a moment, he thought it was Pyxis, third in command after Betel, the two stalwart supporters who'd always backed Arcturyx.

He turned to find the raven-haired woman, her hand to her breast.

"How dare you practice your chicanery under these eaves!"

"The fact that I can should give you pause. Rescind your order, I beg your leave." And the woman knelt, her head with neck exposed now a swift sword stroke away.

Rage trembling through him, his palm itching for a haft, Arcturyx realized what she was saying. And that he was vulnerable were she to wish him harm. "Belay that order," he said, his guards within feet, their blades glinting.

The woman waited, her head bent, her milk-white neck visible between raven-black strands.

Arcturyx breathed a sigh. "Forgive me my precipitate decision. Shall we try this over? Tis a trying time for all."

"Indeed, Lord, and thank you."

He watched the woman return to the place she'd vanished from, wondering how she'd done that. If perchance she'd used a scroll-spell, then indeed her having conjured it under this very roof, inside the Hall of Swords, most certainly caused him deep concern.

"Tis a tragic day a Magux might scrawl a spell in the heart of Swordshire," Arcturyx said. "A thousand years is too short a time for chaos to fade from the memory of humanity. I pray to the stars we do not see a return to such upheaval. Welcome, Lady Magux."

"Thank you, Lord, but Magux I'm not. Were fate but different, it might be so, but my induction into the Crypt of Scrolls was forestalled by the disappearance of Canodex on the very day I might have joined them. Now I stand accused of its theft, proof of which will not be found. My name is Aridisia Myric, but I am neither Magux nor Lady."

"Well met, Aridisia." Arcturyx said. "And well spoken, as though you were practiced in the scripted arts. I might inquire about your interest in the blade-wielding ones. Your manner bespeaks aplomb and grace, your tongue an erudition beyond the humble beginnings attributed to you. Forgive me my earlier outburst. I fear I might have momentarily succumbed to the despair that besets all of our peoples. You are one of thousands of supplicants, whom you no doubt saw in profusion converging on these humble accommodations."

"I am, Lord, forgive me for importuning upon you at this inopportune time, for no accommodation."

"Tis forgiven, quill-miss, as I may beg your forgiveness for my brevity. A great many more importunists await my attention."

"Certainly, Lord. I'll be brief. I seek, Lord High Sage, to clear my name."

"Such a simple task, that seems. Just return the Canodex you stole."

"Would that I could, Lord Sage, had I stolen it. I'll not insult your sagacity by enumerating the barriers that must be overcome. Instead I appeal to the larger circumstance that we both face."

"The object of our reverence bereft from us?"

"Indeed, Lord Sage. When juxtaposed with events in Stonevale, it's clear to me the charge of theft may clearly be laid at another's door, though others may hesitate to defenestrate. None of which exonerates me completely, as no proof exists that I am not complicit. Therefore I seek to expiate any hint of subterfuge, real or imagined on my part, a goal it seems I may achieve if I were to rectify the disequilibration that now bedevils our respective realms."

"How, quill-miss, may I assist?"

"Sanction, Lord."

"Eh? You want my blessing?"

"Certainly, Lord. What better way to restore the dominion of Genesyx than to endorse its recovery alongside that of Canodex and Luxullian? You affiliate with your colleagues in Scrollhaven and Stonevale and engage their resources in your quest to reestablish the sovereignty of the talismans."

Arcturyx looked upon the village girl, a prodigy beyond her ken in wisdom and sophistry, and he held up his hand. He lifted his gaze to the gilded ceiling, the sparkle of precious metals inlaid there in a pattern reminiscent of the nighttime sky.

The walls to either side bowed out to give the supplicant a foreshortened view of the exalted one, making him seem larger than life, the optic deception often mistaken for a prestidigitation trick, their sconces displaying the finest armor and arms of High Sages past, a relief portrait of each above the sconce chiseled from an oval slab of marble, the name inscribed below each bust.

This was the Hall of Swords, which as Arcturyx knew had not been trespassed upon or even sighted by the accused miscreant whose supposed theft of Genesyx had thrown the realm into chaos.

For Arcturyx knew, in speaking with this provincial prodigy, that indeed the theft of not one but three objects of reverence was the work of greater evil than this Aridisia before him or Columba Riverford of Sage ambition, or Marl Gneiss of Adept cupidity, were capable of.

He brought his gaze down to her, wondering that he had not seen in the events of the past five days that which she had brought to his attention. "Your perspicacity merits reward, quill-miss. Alas I may bestow no more than sanction and regret I am not able to provide direction nor protection, as my realm lies beleaguered, in need of its every modest resource. Of these matters the High Magux knows more for the Crypt of Scrolls remains the reliquary of our collective wisdom, documented upon scrolls arcane the body of knowledge that describes the creation of Sword, Scroll, and Stone, and the establishment of Shire, Haven, and, Vale.

"Though Swordshire embodies the strength unparallel of military might, and Stonevale the wealth unmatched of economic accumulation, within the Crypt of Scrolls lies the knowledge unexceeded of erudite enlightenment, and there you shall find the guidance to pursue the scurrilous reprobate who seeks to destroy our lives.

"Therefore, go forth, Aridisia Myric, and with my blessing find this recalcitrant profligate, and restore to us all that which is dear to us. Join together, if you can, with those who stand unjustly accused of crimes they appear to be innocent of, for in you three I sense the resourcefulness to set aright all that has gone awry."

Arcturyx watched her go, her head high and her stride purposeful, and he knew she would accomplish what she'd set out to do, for she was an inexorable being, an elemental force of its own reckoning, mayhap even driven by her very own magic. Independent of the three elementals which buttressed Sword, Scroll, and Stone, respectively.

But Arcturyx knew she would succeed but too late to preserve Swordshire, for even as they spoke, internecine forces gathered within the realm, age-old rivalries long suppressed under the dominion of Genesyx, freed now of their thousand-year restraint, and likely to tear the realm asunder long before Aridisia recovered the One Sword, the One Scroll, the One Stone.

* * *

From the battlement, Baron Caelum Footsore gazed down upon the contingent and smiled. A runner had notified him of their approach and their captive: Marl Gneiss, the accused thief of Luxullian, the One Stone.

Baron Footsore, forty-sixth of his august lineage, cared not one whit whether the fat expatriated Baron from Stonevale had actually purloined the diamond.

All he needed was the impression that he had.

In the mountain behind the estate, honeycombed with mines, thousands of miles of empty tunnel relieved of its ore since the barony's founding nearly fifteen hundred years ago, an army assembled, a formidable host of miner-warrior, the work-hardened people of his domains hungry for better lives, desperate for their day in the sun, inflamed by their Baron's vision of a pampered life at the seat of power.

And all awaiting the one advantage, that slight psychological edge, necessary to imbue their swords with confidence and inflict upon their opponents that one small despair, that this formidable host was backed by the One Stone Luxullian itself, wielded by its thief, the unlanded Baron Marl Gneiss.

No, Caelum thought, he doesn't need to have stolen it in actuality, but those who rule at the Hall of Swords must think so.

Caelum turned to a subordinate. "Have them bathed and quartered in the guest suite, all three of them. And ask them respectfully if they will deign to join the Baron for supper."

He glanced down again as the contingent with its one fat prisoner and two itinerant woodwrights passed through the portcullis beneath him, amused at the semi-imperial reception that they surely were not expecting to receive.

Caelum headed to the north tower, as always to scan the landscape from his redoubt, before retiring to his own chambers and preparing to receive his guests at supper.

Pyxis stood there, scowling balefully, her burnished hair catching the setting sun, scintillating with a greater glow than the cold-streaked sky above.

She looks ravishing and she knows it, Caelum thought, the tug at his loins reminding him of their passionate exploits the night before, theirs a torrid if contentious love, she at least as ambitious as he.

"What the stars are you thinking, Cael? The stain of this thief's reputation will only sully yours. What plot thickens in that turgid mind of yours?"

He chuckled and stepped up close enough to feel the heat of her breath against his cheek. "What possible thought other than to honor him who has wounded our enemy so mortally? The enemy of our enemy is surely our friend, is it not so?"

Her fiery eyes flashed at him and she grabbed below his belt.

"Not now, love, for I've guests to receive. Will you be joining us, Lady Sage Pyxis of Auld?"

She released him and smiled slyly. "Wouldn't that but serve to enhance your stature in this thief's eyes? Nay, Lord Baron

Footsore, you'll get no such sanction from me, for surely you'll fuel your surreptitious fires."

"Surreptitious? I? Never have I dissembled my intent to you. Alas I shall remonstrate no further, though you suspect unjustly, as I know tis not the time for Auld to join with Footsore, though that rumor's rampant now." He grinned and stepped to the crenelation to look out over his domains, his focus always to the west of north whence power that had heretofore contained his ambitions had so recently come.

"The day you stop plotting the downfall of Arcturyx is the day that Auld will join with Footsore."

He glanced over his shoulder at her. On many previous a time, such umbrage provoked a tirade, but not this time. For he had at this moment within his reach the tools and opportunity to do what he stridently denied was ever his intent: conquer the Hall of Swords by force and assume control of Swordshire.

"Tis better that you not attend, Lady Pyxis. If not at sup, perhaps for a midnight bite?" He threw a grin at her.

"Forgive me, Lord, if I decline, for Shire business I must attend. By your leave, Lord, fare thee well, and keep thy hands off the wenches." She grinned as wide as he and brushed his cheek with a kiss, departing in a swish of robes, the sword at her side catching a glint of the setting sun.

She importunes upon me marriages with condition, Caelum thought, her devotion to the Shire far more deep than her love for him. She'll always be her own woman, and though she may take a man to mount, never will she give away her soul.

Caelum turned his gaze northwest, the burning deep in his gut far exceeding that in his loins. I'll always be my own man, he thought in rue contrast, though I may take a woman to mount, never will I give away my soul.

And his heart of hearts he knew that the House of Auld would never join the Barony of Footsore, despite the rampant rumor.

The knowledge brought no sadness, for the Baron would not give himself to emotion without use.

The land below was rich with crop, checkered into the distance, though the mines behind him were the pillar of his power.

His castle stood at the base of the mountains, their rise from the valley floor abrupt, the rearward side of the castle proper abutting the precipitous rise of landscape.

He turned to look at the southeast mountains, where legend told of strange events, his ancestor of ancient times buried in a mine collapse. Much as Caelum gloried in its telling, he gave it little mind, its characters fanciful, especially to him, his ambitions thwarted by magics that he scorned, which he wished berid from the realm, needing only the force of arms to enforce the peace and administer the domains.

Caelum had seen the parlor tricks and impressive prestidigitation by charlatans of facile tongue, and even Pyxis execute a spell or two, but nothing in his experience had convinced him that something more was at work than sleight of hand fit to sway the slight of mind.

His bath and dress a time to reflect, Baron Footsore paid it little mind, the fine silks and light perfumes of little note except to enhance the impression he made, the trapping of royalty doing little to trap his mind.

He presented himself to his dining hall at the appointed hour, his robes precise, his coif debonair. "Lord Baron Gneiss," he said, stepping to the obese man crisply, dissimulating his disgust of girth. "Forgive the rough handling my guards subjected you to, my apologies for the indignity. The commander has been punished."

The commander had done just as ordered and might still be punished if the need to impress the outlander arose.

"Lord Baron Footsore, so kind of you to ask me to share your repast. I do so admire an efficient force. The money-grubbing mercenary rabble in Stonevale who purport themselves as soldiers are as like to flock to the highest bidder as to stab their kin for shekel."

"Tis an art," Caelum retorted, "to command loyalty with minimum expense. A draught of brew or goblet of wine, fellow Baron?"

The big man demurred. "But I demure not at beer or wine, Lord, but only at the honorific."

"So sad, those events of distant lands, a mistake I'm sure to be rectified soon, I would think. Unless of course … " Caelum threw one eye wide, the brow thrust up under his short shorn bangs.

"Unless what, Lord?"

Well if he won't think it himself, perhaps he can be led. Let us see how tractable he is, Caelum thought. "Well, Lord Gneiss, a man of your esteem would naturally deny any such involvement in that nefarious a deed, of course. But if by chance it became known by other means … " He let the silence stretch.

"If what became known?"

"Its location, of course, but there I go, saying the obvious. Forgive me, Lord. An enemy who thought they faced Luxullian in battle is one on the verge of a rout, now, isn't it?"

"Most would quail and soil themselves, indeed." The brows drew together. "But what army would think that?"

"Yon lies the Hall of Swords, considered the most impenetrable and unassailable redoubt besides the Vault of Stones itself. Yet you delved the depths of the latter with but the crook of a pinky."

"I swear I didn't—"

"It's enough for others to think you did, eh, Lord Baron? Listen, my armies and your reputation—they'll surrender the Hall at *hearing* of our approach! What do you say, Marl, my friend?"

"Well—"

And now for the coup de grace, Caelum thought, hoping to seal the deal. "And just think, a swift strike to the northeast while those wheedling scribes lay vulnerable without their precious Canodex! And thence to the Vault to lay claim to the largest hoard of wealth these lands has ever known. All of it, Lord Gneiss, for the two of us!"

Caelum watched the thoughts work themselves through the fat Baron's brain, the beads of sweat glistening from the brow, the sightless stare seeing their jointly-led hordes smashing through all resistance, obliterating the enemy in their tracks.

"And for the first time," Caelum whispered, "All four corners under one rule!"

A slow grin spread across the Baron Gneiss' face.

A thought seized Baron Footsore. "But first a little spelunk into the mines of the Footsore Barony!" Now why did I say that?! Caelum wondered, intending to say nothing remotely similar. "A jaunt deep underground to show you the resources available to the estate." Caelum Footsore was furious! He'd neither wanted to say that, nor had he any wish to take the Baron Gneiss anywhere except to war.

Caelum felt his brow sprout beads of sweat. I retract that, he tried to say. "Only for a few hours, Lord Baron," he said instead, his voice nonchalant, his terrified helplessness rising like a methane fog through the semiconscious parts of his mind.

I will say I'm jesting! he told himself, his own voice in his mind screaming the words. "Not a spelunker, Lord Gneiss? Not to worry—we'll have miners with decades of experience with us." What am I saying! Caelum wondered, the pressure building at his temple, the sweat dripping from his chin.

"We leave at first light, Lord Gneiss. A servant will wake you in good time, and we'll eat a hearty breakfast before we leave, I assure you. Tis well to rest up now, and eschew any nighttime companionship that you might be offered, as you'll need your strength on the morrow."

Caelum Footsore took his leave, a horrific pressure pushing him to order preparations for a morning soiree into the heart of the honeycombed mountain, and all the while his body made those arrangements, his mind screamed in helpless protest that he was going to do no such thing.

A scream that only he heard in his head.

Chapter 7

Columba stared at the High Magux Ravenna Cithara in alarm. "I have to do what?" Immediately, he apologized for not addressing her properly.

The cottage where he'd stayed the night was located in the rear of the compound containing the Crypt of Scrolls, the design and decor intended to delight the visiting scholar, a rostrum for writing complete with quills, parchment, and ink, looking out the window onto a picturesque garden of wildflower.

The morning light pouring through the skylight lit the shelves of books with a pleasant glow, and a soft breeze blew occasional puffs through the half-open window, the mourning doves and whippoorwills calling in orchestral counterpoint, as though conversing amiably.

He'd spent yesterday and yestereven chronicling his version of events, and although his narration now on parchment wasn't the artful tone he'd hoped it'd be, it laid out events sufficiently.

He'd had time this dawn to re-read and eat, attend to his toilet and reflect a moment before his host had approached, sweeping up the gravel path like a specter loose from its nighttime haunts.

He'd immediately seen her haunted gaze, the black-ringed eyes pronouncing her lack of sleep, the clothes she wore the same as yestereven, her shoulders slumped with the weight of her geis.

And then she'd said, "You must find your fellow thieves. Lord Sage."

Columba shook his head at her when she repeated the uncommon request. He could barely believe he'd heard a right.

"Hear me, Lord, before you judge."

* * *

In the beginning, before the Sword, Scroll, and Stone, strewn across the four corners were kingdoms large and small, the geography and our cupidity preventing us from joining together and using the magix cooperatively.

Instead we competed, wielding against each other spells we might have used alongside another's. The separations of time and distance helped to divide, but what pitted you against me, barony against fief, province against kingdom, was the singular perception that what we have is never enough.

And in our pursuits of appetites, what once fulfilled us would quickly leave us unsated, and always beyond the hedge, we saw that brothers and sisters of our very own had something more than we ourselves, and though we sought not to covet more, our peccadilloes turned to foibles and our faults to downfalls, and so of course do kingdoms rise, as we cannot resist the agglomeration of power. If only we stopped ourselves at our neighbors' hedges. Alas we do not, and in our hungers, we are voracious, forever seeking more more more.

And thus did those kingdoms rise and fall, grow and shrink, all the while leaving in their wake a populace in fear of the next commander to conquer them or the next wizard to beguile them, never knowing what the next month or season or year might bring.

Into this unstable brew, there arose a new class of magician, one who mastered not just one of the elementals, but they who tamed the natural forces of two magics. And in these Mages, we saw not just greater power but a loss of scruple in how they used it, as though to cross the division between elements also wore through the moral bindings that anchored their reverence for the world around us and all the creatures who were in it.

What they gained in greater power, they lost in compunction.

And in conquering they laid waste to cities, forests, mountains, and isthmuses. Not enough to lay claim to these features anymore.

Among wiser souls it was seen where this might go, and so the scrolls tell of a time that magic from all three elementals was brought together into a single talisman, much like that knife at your waist, the ruby in the pommel wherein even the Goddess of the Water might be summoned to its charms, her beauty unmasked only by its wielder, a talisman forged by a sorcerer schooled deeply in the tripartite, who took a blade, a scroll, a stone, deep into the fires of Warlock's Mount and in the hottest fires on Earth did forge together all three streams into one.

The shock of its creation killed him of course, and left behind a crater that scarred our beautiful earth forever, and if a person goes due south, he'll come upon the Halfmoon Sea, a bay so perfectly formed that one thinks nature could not herself have made this, and right they are, for there lies the crater, that great gorge in the earth, laid waste by the forging of a talisman to satisfy the lustful designs of unfettered power.

So our ancestors sought once and for all to fetter the elements, to separate them into Earth, Air, Fire, and Water, to channel their magics through eidolons of purity, and to anchor each to the three remaining of the once-four corners of the earth.

Yes, one corner destroyed in the horrific blast that gave birth to a singular talisman, sending aloft such thick gouts of smoke that the sun was blotted from the skies for years, and crops withered from lack of light, and ash settled upon everything like a fine coating of snow and the air was fouled, caused respiratory distress and disease, and storms and winds swept the lands at unseasonable times, rivers grew clotted with thick gray mud and overflowed their banks, and the rim of the crater—of course, a rim which became a mountain range—the scorched earth was glassy and hard, melted into place by the great heat it had endured, a sere forbidding landscape that was, where nothing grew, and the only relief to the weary eye was the water's edge, and huge amounts of water too, so much it's said that coastlines changed all around the world.

Further to limit these talismans, their creators laid down circumscribed areas they might extend to, the boundaries today of Swordshire, Scrollhaven, Stonevale, for they knew that human ambition would batter down any other containment, and while these talismans of Sword, Scroll, and Stone have not rid the human heart of its cupidity, they certainly have reduced the breadth and expanse of its dominion. For built into each is the credo that the one elemental funneled into that talisman is the one true power and that all else is to spurned and derided.

The ancients brought us a thousand years' peace.

* * *

"Which has now come to an end," Columba said, watching the old crone carefully. Her inward gaze told him she was a great distance away. He considered her admonition that he must find his fellow "thieves." What could three outcasts do to restore to their rightful places, the Sword, Scroll, and Stone that clearly had been absconded by a single person or entity, gathering unto themselves the sacred powers allocated long ago between three lands for the purpose of keeping them separate.

"Nay, say that not," Ravenna admonished. "'Tis not for us to predict the future! Yes, we're challenged by the theft of our talismans but we don't yet know its result. And we certainly shall not yield to despair. Questions you have, I'm sure, among them certainly: What leads me to believe?

"You were there when Genesyx was stolen, and someone chose your arrival to facilitate their thievery. Accused you stand of that very act. The same happened here and yet had I not been so despairing at the disappearance of Canodex, I'd have realized the same of Aridisia, an admirable soul whose grace and aplomb will serve her well. Though I've little knowledge of this Baron Gneiss, I suspect something similar occurred in Stonevale.

"Each of you for similar reasons has more motivation than anyone to recover the talismans. Your reputations depend on it. You may as well become the wastrels you stand accused of being should you fail to secure their return.

"Although I suspect there's more at work here, you three have the talents needed to restore the balance. Sword, Scroll, and Stone is more than just the order by which we live. They are the strength, wisdom, and wealth that will guide our race into its future.

"Now, I have brought you all the supplies you'll need and a guide to take you toward Stonevale. Find the trail of your two colleagues and bring together your inestimable talents." She gestured out the window.

On the stone path stood a burly man with an axe strapped to his back, beside him two packs bulging with accoutrements.

Columba followed her from the cottage.

"Columba Riverford, Samshad Woodwright," Ravenna said.

The two men shook, Woodwright easily half a hand taller.

"Just call me Shad, Lord Sage," Samshad said.

"And just call me Columba, or Collum for short, and leave aside the 'Lord', for lord I'm not, its reasons unfortunate. Now, you, Sir Sam, are a fine specimen and grateful I am to have you with me. I can tell by the calluses at hand that you work the wood."

"That I do," Sam said, "and by that token, you're no softpaw, either. A fast blade and strong arm will be a comfort where we're going."

Columba could tell they'd get along.

"Now, as for other fortifications," Ravenna said, turning Columba toward her.

He felt the draw of her gaze and knew.

She unrolled a small scroll and scrawled something brief. "This should help." The pin as slim as his pinky and no longer than the same, the scroll fit neatly into his breast pocket. "Use this only in extreme distress."

Columba nodded. "You have shown me kindness beyond compare, Lady High Magus Cithara. I am grateful for all eternity." He bowed to her.

"Pray bring back to us our Sword, Scroll, and Stone that we each may have that eternity available, Lord Sage."

Columba rose from his obeisance. "That I shall, Lady, that I shall."

* * *

Aridisia reached the top of the trail where the Wizened Forest began.

She stopped and surveyed the trail downward, quickly losing it in the thick undergrowth ahead.

The change in terrain was palpable, the cold draughts one might feel ushering from the mouth of a deep dank cave brushing her cheeks like the wings of bats, and yet at her back, the pleasantly mild breezes of Swordshire pulled playfully at her hair.

"A bit intimidating, isn't it?" Berenice Longblade said.

Aridisia glanced back over her shoulder. She and her new companion had traveled all day northeast from central Swordshire, climbing a slow incline toward this summit, the trail growing ever narrower and ever more faint as they ascended into ever higher elevations, as though the undergrowth itself were trying to obscure the path.

That morning, as Arcturyx Longblade had bade her farewell, his daughter had approached. Younger than Aridisia by a year, she stood as tall as Ari and as wide across the shoulder, but unlike Ari she clearly looked the swordswoman, her muscles toned and posture straight, her gaze full with confidence.

"I thought perhaps you'd like some company," Arcturyx had said, a nod toward his daughter. "As committed as any to restoring Genesyx to its place. Aridisia, this is my daughter, Berenice."

The thought of taking the high road between Swordshire and Stonevale, crossing central Scrollhaven to get there had sounded daunting to Aridisia, as that meant crossing the Wizened Forest, a forbidding land of old growth, so ancient that the trees wore beards to their roots, and the putrefaction of fungus-eaten mulch pervaded the air, and the near-silence was reminiscent of a tomb.

But the chaos now rampaging across the outlands, brigands raiding deep into Shire, Haven, and Vale, bloodthirsty cutthroats raping and pillaging where they willed, now caused even the hardiest of traveler and the most sagacious of wizard to seek reason not to venture forth at all.

For quickly on the heels of refugees from the perimeter lands of each three realms had come the vermin who without a host to prey upon could not long live, left to their own devices, the parasite requiring a host. And behind them had come the scavengers to loot among the leavings, and behind them finally like lobster on the ocean floor, the wastrels, miscreants, and scurrilous brigands who knew not reason but only lust. And thus to these depraved and heartless souls had the outlands been surrendered, their ranks swelling as the rule of law receded to the immediate surrounds of Shire, Haven, and Vale, the theft of Sword, Scroll, and Stone seeming to have deprived even good kind folk of reason, compassion, and benevolence.

Thus the low road had descended literally into the chasm of inequity and debasement.

So despite the forbidding path that now was left to Aridisia, she really had no other except perhaps to sail round, but neither ship nor crew with bravery enough to venture past the Warlock's Mount to the south or the snow queen's ice palaces to the north could be found, especially not for a commensurate price with the meager purse at Ari's belt.

And when the High Sage Arcturyx had proposed that his own daughter accompany her, Aridisia had nearly melted with relief.

"An apprehensive journey," Arcturyx had said, seeing her response. "Particularly one through Scrollhaven, where you are still forbidden. If chaos casts its shadow on the borderlands of Scrollhaven as surely as it does here in Swordshire, the Lady High Magux Cithara's order banishing you will be the least concern of theirs."

Thus she'd accepted without reservation the companionship of the High Mage's daughter, herself as formidable as the forest they now faced.

"I've never been in such thick forest," Berenice said, looking the least formidable that Ari had seen her throughout their day of travel together.

Though fast as any, Ari had had to strain to keep pace with the hardier swordswoman. Well, Ari'd thought, when practiced with the quill, the heart and lungs beat not so shrill.

"What do you suppose is the best approach?" Ari asked.

"To penetrating that?" Berenice pointed to the thick growth that their dwindling path disappeared into, the canopy overhead so lush that only the setting sun behind them delivered light into the thick rich gloom. The younger woman shrugged and lifted a thumb over her shoulder. "Saw a clear patch fifty feet back. Let's camp there and wait til morning."

Aridisia weighed the relative dangers of crossing an unforgiving forest against the urgency of their mission. Perhaps an hour of daylight remained, a fact not evident even a hundred feet ahead, where perpetual gloom appeared to have settled permanently. She whipped out a scroll.

"Luminificate to darkness abate." And she scrawled the sword across the parchment. Aridisia watched carefully as the spell lit the surrounding foliage. The ball of spark wove between oaks with moss-slathered boughs above ferns whose splays of leaves were tangled in thick webs of silk, spiders the size of fists skittering from the sudden light.

"I'm no woodswoman," Berenice said, "but I'm willing to bet that those spiders know no better and don't fear us."

Ari nodded, suspecting few people ever came this far, and thinking that those who'd reached this point like as not had turned back. Her ball of fireflies wound itself past a few more trees and left behind a darkness more gloomy. "All right. We rise at first light with a beacon I'll fashion tonight to insure our direction stays true. Did you notice the breeze coming up the path?"

"The one that carries the stench of rotting wood?"

"There's something else upon the wind, like brine."

"As would make sense, as north is ocean, and the cliffs above them so precipitous that a person might step out into space before knowing she'd found the cliffs! Also a reason not to traverse a forest like this at night."

Ari nodded and gestured back the way they'd come.

The clearing not but a wide place in the path, they set up camp, chatting companionably, taking turns behind a tree to relieve themselves.

Their bedrolls out and a pot of stew flavored with dried meats aboil, Ari looked up at the stars, the sun long since gone itself to bed, a cricket or two serenading the travelers. Across the stars, she saw waves of mist, and she realized the ocean must not be far at all.

"I wouldn't be wanting to try to find it," Bere said in response to Ari's question, "lest it find me first and pull me down the cliff face." The woman smiled across the fire at her, lifting up her stew in toast.

"To a safe passage through the wood," Ari said.

The two women talked a time, Berenice about the frequent importuners for her father's time, Ari of her natal village, where threshing wheat was to be her fate until she found at the age of four how she might with a scrawl or two do the work of ten fieldhands and twenty threshers. As her talents flowered, her mother took her round for pay, had the child do herself the day's work of many, but in minutes' time.

Berenice seemed genuinely interested, her gaze keen and head atilt as though to look and listen for nuance to which she was unaccustomed.

Not given to attention seeking, Ari found the other's listening gratifying, as though given credence she hadn't found before.

"No one's ever really described their lives to me in such detail," Berenice said at one point.

Their campfire had dwindled and the stars glimmered bright when next Ari realized, her attention so deep on her upbringing and past. She also realized despite her thick bedroll how chill she was, her breath fogging. "I'd better relieve myself or I'll never sleep." She rose and slipped behind a tree.

Then scrambled back into her bedroll, her teeth chattering from just the few minutes out.

Berenice did the same, but instead of returning to her bedroll, she spread it over Ari and crawled into hers. Aridisia welcomed the warmth and soon stopped shivering.

"A tale told among the folk around Swordshire tells of a pair of wayward girls given to pranks and pratfalls upon the gullible and less fortunate," Berenice said, her voice low near Ari's ear.

* * *

Twelve and fourteen were these prodigals, their parents fit to be tied with their desultory deeds—burning bags of dung on doorsteps, overalls stuffed with straw and slathered with berry preserves laying on the roadside, and other perverse tricks perpetrated upon the faint of heart.

So perverse were their parlor peccadillos that the village forced their parents to submit these two reprobates to the High Sage for correction.

Well indeed that they did, for these two families might have found themselves cast out of home.

And for their punishment, these two young girls were sent this way to spend one night wandering lost in the Wizened Forest, adequately clothed against the cold but left to their own devices for a single night.

Now legends be what legends are, the hoarhung trees and gnarled trunks and web-clotted ferns all brought to mind the stories told at dwindling hearths known to leave a child with nightmare, and for these two who had known no grief or strife or fright did emerge in the morn with their eyes so wide and hair so gray that never again did they play a prank.

Now it was said of them for generations next that the spirit of the Wizened Forest watched them over all their lives, for when disease did strike, it left them well, and when drought desiccated the sheep and browned the trees, these two thrived, and when the orthopteran pestilence mowed down crop from ocean to mountain, somehow their fields remained intact.

Never did they speak of their ineffable night at the mercy of elements in the Wizened Forest but by hint and wink they both did say they'd found not terror but peace.

Like many who've survived like tragedy, these two stayed together for the rest of their lives, the two eventually earning the sobriquets of white witch, feared by the local populace far more for their aloof eccentricity in their doddering senescence than they'd been as recalcitrant tricksters in adolescent juvenility.

And as strange as their lives might have been, their deaths were stranger still.

As wont to happen in deep abiding love across many decades, a husband and wife will die prompt proximal deaths, their bond beyond compare. So too did these wizened witches succumb to death if not a day apart then hours.

The village nearby had no knowledge of this but for the oppression that lifted from their souls, for the old gaunt pair, whether perpetrating tricks or not, certainly exuded doom and gloom, but it wasn't til the moon was full that night and from the Wizened Wood marched a host so ghostly that people thought the moss-hung trees themselves were filing past. And to the sisterly pair's house this host did go, their forms obscured under cascading hair, around the waist of each belt.

A stranger host was never seen before nor since, and those few brave villagers who dared to watch saw these hairy folk retrieve the bodies of the two white witches and took their corpses back into the wood where sixty or more years before they had spent a single night to wander the frightening forest.

Tis said even now that the woodsages came to retrieve the bodies of souls that had wandered their wood for decades, the two young woman having left behind their sanity, only to have their bodies rejoined with their souls upon their deaths.

* * *

Marl Gneiss didn't like the look on Baron Caelum Footsore's face. His eyes look like those of someone in a full panic, he thought, his soul on edge.

Initially, upon arriving at the Barony courtyard, ropes wrapping wrists and ankles, Marl had thought his goose was plucked and cooked. Instead the Baron Footsore had greeted him as though a brother, sympathizing with his loss of estates and station, feeding, bathing, clothing him, even apologizing for the behavior of his guards.

Then at the supper, the Baron Footsore had importuned him to join an assault upon the Hall of Swords, encouraging him to imply that he, the Baron Gneiss, actually *had* stolen the One Stone Luxullian and would wield it into battle to storm the Hall.

Such a prevarication seemed banal when assessed against the backdrop of uniting the three principalities under a single government. Marl had noticed how Caelum had slyly evaded saying who would actually rule, but Marl swore to take nothing less than dominion over Stonevale, which had secretly been his ambition all along, much as he would deny it were anyone to ask, all the more vehemently for its being true.

Which had been why he'd felt so offended when the High Adept's daughter Minette Hornfels had accused him of taking the very object of his deepest desires, he had felt so compelled to protest too much.

Thus to let slip that he had stolen Luxullian and to imply he would wield it in battle alongside the Baron Footsore in a joint endeavor to conquer all three principalities that he, Baron Marl Gneiss, so recently stripped of his lands and tittles, might regain those lands, and so much more and acquire for his very own the largest cache of precious gems known to mankind at the Vault of Stones, well, these little impecunities seemed downright insignificant against the backdrop of the larger goal.

And then, the moment he'd acceded to Footsore's scheme, Caelum had gotten … eccentric.

Spelunk into the mountain? Gneiss had wondered, the idea more bizarre than the last, and certainly senseless in the face of their previous discussion. Further, the look in the eyes of the Baron Footsore had set Marl's soul on edge.

As he equipped himself at the mine entrance from among the stores brought there at Caelum's order, Marl looked over at his colleague, who was busy ordering people around in preparation for their sojourn, a servant helping Marl don the oversize one-piece canvas caving suit, which they had sewn together during the night for him. The young seamstress who had taken his measure had then stayed to give him pleasure, insisting that it had been ordered by her master. Now, as she helped him into it, she wasn't shy about testing its fit, grinning mischievously at him.

The company around them was a flurry of activity, for the Baron Footsore went nowhere without his cortege, a veritable circus of footmen, valets, sycophants, and jesters. This pre-dawn morning, the fawning sycophants appeared to have found other pursuits, perhaps deciding that their fortunes might not easily be found inside a mine.

As Marl watched Caelum, he saw the same look of desperation that had seized his face last night at the abrupt change of topic. No one else among the coterie of personnel appeared to notice, either then or now, the look of distress in Caelum's eyes, the frantic darting back and forth of the gaze, the beads of sweat above his brow, the slight flush to his features, and the ever-so-subtle clip to the words, the tone slightly elevated as though his voice were strained.

"Lord Baron," Marl said, the caving suit now snug around him, "forgive me for asking at this eleventh hour, what purpose does our spelunk serve?"

The eyes went left, the eyes went right, the brow scrunched, and the cheeks went flush. "Many purposes, Lord Baron Gneiss, and forgive me if my request seems rash. Within these mountains legends roam, although I doubt we'll see them. No, Lord, tis passing fancy to delve deep and to take my guests on a tour of the labyrinthine depths that have sustained my family these hundreds of generation. Passing fancy is a euphemism and forgive me my dissembling my passion and obsession. I have searched for years for a wraith tis said took the life of a forebear of mine, Baron Cetus Footsore, dead these many centuries in a mine collapse of cataclysmic proportion, buried not by natural collapse but by one induced by this aforementioned wraith."

Marl struggled to match the countenance with the speech, the conflict between them disconcerting, for as the eyes danced about in panic, the voice with but a slight bit of strain was mellifluous as a sonnet. He looked among the loyal followers of his brother Baron and saw not a flicker of concern for Caelum's pronounced distress.

"A two-fold purpose, Lord Baron," Caelum said. "To showcase the source of my family's wealth and to search yet again for this creature who's said to have felled my august ancestor." The Baron Footsore looked among his contingent. "I am ready as the skies grow light." He held aloft an arm and gestured toward the mineshaft mouth.

Without the retinue, Marl might have balked, having never been underground save the wine cellar at the Gneiss Barony estate, a catacomb surely worth spelunking. The initial stretch along beam-reinforced corridor ribbed with conveyor and contraption seemed little different from the cellars, sans their multitudinous caskets. Their appearance would not have surprised him, so familiar was the feel of these caverns, the jagged rock faces not far afield from roughly bricked wall, the rough-hewn beam reminiscent of bottle-filled lattices.

Soon the beam-lined walls gave rough way to stark rock corridor, the lighting more sparse but the lamp-carrying stewards beating back the dark ahead.

The pace though moderate was enough to leave Marl somewhat shy of breath, though he disguised as much given present company. That and the little changing labrynthscape turned his attention inward, the shuffle and huffle of those surrounding him a sussurus under which he disguised his short of breath, the somewhat uneven tunnel floor enough to draw his concentration, the occasional stumble giving angst to his sureness of foot. He wondered idly if the sore of foot that was sure to result from this spelunk was the derivation of his colleague's name.

A trick of light caused him to think the rough-hewn rock had moved.

"Did you see that?"

"See what, Lord Baron?"

"The rock wall there, I swear it moved."

"The legends say these walls do move, Lord Baron. Twas likely a trick of light."

"Likely," he said, hearing faint doubt in his own voice.

The conversation traveled the length of the retinue, their party strung along a fifty-foot stretch of mineshaft. As nature abhorred a perfect circle and eschewed the straight line, so too did their journey twist and turn and pitch and yaw. Frequently the tunnel itself was like a bellows, here narrow, there wide, ceiling low, ceiling high, and rarely was the party tail visible from the head or backwise. The sound of their companions through the transmogrified cavern seemed to Marl to come from all directions, the rock reflecting most of it, and its surface supplying reverberations that left the ear confused. Branching mineshafts reconnected elsewhere, echoes finding their way through the maze a moment later.

An eye closed on the wall ahead.

Marl gasped and startled.

"What is it, Lord?"

"Quick, your light there."

The servant held up a lamp.

The knot of rock looked oddly eye-shaped.

"I saw it close."

"Beg your pardon, Lord, it's rock." He took a pickaxe and plucked the eye-shaped rock from the wall. "See? Mayhaps, the Lord Baron whiffed the mine gasses? Tis an affliction we've all suffered, one time or another."

Even so, the prickling along the spine felt as though the rock gaze followed him even after. In addition to the voices echoing through the catacomb, so too did other various sounds, a trickle of water, the clatter of stone. All around these sounds were, where Marl had expected silence. Sometimes even the howl of wind through crevasse.

Further perturbing him were the constant changes of temperature. In some, the still of air thickened around him like some beast trying to suffocate him, the sweat pouring off him in these radiately hot passageways. In others, the teeth-chattering chill and hoar-frosted walls sent spikes of cold up through the soles of his shoes.

And all the while they wended their way ever downward, each descent giving way to another descent, Marl's thighs aching from the unusual use of these muscles.

In one narrow passageway, he saw a stream of dust sift down from the ceiling.

"Is that normal?" he asked the gristled miner walking beside him.

"Aye, Lord Baron, as these mountains are constantly moving."

"Aren't you afraid the ceiling will collapse?" He glanced nervously over his shoulder, his eyes on the ceiling behind them as though his mere vision might pick out the weak spot.

"Afraid? All the time, every day, and every day that goes by when I emerge at its end to see the setting sun, I thank the stars for my reprieve, and it's a fool who comes down here without a fear."

The ceiling crashed and Marl nearly pissed himself.

A call went forward, and Marl waved away the dust, retracing his path into the rubble, looking for survivors.

He pulled one man free who like as not had died instantly, a jagged rock buried in his forehead.

"Leave him," the gristled miner said, holding his lamp to dead man's face. "He'll appreciate a second burial topside. Help me with these two."

Together they pulled two others from the rubble, both sputtering for breath and very much alive. Handing these two off to others, Marl and the gristled miner searched further along.

"Seems I remembers one more behind us."

"Here he is." Marl saw a swatch of tunic sticking from beneath a boulder. "Help me with this."

The miner shook his head. "Must weigh thrice you and me."

"We have to try!" Marl slapped his arm. "Help me out."

The older man nodded. "You're right. Here goes."

They both bent and found a grip and heaved with all their might. Marl felt the hot sweat pouring off him, and the legs, although they'd known little climbing, had borne more weight throughout his life than their due, toughening sinew and bone beyond the norm. Spikes of pain like hot nails shot through his thighs and calves, and he roared.

The boulder tipped and rolled aside.

Marl fell away, gasping for breath, and realized as he catalogued his aches that scraped hands and knees were the worst. I could have broken something doing that, he thought.

The miner was dragging someone from the pit.

"Go on, I'm a bit shook is all," the young voice said.

"Pavo! Oh, Pavo, you're all right!" A bent old man scurried out of the dark and embraced the young boy.

"Sagit Smoothgrain?" Marl asked. "What the Warlock's dusty balls are you doing down here?"

The old man cleared the dust from the whisker that trailed on the floor. "I could tell you were fated to higher destinies than the cynosure of your debased beginnings."

"Marl! Phenomenal!" Baron Footsore patted him on the back. "A noble deed I'd not have expected from you. Well done."

A spark of bewilderment died when Pavo threw his arms around Marl. "Thank you, Lord Baron. I'm forever in your debt. My life is yours, to dispose upon as you please."

Overwhelmed, and little accustomed to any praise, faint or otherwise, Marl laughed and hugged the boy back. "You're welcome, Page Pavo, but you owe me nothing."

"Weren't but without his strength," the gristled miner was telling the Baron Footsore, "that boulder won't have budged." And he shone his light on a rock easily twice Marl's girth.

As Marl recovered his breath, Baron Footsore dispatched a trio to take the dead man topside. "All else well and good?" he asked among the retinue. "A minor setback, is all. When you're recovered your breath, Lord Baron Gneiss."

Marl looked up into the enlarged cavern laid bare in the ceiling collapse.

He gasped at the scintillating rock. "Shine your lights up there."

A constellation of gems cast its refulgence back up on them.

"Finder's right!" declared Sagit Smoothgrain. "Baron Gneiss claims finder's right!"

"Of course, good man," Baron Footsore said jovially, his magnanimity hollow with dissimulation. "Twenty-eighty as always."

"Tis fifty-fifty and you know it!" Pavo said.

Marl wondered what they were talking about. "What's this, Smoothgrain? What's finder's right?"

"Swordshire law decrees that a finder of a cache or horde or seam worth more than ten thousand shivs be granted finder's stake of half the cache." The old man, bent down by the ages, had to turn his head to one side to see the glittering ceiling. "This is easily dex times that."

"Maybe pent at most," Footsore muttered. "Mark the seam and let's get going. We'll need to stabilize the ceiling before we can mine it, of course." His eyes ran across it as Marl's had earlier as though to spy out weakness. "Let's go."

And the company resumed its journey, sans four members, nearly no one broaching the one man's death. Marl supposed they had their ways, and as frequently as columns collapsed or ceilings caved, the toll among them was likely horrific. Best not dwell upon the loss, he thought.

The page Pavo seemed to stay close, throwing a frequent grin Marl's way.

The gristled miner hovered too, frequently pointing out features to Marl's untrained eyes. A while later, the man said quietly, "That were bravery, out and out, Lord."

"Eh?" He wasn't sure he heard right. "What was bravery?"

"Charging in under the cave-in like that. Wouldn't have done so myself except as you'd gone in already. Mighty brave, Lord."

He hadn't felt brave, having nearly wet himself when the ceiling had crashed just feet behind them.

"Tunnel collapses like that happen in waves. The most unstable time is right after a collapse. When we're tunneling or mining, our first priority is stabilizing the area. Only then is it safe to search for survivors."

Hiking along ever downward, Marl considered what he'd done. He'd never thought himself as brave. All his life he'd oft been the butt of tirades against the pusillanimous. He reflected in the glances of those walking near the admiration he beheld in their eyes, and it was with awe he felt their regard for him.

The Baron Footsore called a halt where mine encountered cavern. Stalagmites stabbed the air above and stalactites thrust their spines toward the ceiling. A crystalline lake reflected the toothy cavern. Somewhere trickles tinkled mellifluously.

A fire soon roared, a rock burnt magically, and the sizzle of steak grew loud.

Pavo pulled Marl over to a shelf he'd outfitted with their three bedrolls, the woodwright's a bit apart from the other two. "I've got us set up already," Pavo said, gesturing to show his handiwork.

"Fine job, boy," Sagit said, lowering himself delicately to his bedroll. "Old bones like mine a bit tuckered from the pace. Wake me when the meal's ready."

Pavo glanced at Marl, then back at Sagit.

Marl wondered at the Page's silence.

"May I?" Pavo asked him.

Marl shrugged and nodded, finding a rock nearby for sitting. The sound of camaraderie from around the fire was comforting, which Marl savored as a starving man might food.

"That was brave," Baron Footsore said later in a moment of candor, the eyes somewhat less panicked.

High praise from a fellow Baron. Marl's heart soared.

Belly full and soul replete, Marl retired, the boy laying beside him, and the sleep he slipped into was more restful than he remembered in a long, long while.

Chapter 8

Columba Riverford and Samshad Woodwright looked along the paltry trail and hesitated.

All around them soared frost-tipped mountains, towering escarpments of cold bare stone, their sides so steep as to defeat the purchase of all but the hardiest of vegetation. To their immediate left was one such mountainside, scales of shale themselves holding for dear life to the mountain lest they too be cast into the abyss below.

The abyss below but inches away on a trail treacherous for a mountain goat, Columba shook his head. "I can see why travelers often take the low road."

"Tis clear why few come this way anymore." The big man perched on a small trail looked dangerously close to falling from being top-heavy alone. "I'd have thought we'd reached the mines of Stonevale ere too long."

Although forbidding, the Escarp Mountains were shot through with mines, thousands of years of digging for valuable gems that formed the basis of the Stonevale economy. For in those stones was the magic of the Earth, where to the Valer wealth derived.

Give me fire any day, Columba thought, seeing no beauty in the forlorn, forbidding landscape. "Well, Shad, what now?! I can see the faint sign of this very same goat trail over there, but it's getting there of concern to me."

"We've come a ways since this morn," Shad said.

The sun near setting, the two of them had traveled into steepening spire upon dwindling trail, even the air feeling more and more rarified. All the day yesterday, they'd hiked from central Scrollhaven to the southeast, the gentle, verdant valleys thick with scents of honeysuckle and rose, the air alive with calls of birds, the sky so blue with life and love.

They'd camped the night at a mountain base, its side nearly devoid of growth, as though to tell the travelers what to expect beyond. The next morning they'd set out into the rocky wilderness taking what appeared a well-trod trail.

And by late afternoon had nearly reached its end.

Samshad scrutinized the mountain above them.

Probably for some sign of shelter, Columba thought, knowing he'd welcome even a slight overhang to shield his head from the coming night. Twas clear Shad too thought it too late to turn back, this featureless landscape as welcoming as a bear with a toothache.

"What's that?" Shad said.

Columba followed the outstretched arm.

A pale splash of stone against the darker, weatherworn mountainside.

"Mine tailings, mayhap?"

Columba shrugged, little schooled in mine lore, his people having threshed the wheat. "How do we get there?"

Shad scanned the mountainside, his gaze traveling left to right and right to left in methodical fashion. "There, a faint trail, just a small sign that people have passed this way before."

Columba picked out the detail, no more than a slight indentation that wended its way down toward them. "By the stars, I wouldn't have seen that."

They picked their way up the mountainside, each step treacherous, the loose shale threatening to pitch them into the abyss.

The tongue of tailings longer than it had looked from below, Columba was sweating and swearing when he reached the tunnel mouth, his breathing harsh and labored.

"Bit of a climb, eh?" Shad asked, also looking flush.

He peeked over the ledge. A lot farther than it had looked.

The shaft they'd found was hewn roughly, no larger around than a miner might crawl.

"Ventilation," Shad said, "by the looks of it, anyway. What's that contraption?"

A pulley wrapped by a cable protruded from the upper lip. As they watched, a bucket emerged on the cable, tipped itself over on a stop, and tailing poured over the edge and down the mountainside, the pulley squeaking plaintively.

Columba looked into the shaft, which angled down into the mountain. "We'll have to climb down that?"

"I wouldn't call it climbing." Shad leaned close. "Plenty of fresh air." The gusts emitting from the tunnel blew the hair away from his face.

A second bucket emerged, dumped its tailings and slipped back into the tunnel.

"Someone's filling them from the other end." Columba shrugged and lowered himself into the shaft, the angle gentle enough that he didn't slide, but great enough that a crab walk wasn't comfortable.

Until the next full bucket of tailings clipped his knee.

Grimacing with pain, Columba shouted up to Shad, "Watch for the buckets!" He shimmied down the shaft, the light from above receding.

Every fifteen feet was a pulley wheel, squeaking in complaint, full buckets passing upward, one every few seconds, empty buckets passing downward.

Soon it was so dark that Columba couldn't see the approaching buckets. I wonder if the knife has any magic to it, he thought, and unsheathed it.

He hadn't given it much thought since acquiring it from the curmudgeon who'd tried to kill him with it. And he didn't lend much credence to the tale told him by the interlocutor on his way to Scrollhaven.

"Disparage the dark and benight the light."

The ruby embedded in the pommel flared to life, the lurid red glow somewhat disconcerting.

When pronouncing the spell, he'd thought only of the knife blade, whose working marks clearly indicated its sword-based metal. He hadn't expected the ruby to respond to his invocation. Odd, he thought, I didn't know I had any talent with stones. His magic had always derived from blades. The prohibitions against mixing magics weren't as deeply inculcated in him as a true initiate into the Hall of Swords. Columba had heard their frequent denouncements of Scroll- and Stone-based magic, and the teachings that proscribed their use were promulgated heavily throughout Swordshire, but Columba himself had fallen short of actual induction into Sagehood and had not yet taken the vows eschewing the use of paper or rock.

The glow from the ruby sufficient to navigate by, Columbia resumed his descent.

The narrow tunnel soon leveled out, and he emerged into a cavern where a drudge filled buckets at a desultory pace.

"Fill buckets all day, that's all I do," Columba heard him mutter.

A glop of tailings rose from a slag heap and slumped into a bucket, which then lifted and set itself on the pulley cable. A bucket leaped from the cable and settled beside the slag heap. A glop of tailings rose from the slag heap and slumped into the bucket, which then lifted and set itself on the pulley cable.

The desultory drudge waved his left arm at the big pulley wheel each time he filled a bucket, then waved his right hand in elaborate gesticulation at bucket and slag to fill one with the other.

Columba brushed himself off and glanced at the slag heap, which rose inside the cavern to heights he couldn't see. The poor wretch had a Sisyphean task. Little wonder he performed it desultorily.

The glow from the knife alerted the drudge. "What's that now? A visitor? Greetings, Lord Adept, didn't see you." He bowed elaborately, in such profusity it would have been mocking had he devoted any intention to it. "Vaculite Gravelspit, pleased to meet you, Lord Adept—?"

"No adept I am, Gravelspit. Columba Riverford, I am. Seeking a safe, easy way from the mines is all."

"Well, Riverford," he said, his glance going over Columba's shoulder at the shaft he'd emerged from, "t'isn't an easy way to enter them to start with. What'd you do, come from the land of those faint-hearted quill-pushers? I don't see one on you, which bespeaks a spark of smarts, anyway. That a sword at your side? You ain't a black brigand, are you? All meat between the ears? You've the looks of it."

"Just trying to find a way out, Gravelspit."

Shad shimmed from the tunnel and patted himself off, then stood to his full height behind Columba.

The drudge raised his gaze to Shad's full height. An arm mutely pointed the way.

Columba set off in that direction, thanking the man. The cavern ended in a passageway, which connected with a corridor whose floor was lined with two strips of steel, two bands of thick metal an equal distance apart running both ways along the corridor.

A great rumbling approached, and Shad pulled Columba from the corridor just as a train of bins trundled past, their contents brimming over the sides, leaving the patina of dust behind, the roar deafening.

"Methinks Gravelspit sent us to our deaths."

Columba glanced the way they'd come. "Didn't impress me as having the guile. Those bins are headed where, do you think?"

"Smelter or sifter for processing," Shad replied, a grin splashing his face. "Problem is stopping or slowing them long enough to board."

Another set of bins rumbled past, the vibration tickling Columba's feet. "I'll take care of that." He gestured Shad over and stood between the metal rails.

A rumble began to tickle his feet.

"The wheel spins to stop these bins." He slipped out the knife.

The brimming-over bins rocketed at him, the front bin lit by a bright red beam.

"Look out!"

The bins froze but an inch from impact.

Columba wiped the sweat from his forehead.

"Come on, before the next one comes," Shad said.

He scrambled in between the first and second bins, while Shad climbed atop the second one. "No, in between, you'll see why." Columba gestured, hearing the approach of the following bins. "Away, I say!"

The ore train launched into motion, its four bins heaped full. Columba stood on the articulated connector, a hand on the bin ahead and the bin behind, crouched down to bring his head below the peak of the bin ahead. He couldn't have brought his head any lower.

The train swung into a cavern webbed with scaffolding, then shot into a dark narrow tunnel whose ceiling clipped the top of the piled ore, sending a spray of dust and rock across Columba. He heard Shad complain in colorful language. Had the other man stayed atop the bin, he'd have surely been scraped off by the low ceiling.

The pitch and sway of the ore train might have been disconcerting. The noise was overwhelming, the metal wheels on metal tracks squeaking on every turn, parks scintillating in sprays from the point of contact.

The tunnel wall fell away on the left, a precipitous drop replacing it. Columba got a glance of a mean, roiling river below and sheer rock canyon walls.

The ore train lunged to the right unexpectedly, hurling Columba to the left. He caught the bin lip with both hands, and his body swung out over the precipice just as he saw the tunnel ahead.

Somewhere, someone screamed.

He yanked himself with all his strength and his feet somehow found the bar between bins as the tunnel swallowed them, the wind-whipped dust spraying fire particles into his hair teeth and eyes.

The bins lurched left but he was ready, the tunnel was racing past inches away, his momentum pushing him toward it like some giant hand.

The bins began to slow on a slight incline.

Why would they go up? Columba wondered.

In the tunnel ahead he glimpsed empty sky.

Uh oh, he thought.

The bins pitched forward, the track pointing down, and the tunnel disappeared. Open sky all around, he glanced ahead.

A straight track at least a quarter mile, seeming suspended in midair.

At its end an ore-pile, towering over a hive of activity.

The set of bins ahead of theirs hit the end of the track and disappeared, hurling their ore onto the pile, launching gouts of dust into the air.

Their bins picking up speed, Columba glanced back at Shad. "Get ready to jump!"

The connector vibrating under him, the metal wheels complaining with sparks, Columba set himself as their bins hurtled downward, picking up speed.

He leaped, and the bins disappeared from under him, the loads of rock flying at the ore pile just below him, the top of the heap coming at him too fast, he saw, too late.

His feet plunged into and through the peak, the softer lighter silt giving away to his momentum, and he slid down the far side on his behind, taking with him an avalanche of rock and dirt.

As he slid to a stop two thirds down the side, he looked back and up. Behind him, Shad tumbled like a rag doll down the slope toward him.

"Stumble, rumble, foil and scumble, mind my words and stop his tumble."

Shad slid to a stop beside him. "Thanks for that, much appreciated. My fate would be scrawled on my back-side without it."

"Might still be yet, before we're through." Columba gestured at the mine personnel gathering at the base of the ore-hill.

A stately woman bedecked in jewels stepped through the crowd. "We've been expecting you, Sage Riverford." To the big man beside her, she said, "Bind and gag them."

* * *

Aridisia felt the eyes upon her back the instant she stepped into the forest.

And they might as well be daggers, she thought, the malevolence in them deadly.

"If eyes were knives then looks could kill." Berenice looked back up the trail, their erstwhile campsite still visible.

Aridisia looked ahead, the thick forest looking impenetrable more than ten feet ahead. The trail appeared to fade beyond that, but with each step she took, faint signs of the trail appeared.

As though I'm supposed to think the trail peters out, she thought, dismayed.

And just ten minutes ago, as we were starting out, I felt so hopeful.

Little mystery, as the night had fetched its own delights, the cold notwithstanding. Ari threw Bere a mischievous glance. The other woman returned it, a slight blush touching her cheek. Ari felt her own flush flame in response. Wordlessly, they turned their attention to the trail.

"Given how close we are to the great cliffs," Berenice said, "we'd be prudent to tread carefully anyway."

"And just so the trail itself doesn't lead us far astray," Ari added, fishing out her scroll. "Though forest conceal, trail reveal," she said, scrawling rapidly.

The trail appeared no more prominent through thick underbrush, soggy with morning dew.

"There's heavy magic at work here." The prickles along Ari's spine intensified. "Beacon feast, beckon east." A cloudy ball of glitter rose from her parchment and floated to the east, the direction that the trail appeared to be going for now, faint though it was. "At least we'll know if we're going the right direction," Ari said.

"Tis good, for though we have daylight, I've yet to see the morning sun. Here, I'll take the lead." Bere slipped past her on the narrow trail, brushing Ari enticingly.

Following the woman, Ari struggled to keep her attention on the woods around them, the warmth in her middle stoked by the sight of the delightful creature ahead. Although a year younger, Bere seemed far older, as though precocious in things Ari could not fathom. Further, the relative privation of Ari's upbringing, although a treacherous climb that had lent her strength and courage, had left her hungry for other appetites. Bere had lived in surroundings plentiful, and had guided Ari to places in her soul she hadn't known. She seemed to have a wisdom derived from exploring pleasures accessible only from within a cocoon of plenitude. The other woman's muscles rippling tauntingly beneath tunic and breeches ahead of her, Ari had to tear her gaze away, lest her hands leap ahead to grope what her eyes fondled longingly.

The gnarled oldgrowth oak around them, beards of moss from every branch, grew so thick that the trail could not stay straight. A forest this thick would naturally be dense with sound but not so, for even the breath of her companion was inaudible, the silence heavy, as though the birds were afraid to sing and the wind itself afraid to blow.

Working their way generally eastward, the pair of travelers were quickly soaked nearly to the waist as they slipped along the slim trail, the dewy undergrowth brushing their clothes as they passed, as though to hinder their passage.

"What's that?" Berenice asked.

Aridisia looked.

A bearded trunk stood in their path, as though it had just planted itself there.

"I thought I saw eyes at the top, and just below that a smile."

Ari grinned. "Looks like a lopped off treetrunk, if you ask me. Odd texture to the moss, though, wouldn't you say? Like hair, almost. Hey, what are you doing with that?"

Bere had just drawn her sword.

"No, don't. Let me." Ari pulled out her scroll. "What is concealed, be revealed." The quill flew and the letters settled on to the parchment.

A breeze stirred the leaves at the foot of the trunk, and soon a small dust devil tugged at the hairy strands of hoary moss. The spinning winds approached waist height and arms burst from the trunk.

"Oh, dear me, can't have that." The arms held the hair in place below the waist. "The risk I take when I remove my belt." A face emerged from the hair. "I knew I shouldn't have taken it off."

He looked at Bere. "Are you going to use that toothpick or just bluster and threaten? You don't stand a chance, you know." He thumped his own mid-riff. "Rock maple."

"It's one of them!" Bere said, blinking rapidly.

"But who are they?" Ari realized she was being rude. "Who are you?"

"Me?" The voice was light, and the eyes danced between thick gossamer strands. "Cincinatus Ripplebark, the High Magician of the Wizened Forest, but you're not asking name, are you?" The brow bark wrinkled, a mossy eyebrow rising.

Ari shook her head, not sure whether to be afraid or intrigued. "No, but forgive me. I'm Aridisia Myric, Late of Scrollhaven."

"And by the look of the quill in hand a Magux too, eh?"

"Aspiring," she added with a shrug, irritated at having to explain. "And this is Berenice Longblade."

"Sage Berenice Longblade," Bere added.

"Tis mighty magic you both must have to reach this far," Cincinatus said, "For tis might magic that haunt these regions. Now as to your question, not quite who I am but what is the nature of my peoples and their circumstance that lands them in these tree-fraught environs looking very much like the rooted brothers and sisters who stand so stately nearby. Perchance as the mystery of your penetrating our impenetrable forest will avail you the impenetrable mystery that stands before you?"

Ari contemplated him, this Cincinatus Ripplebark, whose very countenance obscured by moss-like hair begged the questions brimming over the edge of her mind and down her face. "What mighty magics do you cite? And what mysteries lie obscured by the thick overgrowth of your circumlocution? What esoterica do you expostulate in your word-fraught soliloquy?"

A branch arm laid its spidery twig fingers upon the hoary breast. "You impugn that I hide right in front of you, as though my closing eyes may render me invisible to you? Nothing could be more remotely false, except perhaps the truth. But spare not, spare not, and if I might join you anon on your sojourn, so too might your journey be a bit better borne and a little less boring. May I?" And Cincinatus stood aside to reveal a clear straight path through the woods behind him.

When circumstances conspired to provide opportunity, and fate lent a hand to push a person along a path, woe was she who tried to turn aside, for destiny awaited, whether a person assented or capitulated, and she went that way willingly or not, walking face first into the future or dragged by the lapels of the past.

Aridisia looked along the path but once. "Let's go."

Once past Cincinatus, she saw instantly not a thick impenetrable forest but families of Ripplebark's ilk, enjoying their wonderland beneath a canopy of old-growth oak.

Clumps of horsegrass neighed softly in the morning breeze, the scents of honeysuckle and rose, redolent of the High Magux's garden outside Scrollhaven, the slurping of bear bees lapping up the honey, the flapping petals of butterfly lilies scintillating in the dappled sunlight, the chirping of green-wing blue jays flittering from branch to branch, the chattering of squirrel bats hanging from the undersides of moss-slathered boughs, and the chattering of Ripplebark children playing near their caretaker's roots.

Above the path sparkled Ari's eastern starguide, pointing truly east, the path ahead as straight now as it had been crooked before.

"What magics have these woods, Ripplebark?" Ari asked over her shoulder, her stride long and pace confident.

"Magux Myric, you surely must sense some of it, yes?"

"Indeed I do, for it pushes back against mine own, like a giant hand. Earlier you intimated these magics might be revealed with the nature of your peoples. What do you call yourselves, Ripplebark?"

"Our name for ourselves indeed is esoteric, for we call ourselves *Araucaria araucana*, the Monkey-Puzzle Family. Tis a pun upon ourselves, a private joke that blends our simian similarity with the curse laid upon our people so long ago."

* * *

He came from Warlock's Mount, his eyes burning like midnight coal, his breath hot enough to shrivel the leaves off a tree, his face so full of scorn that even the sun was afraid to shine on it, his voice so deep it sounded as if it came from the deepest mine.

He said his name was Travert Crepitans Pictor, but we were all sure it was something much more evil. He wore a sword burnished bright by the sky, wielded a quill adorned with the lightest of down, and sported a diamond the size of your pinky. He said he came to establish an outpost of his own in the Wizened Forest, where our peoples had lived peaceably for two thousand years.

How long ago all this transpired, no one is sure. The passage of time has become unremarkable to our ilk, abiding the centuries like our leafy brethren in quiet contemplation. Tis said a tree always stands in prayer. For us in our altered forms more the meditation of millennium. Were I to suppose, I might be disposed to say fifteen generations as your folk pass the time, two or three of ours since we were thusly cursed.

Blessed, cursed, or somewhere in between, for tis true we live now as much the same as we did then, an insular folk, disinclined to venture far and husbanding our resources, our needs simple, our ways frugal. With gentle care do we tap our resources. Given our thick bark and long hair, we've little need of shelter, and our food the mulch beneath our feet. Among us you'll see those in repose their feet fixed while they stand rooted, drawing nutrients from the soil. A week or two thus rooted, and then they draw up those roots and roam free for a commensurate time.

Cold? Oh we know the cold, and we draw our fluids into our trunks when the weather goes chill and the warmth flees south, our leaves fall off and blanket the ground, our extremities going dormant as the sleet and rain whips off the northern seas, and when the rain freezes in our branches it becomes bone-crushing cold, but like our limbs, our nerves have gone dormant and we're mostly warm deep in our trunks.

When the summer comes and our branches bloom, our leaves proliferate and draw in the sun, our days are glorious and nights alive with the sounds of crickets and of course with love.

Oh, but there I go distracting myself with earthly delights while my audience wonders what tangent I've taken.

So this Sorcerer who declares his name Travert Crepitans Pictor and whose look declared the evil in his soul ventured among us to inveigle us with promises of comity and praises of blandishments to persuade us to allow him to build a colony on our lands overlooking the sea. He assuaged our concerns with assurances of recompense and was vague with his purpose in wanting our lands as locale.

Why did we believe him? It would be simple to say we don't know, to dismiss the decision as an ill-considered choice and to cast upon our forebears the aspersion of hindsight, and to ask with all the cynicism implied, "What were they thinking?"

But that would disregard the enormity of his suasion, this scurrilous scofflaw whom we now call by first name, Travert.

Why grant him that honor, as though he were friend and companion? Perhaps because we came to trust him as such, for this was a time of great cataclysm and turmoil, when the seas battered our poor dear cliffs mercilessly, when the waters seemed far colder and the summers much hotter, when spring and fall were but a blink in between, a typhoon might follow a snowstorm, whenever the difference of temperature between night and day was like the difference between … well, night and day.

A great battle was forming beyond our insular little realm, one which we neither invested in nor cared much about, and in our ignorance of these other forces, we succumbed to the wiles of this charlatan sorcerer, for he was an exponent of the ethos that all magics be harnessed and put to the use for which its wielder intended, a power unchained from its elemental sources and unbound from the incantation which serves to shroud and to contain, for that which requires a couplet to summon may not be invoked unrestrained. Arrayed against him more than a millennia ago was a coalition of practitioners—Sages, Mages, Adepts, Thaumaturgists, Wizards, Augurists, Clairvoyants, Conjurers, Enchanters, Witches, Occultists, Archmages, Theurgists, and Alchemists, all seeking some balance in the magics they marshalled, each seeking to set their own access to magic but each yearning for some limit to the chaos around them.

How the Wizened Forest remained aloof from the tides afflicting all four corners is yet a mystery, but it was not by magic that our isolation was punctured. An isle of calm amidst a sea of storm was sure to draw the envy and ire of the hurricane-battered oceans. For outside our peaceable realm, war did rage, hundreds of kingdoms expanding and conquering with force of arms until they too were conquered by a neighbor with greater force of arms—or force of magic. For a king or queen might enlist a conjurer who would put into battle a fearsome host, and this pair might pursue a campaign to harness nearby kingdoms, until they either had a falling out or the venal conjurer might be gelded to switch sides, a treacherous proposition, for the new owner of this freshly-bought conjurer might never know when a higher price might be in the offing. For too in time these venal magicians became warriors and laid waste to opposing hosts without a phrase or grip, and found themselves conjured away by a mage with a commensurate power, these multi-talented magicians building their mastery of the many magics and combining their powers to bring to bear ever greater destructive energies and engines, the like of which had never been seen between the four corners.

And thus a small group gathered, witness of this terrible destruction, and set their minds to untangle this imbroglio, their goal to make haven and banish forever the scourge of war. And their ethos was that in the not-too-distant past, the magics had been invoked with restraint, the goal never to obliterate the enemy and often not even to dominate but to alleviate some condition or ameliorate a suffering, give succor to the poor or mind the sick. That aggrandizing of self had come much later, that grasping for power, the bald cupidity, the brazen effrontery of these plexiform practitioners to hoard beyond reason the fruits of their many talents was a recent phenomenon. That those of singular talent eschewed the profligate debauchery evinced by this Hieratic oligarchy, and therefore how might they reign in this excess, and these few mages of singular mind set cast about for the means by which they might restore an order to the chaotic land.

Twas no surprise they fixed upon a curious foible in the distribution of magic, that the elementals appeared to wane strong in one place and wax weak in other, the fire to the west, the wind to the north, the stone to the east, and the water to the south.

And this conclave started modest, finding exponents in each region, ones willing to eschew the powers not predominant in their lands, and they each established schools, institutions focused on the refinement of that craft. In the east emerged the Vault of Stones, theirs the first to coalesce around the elemental magic Earth, whence all precious gems do come, and those who attended were inculcated with the principle that the purity of their energies lent them strength. To the west evolved a clan of warriors whose harness of the elemental fire was manifest in the Sword, which was forged from fire, and like their eastern colleagues they too inculcated in their ilk the purity principle, eschewing the other magics in favor of the fire. To the north there formed a clique those worship of the wind was manifest in the sails they sent aloft, sails made of paper with frames of very light wood and shaped like birds whose paper tails descended like furloughs for miles, and on these papers tails they wrote their incantations.

Alas but to the south where the water coalesced the strongest, no society was founded, and these obdurate occupants continued their wicked plexiform ways, the steeps sides of the Warlock's Mount the off-used battleground of these pugnacious prodigies.

The formation of these principalities to the southwest of east of the moss-haired folk was welcomed by the erstwhile denizens of these fecund domains as the turmoil beyond our lands clearly began to subside.

Twas when these nascent states were young that this devil from the Warlock's Mount did come with blandishments and entreaties to request from us a spit of land to colonize. This Travert Crepitans Pictor, as he named himself, did convince those forbears of mine of his putative intentions, and once ceded, he would neither relinquish nor relent, in spite of his misuse of the land we'd lent him.

For on this spit, he caused to be built a factory whose noise and stench did foul our environs, and whose effluents blackened our rivers and poisoned our soils.

When it became clear he'd betrayed our trust and would not remedy the foulness he had caused to be created among us, we fretted and muttered amongst ourselves, our humble natures preventing our posing more than a weak "would you please" which he brushed off as a horse might a fly.

Now this belching behemoth amidst our pastoral glades was more than an eyesore, as the copses around it began to wither and shrivel, and even the earth beneath them to get sucked into bottomless pits, and ere too long did squadrons of tar-body soldiers march away as though hatched somewhere deep in the bowels of the earth, fearsome beasts twice and thrice the size of us and all grotesque of physique and form, their countenances horrific to look upon, the fear they instilled as each one passed enough to send the frail among us into their final spasm of illness. Just a glance from one did suck the life and bravery from our hardiest of people, and leave in its wake an inextinguishable fear that might set a person shaking for days.

And if that weren't enough, the graves of our dead turned up disinterred, as though some horrific creature were unburying our dead to consume or transmogrify their bodies.

It was more than our gentle folk could stand.

We gathered our host and marched toward this foul blemish upon our land, this fulminating, crepuscular, suppurating boil brought forth upon us by this buttocks of a scoundrel, and we unleashed the power of our stately tree, these fabulous ancient oaks so wise and long-lived that their hoary beards reached the forest floor.

As our magicians in their entire hurled the might of the Wizened Forest at this abomination amidst us, he appeared. Travert Crepitans Pictor, himself, clad in the black-as-midnight robe he always wore, as if he'd just returned from a wild noctivagent sojourn, the wild look of incensed injustice in his eyes. And he erected this odd-looking lattice, a magic lattice of course that enveloped the foul factory and absorbed the blast inflicted by our fair sages.

The lattice became a pillar of light so bright we none of us could look upon it and a great wind rushed inward, blowing our waves toward it, each of us tightening our belts against the vortex, a tower of dust shooting forth from the apex of the light pillar, directly into the sky. And dark clouds roiled with turbid delight as they gathered menacingly above us, shot through with crackling light, rumbling like a slumbering monster rudely doused at an inopportune time, and then—

—well, no one cared to describe the next event, the horror in their eyes and minds too traumatic to recall—

—gone.

Just gone.

The pillar, the foul factory, the devil's minion, all his myrmidons.

Just vanished.

And in their place just one thing.

A belt, its buckle of burnished sword steel, a small ruby in its center, and visible through the back a scroll so tiny that the writing could not be read.

Our need for belts obvious, it seemed a gifted to our erstwhile leader, the High magician, Aristata Longaeven Pinus. And of course the fool put it right on.

And imprisoned our peoples forever, every High Magician compelled to wear that belt in turn down through the ages unto this very day.

* * *

Ari looked over at Cincinatus Ripplebark and frowned.

The path here ascended toward a ridge which appeared to circumscribe the Wizened Forest, for beyond the ridge she saw no trees.

Ripplebark seem so deep in thought that he almost didn't notice.

"Wait," Bere said, pointing over the lip of the ridge.

Ari stopped.

In the bowl spread before them, shale-lined sides sloped swiftly down to a shard-filled center.

"Twas here, wasn't it, Cincy?" she asked.

"Yes, indeed it was." He seemed to emerge from his reverie. "It doesn't hold its former terror, this blight upon our forest. Not since …" He glanced toward his waist.

Ari felt her brow furrow. "Since what?"

But no matter how she pressed him, he said no more about the what, not even as he led them around the rim of the circular glass-lined bowl, the shale around it a deep black color, almost the black of obsidian.

He led them to the far edge of the Wizened Forest. "From here on out is Scrollhaven territory, if they've the magic anymore to exert their dominion."

And Ari and Bere left the old wooden wizard standing sentinel atop the ridge, a modest leather strap with a dull pewter buckle holding his body-length hair in place, his aspect blending in with the screen of trees behind him, as though camouflaged, the wind stirring his branches.

It wasn't until they'd lost sight of his hirsute form that it occurred to Ari a simple thing he'd said.

"Didn't he say he was the High Magician of the Wizened Forest?"

Bere shot a glance at her. "I believe he did."

" '… every High Magician compelled to wear that belt in turn down through the ages unto this very day.' " Ari shook her head.

"It's buckle of burnished sword-steel, a small ruby …" Bere repeated.

"Then why wasn't he wearing it? Why wasn't the High Magician of the Wizened Forest wearing the belt with the burnished sword steel buckle, a ruby in its center? What wasn't he telling us?" Ari asked, glanced back as though to read his face from many miles distant.

* * *

Pavo Pagewright winced a little with each step, the center of his soreness between his mid-thigh and lower back, an area that was also the source of a languid warmth that radiated in gentle waves throughout his body.

The Baron had resisted at first, but with a little oral persuasion had soon acceded to Pavo's blandishments, and the pleasure had been mutual, the joy Pavo had felt being far in excess of the discomfort at the Baron's largesse.

Pavo glanced over at Sagit Woodwright.

"I know that look," Sagit muttered, his words barely audible under the voluminous wheeze of the Baron behind them.

"Jealousy is unbecoming upon you, Lord Sagit," Pavo muttered back, grinning mischievously. "Besides, his good fortune is fortunate for us, eh?"

Sagit frowned and hurried ahead, leaving Pavo in the Baron's company.

"What was that, Pavo, eh?" Baron Gneiss said. "Not a little jilted, he looked." The deep low rumble of the Baron's laughter boomed around Pavo, a laughter he was sure did reach the old man's ears.

"Tis not a thing to trifle, Lord, pardon my saying so. We have a saying in Swordshire: 'Be friends with the friends of your friends.'"

The Baron chuckled again. "We have a saying in Stonevale: 'Hold your friends close, and hold your enemies closer.' Might be wise to have Lord Sagit at our fire again tonight, eh? And if you've the energy, show him the kindness you've accorded him in the past."

Pavo looked at the Baron appraisingly, revising his initial opinion. Smart about people in ways I wouldn't expect, he thought.

The rigors and boredoms of travel set in, and Pavo let the lassitude of the night anesthetize him to the drudgery of the day.

Not that here, deep underground, a person could distinguish between them.

It seemed to him from the small talk of their companions—veteran miners and spelunkers all—that they were deliberate in their choice of when to sleep, when to wake, when to eat, and when to break. Pavo had noticed the timing yesterday, the first day of their grand spelunk, that within a half-hour of his noticing his hunger, they stopped to eat, not once but twice, that when he yawned, the camp seemed to seek their bedrolls en masse, that when he woke, the camp also seemed to stir from slumber.

Without external signals to alert them to the changing rhythms throughout the day, these troglodytes appeared even so to detect those signals somewhere.

Perhaps from their own bodies, Pavo thought.

The low light and dreary travel were punctuated by the occasional bit of overheard conversation, and although normally a loquacious lad, Pavo found the looming rock walls intimidating enough that he felt his usual constant prattle might offend, as though by remaining silent, he might prevent their collapse.

The first time he saw a face in the rock, he dismissed it, remembering the tales of mine gasses that might make a person hallucinate. The next time he attributed it to the low light, his mind wanting to add features to the boring patternless rock. He'd heard talk in other places that the mind supplied information where oftentimes was only deprivation.

The third time, he said quietly to the Baron. "You see that?"

"I swear I didn't," Marl replied.

Pavo couldn't make out the Baron's expression in the dim flickering lamplight. "Swore you didn't take Luxullian, either."

"Think I'd be down here if I did?"

"I think you'd be ensconced in the Vault of Stones if you had, winking at the wenches and pawing the pages."

"Quite the opposite would be my druthers, despite the enjoyment. Where'd you learn that, by the way?"

Pavo grinned then stopped. "There's another."

The face on the wall flickered out of existence, the miner behind them holding up a lamp. "What's the hold up?"

Pavo and the Baron shrugged at each other and stepped past the variegated surface, where multiple nodules might have given the impression of a human face.

"We gonna have to send you two topsiders back up?" the miner asked, looking between them. "It's the only cure for mine-gasses."

"The page and I are fine, thank you," the Baron said, his tone affected.

"As you will, Lord Baron."

Pavo and Marl watched him slip past them. "When's lunch?" Pavo asked.

"At lunch time," the miner said over his shoulder.

"Friendly people," Pavo said some time later.

"Sends all his folk to charm school," the Baron quipped.

Pavo giggled.

Soon the coterie halted for lunch, and the Baron Footsore invited the Baron Gneiss to dine with them at a wide place in the cavern.

"Who's the boy?" Footsore said, when they appeared. When told, he gestured him forward. "I thought you were journeyman to the master Sagit Woodwright."

"It was, until the Lord Baron saved me. Now I owe him my life."

"Found yourself a sycophant, eh, Lord Baron? Helpful to have one or two around for contrast. Over here, Lord Baron is a map of this particular set of caverns." The Baron Footsore poked his finger to an area well west of the map. "There's where we came from." He gestured far to the east. "There's where were going, another two days underground. By now you've divined we're staying on a routinized schedule. Without external signals for sunrise, noonday, and sunset, we've got to establish our own, otherwise we'll overextend ourselves, thinking it's still day, and we'll soon be delirious with lack of sleep and be drunk as though with mine gas."

The Baron Footsore directed the Baron Gneiss over to a table, bidding Pavo to fare there, sitting under the map.

At a signal from Marl, Pavo stilled his protest. Glancing between the interlocutors and the map, Pavo nibbled sullenly, knowing his presence at their table to be a breach of protocol but resenting his having to eat to one side anyway. He wasn't their equal and he never would be, and if the Baron Gneiss had invited him to dine at the same table as though he were aristocracy, Pavo would have declined, for a page to accept such honors, even when offered, would have earned him the deadly wrath of the other nobility, and that of his fellow laity. And the latter would certainly main or kill him at the earliest opportunity. He ate stonily, a cold breath of air from the right blowing a wisp of hair into his face.

Watching the fat Baron and the well-proportioned one trade stories of repast past, Pavo ate scantly from the meal brought him, noting how the ruby in the Baron's belt buckle glowed slightly with its inner light. He examined the Baron Footsore while he ate, looking for those signs that the Baron Gneiss had told him about: the darting eyes, the shine of nervous sweat on brow and upper lip, the tightly controlled voice thick with forced nonchalance. And as the Baron Gneiss had told him, none of Baron Footsore's coterie appeared to notice his discomfiture.

Pavo watched the two Barons eat heartily, while he barely picked at his food. Positioned where he was near the map, he couldn't help but trace its lines, the honeycomb of tunnels fascinating in the way they connected at multiple places.

Traveling through the maze was disconcerting for the way sound seemed to travel in many directions, oft reaching his ears through a side passage first, despite the speaker's being just a few feet away, as though the side tunnel had snatched the sound from the speaker's mouth before it was even uttered.

Pavo turned his gaze again to the map. To his schematic-trained eyed, he knew instantly it had changed. Long years interpreting the Woodwright's sketches and schematics, Pavo memorized them instantly and translated their designs into the final form that they were intended to represent.

So he knew that the map had changed and where.

He started, almost tipping the food from his lap. A glance at the Barons, the two men deeply engrossed in a discussion on the perfect female build. Annoyed, as he knew he was more cute than any woman, Pavo dared not interrupt them.

A warm gush of air from his left brought the faint odor of sulfur.

"Smell that, Lord Baron?" Footsore said to Gneiss, his face lit by the eerie red ruby glowing at Gneiss's belt. "Like the hot breath of Warlock's Mount. Ever been there? More's the pity. Desolate mountainsides, stone that sounds like glass when you walk upon it. Not a lick of greenery all the way to the top, and there, at the peak, a caldera with a stench so foul it'll suffocate you."

Pavo sat back as a Captain approached. "Pardon, Lord Baron, but the men tell me that's the scent of doom and they advise—"

"Balderdash!" Baron Footsore thundered.

Even from several feet away, in light too dim to read by, Pavo saw the terror plain in the Baron's face.

"Onward, foul scallywags, or has the meat between your legs shriveled to nothing at all! We move out in ten minutes and any who choose to object may lay themselves before me to have their testicles removed, for clearly any such eunuchs have been emasculated already. Ten minutes!"

The narrow tunnel exploded with activity, and in five minutes the coterie was moving, Pavo hanging back, the two Barons now side by side, leading the way further downward, into the increasing heat.

The old miner who'd helped the Baron Gneiss to extract Pavo and Sagit from the cave-in settled into step beside the boy. "Tis a grim day when one's own Lord throws caution to the hurricane and orders his whole contingent to their deaths," he muttered, his voice so quiet that only Pavo heard him.

He looked at the old miner sharply. "Pavo Pageboy, and Woodwright apprentice."

"Phenocry Sunkenshaft, just call me, Phen." They shook. "Pleased."

Pavo thanked the man for pulling him from the bubble yesterday. "Why would he order it if death is all that awaits us?"

"Thank the Baron Gneiss, as I'd not gone in if given the druthers. Tis a fine line between bravery and foolery, and by the stars I can't say as I know the difference." Phen glanced the boy up and down. "Don't look any worse for it, I'll say. Anyway, never seen the man so obsessed. The Baron has a passion for spelunking, been at it for years, but he's always listened to his Captain, how he maintains their respect, it is. Not like the Baron Footsore to order us headlong into hazards—not at all."

Sweat tricked down Pavo's back. Despite the warming breeze that they walked into, he shivered.

"The way he behaves reminds me of someone not so different, at the legends would have it."

* * *

The legends? Not but a collection of tales at firesides each night to give the children nightmares and indigestion. Aye, but there's always the kernel of truth buried deep in the legend, and who's it for us to say what's true or what's rued?

Before, my folks fished the seas off the western coast, and I'd be fishin' there too but for the strange storm that came out of the sea from half a world away and blackened the sky for months, and set my ancestors adrift inland.

Aye but I'm distractin' myself, I am.

Among the fisherfolk they tell the tale of a merman crowned upon his head with a tiara of sharkteeth and his legs of course the tail of a fish. So strong he was that he walked upon those tailfins, tis said. Once well, of course.

Such creatures rarely show themselves, but tis told the tales of their taking the fisherfolk from the very gunwales of their craft and dragging them deep to take from the fishermen the seed they'd sew with wonton abandon were the mermaids willing.

Oh, there's like tales of mermen and fisherwomen, but among our folk, such malformed child is cast directly into the sea.

There I divagate again!

Where was I—oh, yes.

Came aground one day, this merman, a grievous wound to his side, and embedded deep in the wound a knife. A village waif had found him there, laying half out of the surf, unconscious, the wound bleeding but slowly, the flesh suppurating a foul smelling puss, half green, half yellow.

Our reverence for the life aquatic lent us mercy and compassion, and for this deed we were fully repaid, for among us were those who swore that a magic as foul as the stench must be at work for the knife to remain in the wound as thus but spare the merman his life, an evil magic meant to make him suffer, the necrotic flesh so rancid that it should have felled him with sepsis.

The knife was curious of make, its blade and haft a dull pewter, and set at the base of the pommel, where hilt met blade, was a small sapphire, the kind that refracted light to a point, and seemed to glow with a light all its own, and the butt of the haft looked too different, as though it detached in some arcane way.

The villagers carried him ashore and built a small aquarium for him that he might breathe, and tried to nurse him back to

health, but the knife remained in his side and the wound continued to fester. The merman remained delirious with brief periods
of lucidity, barely able to communicate his needs before slipping
back into his nightmarish lassitude.

How they debated removing the offending object from his
side, all day and nearly all night, they discussed it, nearly to distraction. No, it will cause his death, some argued. He'll die anyway if it's not removed, argued others. None among us know of
such things and can't know, yet others averred. Send for someone who does, one versed in the healing arts, muttered one. Days
away, countered others. A wise one among the villagers worried
that the knife's removal would bring upon the village the curse
that lay upon the Merman.

Days and days they went round and round, and still they came
no closer to squaring with a decision. The situation remained
uncertain until the day the merman decided it for them.

The day woke gray, a storm to the west and approaching land
slowly. A big slow storm, one seen once a lifetime, deep dark
clouds hovering at the horizon, streaks of lightning shooting in
spasm, a phalanx of cloud that seemed to move neither north
nor south but grew slowly taller, a sure sign that it was destined
to make landfall upon the village itself.

And just when it seemed the storm was about to fall upon
the village and pummel it to pieces, the merman emerged from
his delirium. "Bring me to the water's edge for the sea sends its
storm to claim me."

The first full coherent sentence we'd heard from him, his
speech until then a salad of syllables with a few meager meaty
words mixed in. A full sentence sated us as though a banquet,
and they hauled him to the water as he bade, the wind now
whipping whitecaps towards them, wisps of moisture stinging
their cheeks.

And in this typhoon, the Merman raised himself out of the
tank by its sides and hurled his gaze at them.

"Remove the knife from my side and free my soul!" The tiara of sharkteeth declared his majesty, and in that moment it was clear he was King of the Sea himself, exuding command as though sanguine. He leveled a commanding finger at one poor soul, a young woman of fair countenance who among them had devoted exhaustive hours to his care. And perhaps because of her fatigue and the time she'd spent in delicate study of his comely countenance, she obeyed.

Antlia Catchmonger was her name, one now revered by coastal folk all along the western shore, for as he commanded her to remove the offending knife from his side, the full fury of the hurricane fell on them all, lightning striking the nearby trees and setting them alight, the thunder deafening, and the hail as big as fists pulverizing the villagers.

Antlia grasped the hilt, set her foot to the aquarium side and heaved with all her might.

Yes, it came loose, and the storm ceased in moments, the king Merman falling back with a gasp, a single gout of bladeblood gushing from the wound, which the sealed without a scar.

But as Antlia reeled backward, the hilt in hand, the whirling storm wrapped around her, spun her so fast all was a blur, and spun her into the shape of an eel, which danced across the sand on its tail, an eel as big and fat and round as the jungle snakes of Halfmoon Sea.

The Merman King leaped from the tank and hurled himself upon the eel, was himself caught in the spinning, and the combined blur spun toward the sea, whipping the now calm surf into another type of froth, the eel and merman locked in combat, their fight taking them farther and farther from shore, the fight pausing now and again, the young Antlia now transmogrified into some vicious sea monster, the merman king fighting valiantly even in his weakened state to draw the monster out to sea.

Soon enough but a blot on the horizon was all they could see and then that too was gone from sight.

The parents and siblings of Antlia were distraught, and though the comfort of fellow villagers did assuage, it could not return to them their fair girl, the light of their lives and as pleasing to look upon as the rising sun.

Though the storm had subsided within moments of the knife's removal from the Merman King's side, a gloom began to gather, this one far more subtle than the hurricane that had beset them, this a gradual thickening taking months to coalesce.

This gloom did thicken and cast a pall more morose than the malaise of grief that the village endured at the loss of their dear Antlia, and across the months of thickening gloom, the rumor started that the village was cursed. For but a few miles north and a few miles south, the sand sea and sky behaved as it they held a grudge and did oppress the village under such a veil that even the fish fled the sea offshore and the plants grew sallow from lack of sun, the birds had ceased to sing and even the air was afraid to blow.

Soon, the villagers bereft of their sunny daughter and of the sun itself debated what to do, some so hopeless, they lay somnolent in their beds all the day long and some so panicked they wept all the night.

Without hope of reprieve after a year, they left the village and went inland, leaving behind all their belongings, most with barely the strength to carry with them their fellow villagers without the will even to walk.

The Barony of Footsore gets its name not from the miles of tunnel that catacomb its mountains, but from the wearing trek undertaken by the demoralized villagers that left them heartbroken, helpless, hopeless, and footsore.

Chapter 9

Minette Hornsfels, daughter of the Lord High Adept Gabbro Scoria Hornsfels, and herself an Adept in her own right, looked with scorn upon the captive and thief of the one sword Genesyx Columba Riverford.

"What do you mean, you don't know where it is? You stole it, thief, how could you not know where it is?"

The poor wretch—the sinuous rippling muscles admirable anyway—blurted a half-strangled denial, cut off with a cry when her cat-o'-nine tails ripped across his back.

A thrill rushed through her to see his flesh twitch and his muscles squirm.

Now if he would only tell her where it is! she thought.

She stood over him in a prison cell deep beneath the Vault of Stones, itself heretofore deprived of its most valued stone, Luxullian, by a fat pusillanimous wretch who'd presumed to his uncle's estates and declared himself to Baron Marl Gneiss and thus had dissimulated his real intent whilst importuning upon the Lord High Adept at a distracted moment and purloining the one stone Luxullian from under their very noses.

Why couldn't he have been handsome, at least? Minette wondered, the thought of whipping the fat flabby flesh of the ugly obese baron nearly turning her stomach.

"Where is it, blast you?" And she brought down the multi-stranded whip again, his cry sending a rush of warmth coursing through her.

He was laid across a narrow table, face down, his clothes in a pile in a corner, his accoutrements spread out in the next room being inspected thoroughly. Oddly, only the sword that belonged to him appeared to exude any magic, and that a paltry amount, surely such a paucity that they must have laughed at him when he sought admission to the Hall of Swords.

Minette found difficult to believe the tales that this man had foiled the defenses of that thickly-defended bastion and had won a berth as apprentice in the moments before the theft.

Probably flexed his handsome frame to that bitch Pyxis! Minette thought, sweating from exertion.

"Where is she?" came a voice through the catacomb. Her father's voice.

Minette sighed. He always spoiled her fun. She looked upon her prisoner and debated: Insist on whipping him further until she got her information, or turn him over to her father, whose persuasions were much more subtle and far more painful?

"There you are." He bustled into the chamber, inspecting the lashes on the back. "Exquisite pattern, deftly done, but you'll not get the information from him." He whipped out a small diamond. "Columba Riverford, heal self with energy stored."

The wounds magically disappeared.

"Minette, come with me. Guards, get this man back to his cell."

She shrugged, puzzled, and sent the cat-o'-nine tails to its holder. The glow from her apricot-sized sapphire dimmed and died. Tucking it in its belt holder, she glanced into the next room, where his accoutrements were laid out.

The belt with its sheaths still attached was a standard affair, rivets holding the sheath to the belt itself. A few inches farther along was an empty knife sheath.

She looked up at the quartermaster. "What was there?"

"Not sure, Lady. Looks recently used, but no knife anywhere in his belongings."

"Interrogate his friend, and if you don't find it, get someone to return to the mine to look for it."

"Yes, Lady."

Minette frowned and turned to follow her father, bothered by something she couldn't quite name. The dark stone walls seemed to press in on her as she followed the narrow corridor where her father had gone.

He stood outside the cell of the other man who'd accompanied the thief. "From Scrollhaven, a native."

The implications were many. "But why? Haveners don't like Shirees much."

"Exactly. Come on." He led her further along into the Captain's office. "We'll need to borrow this, please."

The Captain bowed and retreated.

The High Adept closed the door and secured it, then turned toward her and grinned. "The Lady High Magux Cithara Ravenna embedded a message in the other man's belongings."

Minette felt her eyebrows climb her forehead. "She's been seeking your downfall for forty years, Father. What poison has she disguised with her honey this time?" She looked upon him, he who so recently lost the cipher that bestowed upon him the power to rule these domains, and yet she saw not a man defeated, but one resilient, responding with his own crafty wiles, rejuvenating the sly trickiness that had acquired him the title of High Adept some forty years before from his slovenly insipid uncle.

Minette had been born ten years after the coup, and thus had been spared the machinations of the blood feud between Uncle and Nephew, but the reverberations on occasion sent a tremor through the Vault of Stones. The High Adept had remained on guard for similar trickery, for one who had usurped the kingdom might in turn have it usurped from him.

The histories were fraught with similar upheavals, and the dominance of the Sword, Scroll, and Stone oligarchies was no guarantee of smooth transitions between rulers. But the tumult that preceded their imposition had consisted of far worse than a nephew deposing his inept uncle.

The Vault of Stones—before the theft of Luxullian—had at least guaranteed the stability of the state itself if not always the ruler who presided over it.

And now that Luxullian was gone, a fact no ruler could possibly hide, the continuity and safety of Stonevale tethered on the edge of chaos while armed bands of brigands raided with even greater bravado into lands formerly protected by the Lord High Adept.

That Stonevale had stood staunch for nearly two millennia was testament to its durability, and its longevity certainly contributed to its having withstood this vicissitude.

Further contributing was the nearly simultaneous thefts of the One Sword Genesyx and the One Scroll Canodex. Had Luxullian been stolen while Canodex remained in the hands of the Lady High Magux Cithara Ravenna, she might well have launched an assault on her neighbor to the east, an assault that surely would have been met with a fierce force of trained warriors, but whose conviction would have been undermined by the loss of Luxullian and the magic that its wielder, the High Adept Gabbro Scoria Hornsfels, would have deployed in the defense of Stonevale.

We've withstood the brigands these few weeks, Minette thought, but we've not the resources nor fortitude to withstand a prolonged period without Luxullian. The denizens of Stonevale had grown too accustomed to peace for that. We're soft! she thought, shaking her head. She looked at her father, her fear on her face. "What will we do, father? Against those disorganized miscreants, we might hold out for months, but not if that bitch Ravenna launches an attack."

"She's as beleaguered as we are, and less equipped besides. Nay, she'll not attack, at least not by conventional means ..."

"So she sends her minions, these two curmudgeons?"

"Nay, I don't think so. Hear the message: 'Lord High Adept Hornsfels, greetings. May the peace of your crystalline contemplations serve to buttress your resolve in this trying time. I've embedded this missive for your perusal in the clothing of this Woodwright. He suspects not what he carries, which if he knew, might expose him to more danger than his ignorance. What he doesn't know he carries cannot hurt him, eh?

"'With him is the purported 'thief' of Genesyx, the One Sword, who quite openly approached me and requested help. In my research into the depths of our sacred Crypt here in Scrollhaven, I did come across evidence to support this thief's assertion: that another was behind the theft of the One Sword Genesyx, and that this agent or agents is responsible for the thefts of your very own Luxullian and my One Scroll Canodex.

"'A fact that should have been evident to me from the outset.

"'Alas I was blind to it, upset in this aftermath of Canodex having been lost to Scrollhaven, a feeling I'm sure you felt in similar measure. In my blindness, I fear I have spurned the one person with the talents to aid us in our quests to recover our talismans. Upon further reflection, I became convinced that their recovery will require the combined talents of all three of these supposed thieves. These three—Columba Riverford, Aridisia Myric, and Marl Gneiss—are the agents by which we will see the return of the Sword, Scroll, and Stone. Toward that end, I beseech you to assist Sage Riverford in joining with the other two, should you know their whereabouts. For all of us—the peaceable residents of Shire, Haven, and Vale—I beg you to assist him.' "

Minette saw the look in her father's eyes. "She's beguiled you already, hasn't she? Embedded a charm in her parchment, I'll wager. Or in her panties!"

"I don't think so, daughter." Her father looked almost hurt at her assertions. He pulled out a tiny scroll. "In spite of her facile use of these in the past, I sense no subterfuge nor even emanation from this scroll. Here, examine it yourself."

She backed away, refusing to take it from him lest it be infectious. Her back against the wall, she kept an eye to the door for quick egress. "You can't trust her for a moment, father."

"I'm afraid we must, daughter."

He might have slapped her, his rejection an invalidation of her hypothesis. "She sends the Genesyx thief with a companion whose garments contain a secrete message intended to suborn your instinctive cautions, and you intend to acquiesce to her demands without question?" She wasn't sure where to direct her alarm, to the missive or to her father's gullibility.

"We both detest the Baron but it was overly magnanimous of us to attribute to him the guile required to purloin Luxullian from under our very noses. Such an act is far beyond his sophistication, and you know it. And to acquire Canodex and Genesyx at almost the same moment?

"Ravenna is right, daughter, a far more sinister agent seeks our downfall. And if it were only the restoration of Stonevale to be considered, I might side with you. But Scrollhaven and Swordshire are equally beleaguered. Yes, I'll die to defend Stonevale, but if either the Haven or Shire fall too, our doom will be writ upon their ashes." Gabbro Hornsfels pulled himself to his full height and turned his glare upon his daughter. "I beseech you, hear me out before you dismiss my ramblings as the misguided babbling of a spell-besotted billygoat!"

Minette shook her head at him and sighed. How'd he know what I was thinking? "All right, father, what are you thinking?"

He searched her face, his gaze probing her soul.

She felt him in her mind, her adoration of him across so many years weakening any attempt she might make to shield her thoughts from him. For long hours in her youth, she had learned from him how to clutter her mind with inconsequentials to prevent the kind of probe that he now explored her mind with, and in his probe, he revealed to her what he had found when he had probed the supposed thief Columba Riverford.

That, no, Columba had not stolen Genesyx, and would not have done so even if presented with the opportunity. Further, Columba was committed to its return to Swordshire and to his service to the Hall of Swords, should they accept him back. Like Gneiss, he was incapable of planning or executing the theft of such a talisman.

"And if Ravenna, High Magux of Scrollhaven, insist that the young woman, Aridisia Myric, could not have stolen Canodex, then I will have to place my faith in her belief."

"So you want me to go with Columba to help him find Myric and Gneiss," Minette said.

Gabbro Scoria Hornsfels nodded.

"Why?" she asked. "It's more than that, isn't it? More than the theft of the three talismans within an hour of each other, more than the chaos biting at the edges of our domains, more than the hortatory bombast of that evil witch to the northwest of us, more than the panic and impending doom that's besieged every one of us to the very core of our beings, isn't it?"

"Yes, dear daughter, it's more than all of these put together. As my heir and she who faces the most to lose if Luxullian remain unrecovered and our three kingdoms do not survive this crisis, you deserve to know the whole of it."

* * *

In the making of the Sword, Scroll, and Stone, a cabal of practitioners united to bring order to this chaotic land. Prestidigitationists of every stripe joined this effort but one, a necromancer named Travert Crepitans Pictor. Such a one in singular held no sway to stop or impede their work, this cabal, and as they focused the elementals energies to the north, west, east, and south, Necromancer Pictor brooded deep in his haunt beneath Warlock's Mount, his minions surveilling the events above ground while he lurked in his volcanic home of sulfur and sweats.

Now as the cabal finished its work and secured the energies of earth, fire, wind, and water, Pictor did attempt one last time to undo their work and release the constraints the cabal had imposed, but his effort was but partially a success. In all but one realm he failed, and was defeated for all time, a thousand magicians to his one, his very soul and essence and being obliterated in the calamitous war.

The one element that he succeeded in freeing in his pyrrhic victory was that of water, and thus he secured for himself the complete control of the seas. In doing so he lost his life, but the end result left Warlock's Mount a pyroclastic cone in the center of the Halfmoon Sea.

The other three realms were preserved and maintained their dominance until today.

Nay, you're right I don't believe we've heard the last of this Necromancer, Travert Crepitans Pictor, for as is his wont, raising the dead was his talent, and a magician of his inestimable talents would like as not raise himself from the dead.

Know I this of the certainty of the rising of the sun?

Of course not, but there were signs.

A gadget-maker to the south whose confabulations awed even the mighty, and whose contraptions were sought by the wealthiest among us, and whose cupidity proved the doing of his own undoing.

A thaumaturge who sought to persuade even the reclusive folk of the Wizened Forest to bend to his will and very nearly succeeded.

A Neptunian nymph who suborned even the King of the Oceans to her guiles and charms and who but for fortune would have taken his life even as she was charming the life in his loins to join with the life in hers.

These tales are told in the far reaches of our four corners, tales whose scraps I've heard from each of the guilds in all our lands, for the time I've spent wandering has filled my mind with fantastical tale of a thousand threads, which when each complete does weave together a forbidding tome, a palimpsestic scroll, a variegated gem, a multi-alloy sword.

And Columba Riverford, our supposed thief, finds himself in his own mind going back to an encounter with a curmudgeon of the lowest sort, a debased character little worth the breath I waste on him, but one whose humble beginnings went astray when he was struck aglance by a falling tree.

Now Dorad Fallentree was pitiable to behold, an ugly wretch with a lopsided head and a grin to match. Now his fate after being struck might have come about much faster had he not happened upon—or had happened upon him—a little twist of fate in the form of the Dam who lived in southwest Scrollhaven, far too close to the badlands for most, but her small cottage unmolested by roving brigands who sought succulent old women more vulnerable than she to prey upon.

Now as Dorad was lacking the sense to clothe or feed or house himself, he frequently went unclothed, his unbathed self raising a fetor that caused a skunk to faint. As he had no mind to his body, he certainly had a no plan or will to cause what happened next, but even so, after spending a night in the old Dam's roadhouse, he was found outside with a bloody knife, and she was found inside, all stabbed and choked, her wizened frame naked and ravaged.

Not to excuse, but for a deed already done, the poor fool fled and prowled the hills between Scrollhaven and Swordshire for years afterward, having acquired a sudden cunning quite beyond the ken of his misshapen brain.

Aye I ramble but hear me out.

Twas that very same Dam, a necklace of sharkteeth around her neck, who settled on the outskirts of Scrollhaven whose roadhouse stood sentinel for the weary traveler seeking that first haven where a soul might be safe from the likes of Dorad, and in that unlikely place this Dam did reside, seems like more than a century. The local legend averred that she arrived one night at the crossroads, still aglisten from the sea, a young woman then, mesmerizing in her beauty, and at the crossroads there ensued a terrible fight, so devastating in its aftermath that no one remembers what it was about.

All the legends can say is that a Sage, a Magus, and an Adept converged, the sage from the west of course, the Magus as you might expect from the north, and the Adept as ever from the east.

Twas like an explosion, they say, and the only creature left standing was the young Dam Antlia, she called herself, the necklace of sharkteeth and the knife in her hand her only adornments.

Like as not it was some distraction, this whirling dervish of ravishing beauty whose countenance was wont to change like a snake or eel or other long sinuous creature.

Suffice it to say the area was leveled, trees flattened and shrubs shorn of their leaves within the area, and a great gout in the earth which later had to be bridged.

But it was there at the crossroads she stayed with nary a care as to who came and went, eventually building a boarding house for the weary, unwary traveler, a place so forlorn and infested that only fools would rush in, a place she eventually called Fools Rush Inn.

Now of the Sword, Scroll, and Stone that each the Sage, Magus, and Adept had wielded, none know the fate, and naught of their remains was ever recovered. Now mayhap the Dam Antlia knew the location of these talismans but that knowledge died with her, or perhaps is buried in the knife itself, which Dorad himself used to kill her.

Where is the knife now, dear daughter? Heaven knows where it might be.

And that alone is reason for you to accompany Sage Columba.

* * *

Bere and Ari stopped at the edge of the world and contemplated their choices.

The jagged cliff-face, should they choose to adhere to its rim, buckled across the miles to the east until it faded into the mists wafting up from the invisible but audible surf below.

Straight below them, Bere glimpsed a sharper white than the dull amorphous fog that roiled against the cliff-face like the cold breath of the Sea Dragon himself.

Bere had been to the northern coast of Swordshire many times, but those were gentler shores in gentler climes, and here the biting cold that blew up the cliff face and worked its chill fingers under every seam of her clothes might have been a giant frozen hand forbidding her descent through the turbid mist to the diaphanated beach far below.

"Stars above," Bere said, shaking her head.

"Surf below," Ari retorted a grin on her face.

Bere snorted and looked inland.

Mounting hills of grass ascended without apparent break toward forest-covered mountains, themselves looking formidable and impassable, although her sense of them was that they would find a way through, were they to try.

Into Scrollhaven proper, where Ari was reluctant to go.

"Boiling pot, frying pan, or fire. Doesn't seem much of a choice." Bere sighed and looked at Ari. "Let's camp here and decide in the morning."

Neither had spoken of the night overlooking the Wizened Forest, but Bere had caught the occasional glance from Ari, the amused bewilderment in her face, the soft subtle glow of satisfaction, and the slight blush at cheek of embarrassed joy.

Although younger than Ari by a year, Berenice Longblade was long accustomed to having what she wanted when she wanted to have it. Before she died her mother had instilled in Bere a healthy respect for her desires, one that included the freedom to affiliate with those who pleased her or piqued her fancy without the need for lasting attachment. Although her lovers had sometimes surprised her with the depth of their desire for her, Bere had rarely become so enamored of anyone that she felt the need to remain involved for longer than a few months at a time. She asked little of her intimates, gave of her passions freely, and soon developed other interests.

Frequently the object of her amours were likewise advanced practitioners of their respective magics, and Bere's sense of Ari was similar, but its quality eluded her. Among Bere's talents was a sensitivity to other's magics, and in Ari she sensed a dynamic force whose inchoate nascence obscured a formidable puissance, the strongest that anyone had registered in her senses since her father.

Ari's power at least equals and may even exceed my father's, Bere thought, watching the other woman carefully.

Ari shrugged at Bere. "I'd rather get down there, first." She pointed down the unscalable cliff face.

"And how will we get down there? Float magically?"

Ari whipped out her scroll. "By sight, by might, set us in sand before night by flight." The quill danced across parchment.

The giant hand that had pushed against Bere, warning her not to descend, did lift her from the lip of cliff and ease her down toward the beach. The cliff face, she saw as she passed it, was far more jagged and unscalable than it had looked from above, overhang and shelf corrugating the otherwise vertical surface, tufts of grass and small bushes clinging precariously to meager purchases, barely able to afford themselves nutrients from the variegated rock.

From the beach, the cliff looked even more foreboding, as though it threatened the crash upon them on the beach, the weight above it pressing relentlessly down.

The soft sand under Bere's feet was at least a comfort, and she realized it wasn't as cold as she might have thought, although the wind did pick the spray from atop the waves and carry it to them as a fine damp mist, the scent of spindrift brine filling her nostrils. The gentle susurrus of the ocean swell, the occasional call of the lonely gull and the breath of wind were the only sounds, the sun to the west barely visible as a white disc through the mist surrounding them.

While the rim of cliff above them had buckled into the distance, the beach seemed to stretch straight to the east without visible break until it too was obscured in the thickening mist.

Bere marveled at the endless sea in three directions.

"Here the cliff bends back around in a slow arc toward the northwest mountain in Stonevale. These cliffs may look straight here, but that's because its curve is obscured in the distance." Ari gestured for them to get moving. "We've a long way to go."

Bere set out with gusto, the wind buffeting her from the left, the towering cliff face to her right. Although the wind was sharp and cold, her exertion kept her warm. She refrained from magic, suspecting she might need it that night, especially if they found no shelter from the wind and cold. Her head down and chin tucked into her collar, Bere walked briskly, turning over in her mind the odd story told them by Cincinatus Ripplebark, the wizard from Warlock's Mount seeming to have capitulated prematurely to the hairy reclusive natives of the Wizened Forest.

And what had he withheld at the very end? she wondered.

Bere stumbled into Ari. "Oh, Sorry, what—?"

Ari stared straight ahead, seeming unperturbed, almost entranced.

Bere looked ahead.

On a rock outcrop protruding from the sand at the waterline sat a mermaid, a tiara of sharkteeth crowning her head.

She'd heard legend of such creatures during a visit to the western shore of Swordshire. Acclaimed to have the power to transform themselves into normal human beings, the Merfolk were renowned for their comeliness. The creature before them was certainly well proportioned in both face and figure, enough to stir both envy and desire in her human observers.

And Bere's sense of the creature's magic was similar to her sense of Ari's, a quiescent volcano slumbering for now in nascent ambiguity.

Bere stared, still fifty feet away.

Ari nodded to her, not taking her gaze from the figure on the rock.

A voice resonant as a bell and redolent of command rang in Bere's ears and in her mind. "I'm a Salina Coralreef, Queen of the Northern Seas, and thaumaturge of water. You are Aridisia Myric, Magux of Scrollhaven, with Berenice Longblade, Sage of Swordshire. You seek the thief of Canodex, the One Scroll, and Genesyx, the One Sword. Your purpose here is clear but your methods murky. Pray tell, Ladies Ari and Bere, what brings you to the edge of my domains?"

How does she know all that? Bere wondered, and realized instantly that the Mermadam had heard her thoughts as though she'd spoken them aloud.

"Of course I did, Lady. From the time you left the Wizened Forest, I felt your approach. One as bright as your companion, the Lady Myric, can be seen from many leagues for those who have the sight. Please, be not afraid, for we have more in common than you might think."

Bere felt the tug of Salina's invitation, as though the Sea Queen had tugged on her hand. Behind it was a comfort and welcome that was difficult to refuse. She stepped forward, instinctively trusting the mermaid for reasons she would have had difficulty articulating.

She found herself facing the rock, Ari right beside her, both of them kneeling. "Queen Coralreef, a pleasure to make your acquaintance."

The tiara-topped head nodded slightly. "And yours, Ladies. Lady Sage Longblade, please convey to your farther my condolences on the disappearance of Genesyx and my sincere wish that it be returned forthwith. Lady Magux Myric, though you shy from the title, few are more worthy to wear it, your talent and skill having brought you through numerous difficulties already. Further challenges await you, and none so arduous as the recovery of Canodex, though I suspect it is closer to hand than you know.

"I see you are cold. Come, let us repair to a place more to your liking, for if the inclination of the sun does remind me, you have nearly reached the end of your day."

"Just so, Lady Thaumaturge," Ari replied. "The chill does cut to the bone in the fading light."

Bere's eyes went wide as the lower half transformed into that of a woman, a lower half just a voluptuous as the upper half.

"My apologies," the Queen said, getting to her feet. "I forgot how alluring this form can be." And she snapped her fingers.

A gush of waster sprouted from the top of her head and spilled down her face and body in an even coat, obscuring the shapely form not at all but covering the skin with a soft frothing foam that puddled at her feet, where the sand absorbed it without a trace. "This way, please."

And she led the way toward the jagged cliff face. Where solid rock had been moments before, a tunnel passage opened, and inside was a cheerfully lit room with oaken floors and quilted walls, a table heaped with repast taking up most the room. Behind it burned a blazing hearth, to which they hurried to dispel the cold.

The Queen watched them both with a detached amusement.

We must seem the desperate lot, Bere thought, eyeing the food hungrily from a spot as close to the fire as she could get without getting burned.

"Please, eat after you've warmed yourselves. I too in this form find the weather uncomfortable." The water still spilled down her face and body, a constant flow that kept her modestly covered.

"You felt our thoughts from leagues away," Ari said. "But how? Rare is the talent that penetrates the murky human mind."

Queen Salina laughed softly. "Tis true the murkiness of the mind, a trait we Merfolk share with our land-bound cousins. Tis not a weakness of their own that allows me glimpse of thy thoughts and fears. Ere anon, I would share what I know but first I must ask: Why do you seek a sword and scroll in this desolate clime?"

Bere and Ari shared a glance. Had she wanted, Bere might have cluttered her mind with inconsequentials or done her best to keep it blank, but given the perspicacity of the creature before her, she knew that such effort was of little avail.

"We seek allies in our search," Ari answered. "We three supposed thieves have both the restoration of our good names and the object purloined in those names to seek. And thus are doubly motivated to right the wrong. Our journey brings us here because my presence in Scrollhaven is an affront to those who accuse me of this deed, and better that we journey through this northern clime than take the brigand-beset south road and mayhaps lose our lives."

"Ah, and in gaining allies you might expose the mystery mage who orchestrated those thefts." The Queen's gaze narrowed.

"But you said 'three'. Two thiefs I know of, but who is the third thief? For reasons obscure, I sense him not."

"Who do you not sense, my Queen?" Bere asked, "Columba Riverford, the upstart Sage, or Baron Marl Gneiss, the upstart Adept?"

"Gneiss you say? And a Baron besides?" The Queen shook her head. "He does not appear to me in any form. Is he such a bad man?"

Ari looked at Bere. "You say he doesn't appear?"

"'Tis a flaw in what I see. Evil intent does not manifest to my vision, and sometimes I am blinded to a fault. A vulnerability of my ilk, 'tis true. More's the evil, the fainter my sight of it. What is he like?"

Bere shrugged, but she saw Ari draw back as though in recoil.

"A fat man with fleshly insatiable appetites. He exudes a fetor of corruption and a paucity of compassion. He carries an apricot-sized ruby and wears a buckle with a ruby in its center, the surrounding metal burnished in an odd way," Are glanced around as though to find an object. "Burnished like the steel of Bere's sword."

"Bere being the swordbearer," Queen Coralreef said, turning toward her, "you would recognize swordsteel, were you to lay eyes upon it?"

"I certainly would, my Queen. It has the delicate imprint of a thousand hammer blows, which no amount of polish or sharpening can truly remove."

"Then seek this Marl, for his absence in my sight does not bode well for the mission before you."

"Forgive me, Queen," Ari said, "but is that necessary? He's a loathsome man."

Queen Salina Coralreef nodded. "Evil and good differ only in the direction of one's intent. And your loathing reflects anxieties regarding qualities you detest in yourself. We are all capable of insatiability. What is corpulence but a desire to escape depravity? What is Saturnalia but the feast that follows famine? When faced with extreme, we all respond in ways we would otherwise eschew.

"I would imagine that this Baron has escaped my purview precisely because the fetor of corruption fills his thoughts and leaves no room for compassion."

* * *

King Victor Sandbar though modest his name was the quintessential hero we all acclaim. So fair was his countenance that his fame did spread onshore, and many were the maidens who threw themselves into the sea in hopes that he might offer them his attentions. A few did drown before he promulgated a law requiring that these besotten human females be carried back to ashore.

Reluctant was King Victor to approach the coast because of this, although his magic was strong and he might have given himself a visage nearer the eidolon of ugliness. As we know, all perfection carries faults and mayhaps his was liking the admiration he inspired, for he was known to yield now and again and frolic in the surf with a particularly comely maiden.

Unfortunately, it wasn't always maidens to which he often was afflicted attention from. Even the married among the human women were like as not to forget their vows and hurl themselves into the sea after this comely man with the bewitching face.

And every married woman has a husband.

The inevitable happened, and the married woman who plunged into the ocean in pursuit of King Victor was strikingly beautiful, and most nearly every man she encountered was as smitten with her as women were with King Victor. Alas had she been Merfolk the tragedy might have been averted, as the two might have married.

The wrath of a woman spurned tis legend, but we all know the unspeakable fury of a husband betrayed.

And this husband, it was said, was himself a power of singular note, his magic strong and his physique to match. Though his countenance was fair, King Victor's refulgent face was the sun in the daytime sky to the husband's moon at night.

On the southern coast of Swordshire, these events took place, and when the husband did espy his wife's discarded garments on the shore and saw in the surf the frolic of the two-backed octopus, he threw caution to the wind, and armed with only a knife, he plunged headfirst into sea.

A knife, yes, but no simple knife. Its haft looked pewter and set at its base where blade met pommel, a single sapphire was mounted, embedded in metal. At the end of half was a screw-on cap and beneath the cap a tiny scroll, the spell upon it written so long ago that the ink had faded and the vellum flaked.

Yes, a talisman that violated the inviolable, a blasphemy reminiscent of our time before the Sword, Scroll, and Stone when the blending of magics wreaked havoc between the four corners.

Tis true we know not where this knife came from, and when the humans sought to identify this husband and wife, no trace or knowledge or relative could be found. There were those who speculated this was a supernatural pair, marionettes in some puppeteer's play upon the strings that bind the magics to their talismans, and foreswear upon the human race to eschew but one of the fundamental forces.

Now tis no mystery that among those four, only water retains its freedom to flow, whereas fire, wind, and earth are now bound each to their respective Sword, Scroll, and Stone. That a great sorcerer did resist the cabal of his brethren to channel the fundaments into these talismans, and in his efforts he did succeed in destroying the talisman intended to encapsulated water, losing his life in the battle.

Thus when husband hurled himself, knife in hand, into surf that frothed from frolic, the two-backed octopus was intent on its own activities and saw naught the danger fraught, and the husband's first blow caught not the King but the wife such a grievous blow that she died in moments. So aggrieved and more enraged was the husband that he turned upon King Victor and plunged his knife into King Victor's side so deep that he lost his grip on the weapon.

The King in his element had the advantage in spite of the knife lodged in his side, and quickly the husband succumbed and was dead.

The blood-thickened waters settling around him, King Victor looked upon the tragedy he'd wrought and remorse inflicted its own wounds to his psyche, and he swam out into the vast expanse of the western sea as far from land as he might go and keened for days on the contretemps he'd created.

Initially it was thought that the knife lodged in the wound was kept there by the longanimous suffering that King Victor felt for having succumbed to his desires. But over the years as even he saw that the circumstance was an imbroglio to which he'd only contributed, not one that he had caused in its entire.

On land, it's known that the pedalist humans found not a trace of either husband's or wife's origin, and could not account for their arrival on the southern shore of Swordshire, nor could they say with any certainty whence had come the knife which abrogated their inculcated prohibition to mixing magics.

There in the vast gyre of a stagnant sea did King Victor Sandbar suffer, his psyche healing slowly but the wound in his side necrotizing in spite of his having the finest of thaumaturge at his disposal. The wound suppurated slowly, the fetor inescapable, the pain so severe that King Victor could be heard keening from leagues away.

The passage of time underwater is not so distinct as it is on land, and thus isn't known how long he lay on the bottom of the sea, his wound seeping slowly, his life bleeding from him like water through a pinhole in the side of a dam.

The increasing pain and weakness he felt were akin to that the amphibians might feel when being rendered for their fleshly legs. Turn the temperature up gradually and don't stir the pot, and they'll sit there until sautéed, but turn up the heat too fast or slosh the broth too much, and out they'll jump.

King Victor was a boiling frog, the wound growing so gradually worse that all he did was lay there, becoming habituated to his pain and suffering.

Word did reach him of a human maiden so pretty and demure she did attract suitors from all the four corners. King Victor having lain on the ocean floor deprived of sensual pleasures for decades did rise, in the faint hope that a glimpse of so fair a woman might assuage his pain in but a moment.

With what seemed the last of his strength he donned a crown of sharkteeth and rose from the ocean floor and to the west coast of Swordshire he swam.

In his time ashore, the Merfolk had no contact, and what events transpired there we have only his recount, of which he have but a penurious narrative, to which he said she was pretty as foretold and ameliorate she did, but the people there could not cure him.

Despairing that he would not return, the Merfolk summoned the support of the sea itself and sent a great storm, and as it descended upon this village, the maid did yank this poison knife from the wound.

Alas that she did, for it turned its poisons upon her, and transformed her into an eel, as thick through its body as plump as she'd been through the hips. Its fury renewed with her energy, the knife resumed its attempts to vanquish the Merman King and thus make way for its master to reign supreme over the fundament water.

But the storm that the Merfolk had summoned carried the evil eel and the knife that drove her round south of Swordshire into the Halfmoon Sea and spat her upon the beach, sans her weakened target, the Merman King Victor Sandbar, leaving a coastline ravaged by wind and storm, headlands eroded and fishing ports smashed to twigs.

The much enervated King Victor did recover but never to his former vigor, and he passed his mantle to me, bidding me to beware the fall of Sword, Scroll, and Stone, for of the knife that had laid him low and wounded him grievous, naught is known, nor of the fair young maiden Antlia, whose countenance was transmogrified into a deadly eel.

Nor is known the whereabouts of the regicidal warlock who plotted to entrap the Merman King, my father, who but for providence would have killed him.

* * *

Sweat pouring off him, Baron Marl Gneiss swore softy and stared ahead in dismay, checking over his shoulder once again for an egress that he knew wasn't there.

The tunnel had collapsed behind them an hour ago, the roiling clouds of dust sending them all scampering headlong down the tunnel in fear of their lives.

Nearly into the open glowing lava beds.

The Baron Caelum Footsore had teetered on the edge for a brief wide-eyed moment, arms aflail.

Then had regained his balance.

"I don't know what possessed me even to order this ill-fated spelunk to start with," he'd said, his gaze clear of the wild panic that Marl had seen in his eyes for three days straight. "Let's turn around immediately."

But the way was blocked, and thus deep under the mountain, there weren't any other tunnels.

If they were to escape, they'd have to dig their way out.

For the past hour, in between trying to calm the panicked coterie, organize an excavation team, and catalog the resources available to them, the Baron Footsore kept apologizing to the Baron Gneiss. "I swear, no matter what I tried to get my tongue to say, all I could do was order the men to hurry up with the preparations. I thought I was going to explode I was so frustrated!"

Marl looked over the glowing lava, the ceiling a half-circle of rounded bumps, as though the jagged edges of rock had been melted into smoothened nodules. Clearly the cavern had once been filled with lava and upon receding had left a hemispherical tube, the cooling lava floor still glowing red and far too hot to traverse, the waves of heat coming off the surface and seeping around the cave-in behind them, where a group of miners worked furiously to clear the cave-in, the stench of sulfur clotting their nostrils.

How are we going to get out of here? he wondered.

"These are miners, dear Marl," Caelum said, seeing the direction to his gaze. "They'll have us out of here in a few hours. Not to worry, my friend. We're a continent to conquer. No idiot cave-in will stop us!"

Marl wished he felt that confident. He glanced back and forth between the lava beds ahead and the cave-in behind. "How long will our supplies last?"

Caelum scoffed. "What's the worry?! We'll feast on our remaining supplies when we return to Castle Footsore."

The contingent commander approached. "A moment of your time, Lord Baron." She looked at Marl. "Alone, Lord, my apologies."

Marl retreated. The remaining members of their group lined the walls, a worried Pavo and Sagit sitting alone in an alcove.

"Baron," Pavo said, pulling him aside and speaking in a low voice, "the miners aren't making progress. The rock won't stabilize under their spells, as though some geis keeps their magic from working. What are we going to do?"

Marl glanced back the direction he'd come. Through the sulfur mist came the Baron Footsore, the look of dismay on his face matching the despair of Marl's heart. Caelum must have just learned the same.

"Come with me, Baron Gneiss," Caelum said, gesturing toward the cave-in.

The air at this end wasn't so fouled with sulfur at least. Marl looked over the miners as he and the Baron Footsore approached.

One by one, they ceased digging and stepped aside, their gazed averted, their expressions ashen.

There was barely room at the caved-in end of the tunnel for both Barons to stand, Marl painfully aware that his bulk filled most the space.

"Have you performed magic upon rock before, good Baron?"

Marl shook his head.

"Tis like any other physical substance. It obeys the laws of magic, but most especially obeys the fundament of earth. You're a disciple of Stonevale, the arbiter of earth and its commander. You of all people can surely tame this obstreperous rock."

Marl began to sweat all the more, despite the significantly cooler temperature here. "Surely, Lord Baron Footsore," he said with more conviction than he felt. He slipped his apricot-sized ruby from its pouch. Its glow lit the tunnel brilliantly. "Stone of rock, these miners mock, but my command wilt thou obey, and open a way." and he thrust the ruby at the rubble as though to blast a path.

A perfectly circular tube sank deep through the cave-in, and the rush of wind told him he'd done it.

A cheer erupted behind him, and Marl turned to grin.

A roar of rock collapsed the tube behind him.

The instant silence was grim.

"Must've lost my concentration," he said under his breath, but somehow he was sure everybody had heard. With a deep breath, he lowered the stone, then gathered himself, pulling the arm back as though to hurl the ruby forward.

"By Gods galore, as eagles soar, I do implore, remove this core!" And he pushed the ruby toward the cave-in.

The tube returned and the wind rushed again but no one cheered.

Marl kept his eye on the tube, his arm extended, the glare of his ruby almost too bright to look at.

"Phenocry!" Baron Footsore called over his shoulder. "You and five miners—get through now!"

The old miner scrambled past them, five others following with alacrity.

Probably wanting to escape their raving-mad Baron, Marl thought, and immediately wished he hadn't.

The tube collapsed on the miners.

Sickened, Marl fell back against the tunnel wall, guilt and shame doing back flips in his stomach.

"Lord Baron, the lava ..." Someone somewhere said.

The excited chatter drew everyone's attention, leaving Marl and Footsore at the death end of the tunnel.

Baron Footsore said something.

Baron Marl Gneiss whirled on him. "What did you ask me?" No honorific no apology.

Footsore's gaze was full of steel. "I asked to see your stone." No honorific, no apology.

Marl didn't like anything about the request—the tone, the lack of honorific, the lack of apology, the effrontery of someone's asking to see his family jewel. He might as well be asking to see my testicles, Marl thought.

But to refuse: Animosity, hostility, possibly even a parting of ways.

Marl glanced at the collapsed tunnel behind him, where six miners had vanished in a moment of inattention. Marl realized sweat poured off him, for to refuse might risk the Baron Footsore's abandoning him in these trackless catacombs.

He also realized that everyone else had made their way to the other end of their tunnel, where the pyroclastic flow of hot molten lava blocked their forward progress. They were alone, and the indignity of Baron Footsore's demand had gone unwitnessed!

And his final realization was that his delay in responding was tantamount to defiance.

"Of course, Lord Baron," he said, dissimulating with a smile, his guts grinding, his palms sweating. Wiping them slyly, he reached for his apricot-sized ruby.

Red rays dappled the tunnel walls, the stone instantly alight, the color and brightness bringing Marl instant comfort.

"Set it there, Lord Baron," Caelum said, gesturing to a random rock shelf protruding from the wall. "I'll not touch it, I assure you."

Marl wasn't assured.

"Listen fool, it would be blasphemy for me to try to use your stone. My own magic would repudiate any attempt I might make. You see this sword?" Baron Footsore drew his blade, its burnished metal glinting in the dim light. "Passed along to me through the Barons Footsore from the original Baron Cetus Footsore, the First, whose dominion over the Barony was granted him by the first High Sage, the ancient revered Ovate Crepitans Pictor, grandfather to that reprobate cur, the apostate Travert, who nearly brought down in its nascence the very structure his grandfather worked so hard to establish. I would be relinquishing millennia of tradition and fealty if I were to try to use that scurrilous bauble of yours."

Marl didn't know whether to be offended that the other had called his gemstone a scurrilous bauble, or him a fool. He decided neither, guessing it was simply Footsore's way of saying he had no use of either, and no fear of either.

Caelum Footsore had never struck Marl as fearful.

So he put it on the ledge as the other man requested.

Footsore perused the stone, its red rays playing across the landscape of his face. Then he brought his sword blade up and positioned it in between his face and the stone, a mere six inches from stone to blade to face. "By the stars, by the scars, reveal to me what you ares."

A nimbus of light worked its way up the blade, worms of electricity writhing within, and a field of electrical tentacles surrounded the ruby, its facets morphing or seeming to morph under the bombardment of electrons.

Marl felt a heat collecting at his belly and caught a whiff of … Smoke!

And the warmth flashed to hot!

He ripped the buckle off, singeing his fingers, and it fell to the rough stone floor, the leather strap smoking, the tiny ruby on the buckle face aglow.

"What foul magic is this!" Baron Footsore trapped the buckle with the toe of his boot, then raised a gaze full of alarm to Marl's face. "Failing to abide by the ancient proscriptions is punishable with excommunication and expulsion. You told me you're faithful to the stone. Do you flaunt them even as you asseverate how deeply you abide by them?" Accusation in his eyes, the Baron Footsore turned the sword blade toward him. "Truth be told, truth behold."

The words leaped from Marl's mouth like so much expurgation. "It carries me across the land and not I it. I know not its mysteries or origins, and I swear I use it not!" And Marl put his hands over his mouth to contain what had already escaped.

The Baron Footsore nodded slowly and turned to look at the ruby.

Marl followed his gaze as though he saw a different stone, a crystal of some type, but no, it was the red of the ruby he'd so gently placed on the ledge.

The brow of the Baron beside him wrinkled then smoothened. "You are fortunate that the High Adept Hornsfels did not see the buckle, else he might have blasted you to Eternity—or wherever else your superstitions would have you reside after you depart this world."

Marl didn't mention he'd acquired it from the bandit Skarn Arkose under circumstances so odd that even he, Marl Gneiss, wouldn't have believed it, had he told himself the tale. Let Baron Footsore believe I've always had it. "Belonged to my uncle, the deceased Baron Gossan Jaspil Breccia Gneiss."

"Dabbled in the black arts, it appears," Baron Footsore said. "Take your bauble and this abominable talisman," he added, gesturing first at the apricot sized ruby and then the still smoldering belt with its hot metal buckle. "Since neither can help us get out of here. As to the tunnel, well . . ." Caelum muttered, "Had to try, my friend, had to try." And he turned and walked away.

It was the first time Marl regretted having the stone. He wished he were rid of it. He hadn't thought as he'd taken the prized ruby from its setting in the underground cavern below his uncle's mansion that he would be responsible for other people's lives. Or for their deaths.

And yet he'd effectively murdered six experienced miners who'd been commanded to enter an unstable tunnel held open only by the concentration of a presumed Adept from Stonevale, one whose pretense was exceeded only by his bravado.

"You did the best you could," Pavo said.

Marl hadn't seen him approach. Everything around him looked distant, as though viewed through a thick veil, and sounds barely reached his ears, snatched away by some unfelt wind. His hands and feet tingled, and his chest felt tight, as though a huge tree trunk bore down upon it.

The sting of utter rejection aflame upon his soul, Marl picked up both objects, the buckle now cool and the belt still serviceable. He buckled it around his waist and looked at the apricot-sized ruby in his hand, relieved that the Baron Footsore hadn't probed further into the buckle's origin, but further dismayed by the dismissive condescension.

He's right, Marl thought, I'm not good for anything.

He looked to the cave-in, where six miners had met their fate because of his inattention. Better that I die here with them than suffer a moment more, he thought.

The Baron Marl Gneiss rose, feeling peculiarly light in both body and spirit, as though less burdened by the bulk of life, as though his decision to atone for the miner's death had somehow ameliorated the horrific suffering he had caused them and the companions whom they had left behind.

He climbed the loose rubble, where minutes before tons of rock had pulverized six people instantaneously.

"Rock divine, take stone of mine and pulverize me complete—"

"Baron, don't!"

The tackle took him to his knees and knocked the glowing ruby from his hand. Marl looked around, wondering what had struck him.

Pavo picked himself out of the rubble, and extended a hand to help Marl to his feet. "I don't know what possessed me," Pavo was saying, slightly breathless, "I've never done anything like that before."

Marl found the ruby along with his feet and rolled it around in his palm. I guess you require that I continue to suffer, he told it.

The glow on the youth's face, Marl realized, was coming not from the now-inert ruby in his palm, but from the small ruby embedded in his belt buckle. Odd, he thought, not having invoked its powers, puzzled that now twice in the span of a few minutes, its powers had been activated.

Pavo had recovered his breath. "You weren't really going to do that, were you?"

Marl didn't reply, gazing at the apricot-sized ruby, the prize gem from his uncle's collection. With it, his uncle might have become Adept at the Vault of Stones, serving the High Adept Gabbro Scoria Hornsfels. Instead he'd died errantly under an avalanche with all known relatives, save Marl. Why couldn't he have of least died in the pursuit of some noble cause, anyway? Marl wondered, wishing he'd had the illustriousness of a noble death to illuminate his ascension to the Barony.

He sighed and saw Pavo there as though noticing him for the first time. "Why'd you come back for me?"

Pavo's face brightened. "The lava—it's cooled, and we can walk on it now. Come on." He gestured and turned.

Marl followed, absent any enthusiasm, abject shame and humiliation still very much in his thoughts, his failure to keep the tunnel open just like all his other failures. Every task he'd ever turned his hand to had gone awry, from shepherding to tree harnessing to grain grinding. He'd proved himself profoundly inept at everything he'd tried, and he'd thought in these last two weeks since arriving at Stonevale with the ruby in palm that perhaps his fortunes had changed, that the bizarre, almost eerie series of bungled attempts at mastering some task or trade had taken a turn for the better, in spite of Luxullian's disappearance, which had been no fault of his, and that he might look forward to sunnier days and more gentle climes.

But as he thought about it, and in particular, recalled that the High Adept had stripped him of the Barony, and that the thief Skarn Arkose had assaulted, robbed, and bound him, and that the Baron Footsore had nearly taken him hostage on this ill-fated excursion to the bowels of the Footsore Barony, Marl realized that the last two weeks had been nothing more than a continuation of the same longanimous lucubration that he'd endured throughout his execrable existence.

Marl realized that Pavo watched him closely, glancing repeatedly over his shoulder as he led Marl toward the previously impassable lava beds. His desire to die as strong as ever, he knew Pavo wouldn't stand idly by if he were to attempt it again. They caught up to the ragtag remains of the cortege, all of them looking at least as desperate as Marl felt.

"I'm not walking out on that!" one miner said.

"You can't get me to do it either, Baron, pardon the impertinence. I'll not do it, I tell you," said a thick-bellied servant.

All eyes turned to Marl.

He felt the recrimination in their gazes. "I will."

All those gazes averted, as though to look upon him might somehow implicate them in his demise, as though they would somehow be at fault if they didn't stop him from what was surely a hot, fiery death.

For they knew, as the Baron Marl Gneiss well knew, that the lava was unlikely to be stable enough to walk on, that it only looked solid, that underneath a thin sheet of cooled rock was a pyroclastic flow that would incinerate him instantly if he were to fall through the thin friable crust.

At least it'll be a quick death, Marl thought. "If it can hold my weight," he told them, "Then it'll hold the lot of you."

No one objected and no one looked at him save Pavo. The boy was shaking he head, big pools of tears collecting in his eyes, his mouth silently saying. "Don't," over and over.

Marl squeezed the boy's hand and stepped toward the newly crusted rock. Little spouts of steam geysered from the rock every few feet.

Sweat pouring off him, Marl stepped out onto the glazed rock. As it accepted his full weight, melodious cracks sounded, like the tinkling of glass, and were greeted by the observers' gasps.

He felt the increase in warmth through the sole of his shoe but the rock gave no more, and he took the next step. Again crackles radiated mellifluously from around his foot but it held.

And the next.

His courage built with each step, and soon, he was striding at a normal pace, the glow of lava seeping through cracks adding to the bright glare cast by the ruby in his belt buckle.

Again mystified that its magic worked without his invoking it, Marl wondered at its properties, for surely such a talisman was at least as valuable as the Sword, Scroll, and Stone.

The warmth against his belly, he knew, was that of the buckle he'd stolen from Skarn Arkose.

He slowed only when he saw no more spouts of steam or glowing red cracks, and he realized the stone floor was no longer warm through his shoes. The passageway opened into a larger cavern, the floor notably uneven and buckled in places, but showing no evidence that magma lurked close beneath.

The darkness encroached, his buckle no longer lighting the way, and he muttered, "Cavern gloom, stone illum."

Brightly colored stalactites stabbed downward from a high ceiling. The same water that had eroded the crevices and recalcified the stalactites had also cooled the lava floor. The steam here caused Marl to sweat, but it wasn't the roasting heat he'd felt in the tunnel he'd just come through.

Multiple voices emerged from that tunnel, followed by Baron Footsore, Pavo, and Sagit, the latter's moustache looking singed at the ends.

"You did it!" Pavo said, his face bright with excitement.

But on the Baron Footsore's face was condemnation.

What did I do wrong? Marl wondered.

"Foul warlock!" Footsore hissed. "Contempt and castigation is all you deserve! Mock the inviolate proscriptions of your Adept calling, but pronounce your innocence no more! How dare you blend the magics of Sword, Scroll, and Stone! Fiend! Duplicitous infidelity to Stonevale is all you can summon? That buckle with the ruby—I felt it emanate the power of the Sword! That was how you compelled me to bring you down here! Deny it, Gneiss, go on! I dare you to refute that you've violated the proscribed practices and applied the magics of sword and scroll these last few minutes. Deny it, fiend!" Caelum had pulled his sword and pointed it at Marl's midriff.

Stunned, Marl bent as well he could to look at the buckle. Intuitively, he knew Caelum right, else how had the rock cooled under him, or indeed how had Pavo, a boy a quarter Marl's size, knocked him from his feet?! "No," Marl said weakly, "But it wasn't at my bidding, I swear!" He put his hands to the buckle to take it off.

"No, you don't!" And Caelum feinted as though to warn. The sword point went astray, nearly throwing the Baron Footsore off balance. "You know not the power you contend with!" He drew back, his gaze narrowing.

"No," Marl said, breathless.

"Stars above and fire below, take this snipe and lay him low!" And he thrust the sword toward Marl's gut.

It folded as though in a mirror and the blade pierced Caelum Footsore's chest. He gurgled and collapsed, the bent blade embedded through his sternum. His eyes alight and fixed to Marl's face, Caelum squirmed and then he died.

The members of the cortege all knelt save Pavo, Sagit and Marl.

Shaking his head, Marl bent to look at the sword, careful not to touch it or any part of the Baron, as though either might be infectious.

Along the "fold," the sword looked perfect, as though it had been thrust through a mirror.

"Incredible," Marl muttered, straightening. He looked among the Baron's followers, many of whom were climbing to their feet.

Their glances went to him, and then to each other.

As though they're expecting something from me, Marl thought.

Chapter 10

Columba looked between Adept and daughter, their exchange of glance inscrutable.

He stood before them, having been fed, bathed, and given back his possessions, and then joined by Samshad Woodwright, who had also been brought up from the dungeons of Stonevale.

He didn't understand the change but felt relieved, not wanting further persecution and torture. The Adept daughter had inflicted excruciating imaginary pain, and he could still feel the burn of her lashes, despite his skin's being unblemished. Further, he had felt her pure delight and mounting ecstasy as she'd applied ever more painful techniques.

Without his sword, he'd lain helpless to her torture.

His sword back in hand, Columba itched to use it, to inflict upon his captors a measure of what they'd inflicted upon him.

A chandelier above them lit the room with brilliant white diamond light. The hall was split by a long stone table, its surface embedded with gems more brilliant and larger than any found elsewhere. Rubies, sapphires, diamonds, and emeralds, and in between—a variegated slew of semi-precious stones. The walls were similarly adorned, and other than the one door through which he'd been brought, the room had only one other door— a gold-barred grate that stood half-open, as though the room beyond awaited occupation, the gold glimmering with ambient light.

"I see that the gold cage door draws your attention," the High Adept said.

Columba returned his gaze to the older man.

Wearing silks woven with stone sequins, the High Adept sat in a chair that nearly swallowed him with sumptuousness, a satin brocade with interwoven gold and silver threads, giving the high back a coruscating appearance. The High Adept's every move threw off another scintillating spray of light.

I'm afraid if he smiles I'll see diamonds in his teeth, Columba thought, wondering what anyone would need with such opulence.

"It is a cage, Sage Riverford, that now lies emptied. What do you suppose that it heretofore contained?" The High Adept seemed smug.

Odd that persons in positions of such power have so little ability to persuade others, Columba thought. He knew that any response from him was likely to be taken as impudence or worse.

"Behind that door stood Luxullian, and in that cage was the prohibition. Do you, Sage Riverford, still abide by your prohibition?"

The words wrapped around Columba's brain and almost forced speech from his mouth. He sensed that like daughter, Father might compel anything from him, except the one thing that the High Adept really wanted.

My cooperation, Columba thought. What arrogance to think he'll ever have that, after the torture his daughter inflicted on me.

"How arrogant of me to expect anything but enmity from you, eh?" The Adept glanced toward his daughter.

She stepped forward from beside the elaborate throne and knelt at Columba's feet. "Lord Sage Columba Riverford, my apologies. I inflicted pain for no purpose other than to gratify my own desires. I'm capable of equal soothing. If there's a way I may soothe your wounds, please by ask." She bent and softly touched her forehead to the stone floor, held it, and then raised herself to sit back on her haunches, her gaze on his face, no hint of remorse in her eyes.

They hope to hook me by my response, he thought, moving his gaze from her face to his, slowly, deliberately. "I beg your leave, Lord, to do only that. May I go?"

"Yes, certainly, and immediately. And I too am sorry that you receive such treatment. Farewell, Lord Sage, and feel free to return at your leisure. I shall see that next time you receive instead a hero's welcome." The High Adept Gabbro Scoria Hornsfels stood and bowed. "Again, my apologies."

Columba was surprised.

No request, no conditions, no obligations.

They must really want my cooperation, he thought. "What do you want?"

Adept Hornsfels tilted his head as though to hear better. "Pardon, Lord Sage, what was that?"

"You want something from me," Columba said. "What do you want?"

The woman laughed and stood, standing close enough that her perfume wrapped him in its heavenly delirium.

If he weren't so annoyed.

The High Adept cleared his throat, and his daughter stepped back. "Yes, well, nothing so refreshing as a direct request, eh, Lord?"

Columba stared at him, waiting. He might have been the High Adept, and Hornsfels the supplicant, their indulgence so apparent.

"Very well, as we've nothing much more to lose than we have lost already." Hornsfels stepped closer. "You seek the other two supposed thiefs, Aridisia Myric and Baron Marl Gneiss. I know as well as you that they stole nothing, that they like you were the victim of a masterful plot to bring about the collapse of our principalities. I know that now, but didn't when the Baron Gneiss insinuated himself into this very room in the moments before Luxullian disappeared. My request is simple: Please tell the Lord Baron Marl Gneiss that his lands and position have been restored to him."

Columba frowned. "You have too few messengers that you can't send one yourself?" He realized how abrupt he sounded, but Columba wanted nothing further from these Valers but a distance of road between him and them.

The High Adept smiled. It lacked a hint of mirth. "If you prefer a messenger, I will send one, but I doubt you'll like my selection. Minette, please go with the Lord Sage Riverford and convey to the Baron, the Lord Adept Marl Gneiss, the news of his restoration to the Barony."

"Certainly, Father."

Columba didn't relish the idea. "I'd rather tell him myself." He was reluctant to have alongside him someone who enjoyed inflicting pain, or who might derive pleasure from watching someone else suffer. Stars above, he thought, she'd as soon let something horrific happen to me out of simple amusement.

"She'll guard you as vigilantly as she does Stonevale," the High Adept said. "Won't you, Minette?"

"Yes, Father." She turned to look at him. "You don't need to worry that I'll harm you, Lord Sage, or for that matter that I'll let something horrific happen to you out of simple amusement. You are our best hope of regaining Luxullian, and as my father's heir, I've the most to lose if you should fail."

Does she read minds? he wondered. Columba watched them both for a moment, realizing that if he didn't take her with him, she was likely to set out on her own and arrive at the same destination as his, not out of any intent, but simply because the person they sought was one in the same, the true thief of Sword, Scroll, and Stone.

Samshad, who'd remained silent, stepped close to him and whispered. "Hold your friends close and hold your enemies closer."

Columba nodded, glancing between father and daughter. Whatever else they might be, they were committed to restoring Luxullian, just as committed as he was to retrieving Genesyx. He realized he could ask anything of them. "I keep any stone she recovers."

The daughter recoiled as though struck, looking to her father as though to object.

His impassive face silenced her. With a slight tilt of his head, he indicated she reply.

Her fingers clenching the folds of her dress, Minette dropped her gaze, and then brought her gaze up to him with an effort. "Yes, Lord, of course."

"I'm in command. Any insubordination, and I'll return you to Stonevale by any means necessary—even if I have to hire a slaver do it."

Blush flushed both cheeks, and her throat worked, but she remained silent.

"Swear to your father that you'll obey me in all things up until the very moment that you return Luxullian to his care."

Her gaze aflame with rage, she looked at the High Adept.

"Do it, daughter, and hold true to your word. Even if Luxullian is recovered before the other two talismans," Gabbro Scoria Hornsfels said, "you must obey Lord Sage Riverford. I'll not see our three Kingdoms collapse because the cause was abandoned before it was complete."

"What about *him*?" She'd found her voice, at last, hoarse and deep, and sounding like someone else's entirely.

"His fate is his own. Should he turn aside before all three are recovered, he will have a geis upon him and all his generations. Swear it, daughter, or tell me now that you're not able to abide by such an oath."

Columba watched her struggle, admiring the High Adept's insights. Tis true we'll need to recover all three to insure there's a future for our domains, he thought.

If any single Kingdom should fall, the other two would suffer the chaos that would ooze from the suppurating wound and might even incur the same or similar inflammation.

"Very well, father," Minette said, her voice a whisper." I do swear to obey the Lord Sage Riverford in all things up until the very moment that I return Luxullian to your care, and to return Luxullian only when the other two talismans are similarly safe." Her face was an ashen mask.

And hopefully by then, she'll have forgiven or forgotten the indignity that I've just put her through, Columba thought, noting she made no mention of afterward.

"Bring your sword over here. Let me examine it."

Columba threw a sharp glance at Minette. "She leaves the room."

The High Adept glanced at her. "Just for a moment, dear."

"Yes, Father. I'll be within earshot."

Hornsfels gestured Columba to lay it on the table.

He did so, and stepped away.

Hornsfels pulled a diamond from his sleeve. "Mysteries cloud, magic unshroud." A light sheen of dust burst from the diamond and settled on the sword. He bent to look closely at the weapon. "Ah, a fine make, the blacksmith Lemnos himself forged this one. But you—"

Hornsfels raised his gaze from the blade. "A hand from the southern wheatfields of Swordshire presumes to own a sword this fine in make. Little question they thought you parvenu." He returned to his examination, working his way up from the haft. He ended his exam at the tip. "Ah! here it is, Lord, A flaw, extending from the point two inches in, cleverly repaired, nearly invisible." Hornsfels straightened and smiled. "Only detectible with the finest of instruments." He held up the diamond. "Probably would hold up in battle, but a flaw nonetheless. Explains how a person of your origins might have obtained an otherwise exquisitely crafted weapon." His smile faded. "What's that at your belt?"

Columba frowned and looked in the direction of the other man's gaze.

The knife Serpens that he'd obtained from Dorad Fallentree, its single ruby winking.

How had he seen it? Columba wondered, then felt mystified at the thought. Why wouldn't he have seen it?

"I inspected your weapons thoroughly," the High Adept said. "I didn't see it among your possessions. Only the empty sheath that it's in."

Columba reached for it reluctantly, as though he battled some horrific reservation. What am I so afraid of? he wondered. The knife seemed thrice as heavy, as though it didn't want to be laid on the table. He withdrew his hands.

Hornsfels drew in a breath. "Remarkable," he said, his eyes aglitter. "You told me earlier you abide by the proscriptions, and yet you carry this in open flaunt of the precepts you've vowed to adhere to." The Adept looked at him closely. "Why?"

The command pulled the words from him. "It isn't mine, and I've not used it, but I carry it because ... " He couldn't quite believe what he was saying, even as he said it. "Because it allows me to carry it, and wants me to carry it." The compulsion released him and left him sweating.

"A truth spell," Adept Hornsfels said. "Forgive me my using it. Truly spoken, I can tell, and something I suspect you didn't even know. Am I wrong?"

Columba knew he wasn't.

"Her Highness the Lady Magux Ravenna Cithara knew not about this knife, did she?"

He shook his head at the Adept, a question in his eyes.

"What is it? Who does it belong to? Yes, the very questions whose answers elude us. And if you'll notice?" Hornsfels gestured at the sword, which lay inches from the knife.

The sword seemed to flicker, almost move of its own accord, as though bending toward the knife. But with each flicker, Columba's brain instantly measured how much it moved, and to his eyes, the sword had moved not at all, like two objects of identical dimension, one behind the other, in changing light, the play of light and shadow fooling the eye to detect motion, an illusory chiaroscuro.

His hand snatched the knife off the table.

"A weapon that dislikes examination." Adept Hornsfels raised an eyebrow at Columba. "Tell me where you got it."

"Soon after I was expelled from Swordshire, I espied a rogue watching me from higher elevations as I traveled the road toward the summit. He tried to ambush me, but I did him instead. He was glib, persuaded me he meant no harm, then hurled himself at me the moment I feigned sleep. Dorando Fallentree, he called himself."

"Dorad, perhaps?" Hornsfels asked. He gestured at the sword to indicate that he was finished.

Columba picked it up, looked closely at the point. Without perceptible flaw. "Perhaps, Lord Adept. Recognize the name?"

The older man nodded. "Wanted in all three kingdoms for a variety of crimes, began his misadventures by raping and killing an old woman at the southern edge of Scrollhaven, a deed so foul we haven't seen its like in the ten years since it happened."

"Any idea where he got the knife?"

Hornsfels was silent.

Columba glanced at him.

A worried wrinkle sat upon the older man's forehead. "Now that you ask, I remember a distant myth of a woman who fought the King of the Sea, a Merman King, and her weapon of choice was a ruby-inlaid knife."

"Perhaps she was its wielder of choice?"

"Exactly my thought," Hornsfels said, his gaze boring deeply into Columba.

The Warrior Sage considered discarding the knife, then quickly dismissed the whole conversation as paranoid fantasy. He turned to look at Samshad Woodwright, who'd observed everything with a disconcerting stoicism. "A barrel full of half-cracked theories, Shad?"

"Sounds a bit farfetched, Lord. Are you sure about bringing her?"

Columba glanced between Shad and Hornsfels. The woodsman was absent the sophistication to be disingenuous, but he knew very well not to be sanguine about taking the High Adept's minacious daughter with them.

"I'd rather have her cooperation than her competition." Columba nodded deeply to Hornsfels. "Bless, Lord High Adept, for all your assistance."

* * *

"Lady Magus Myric, if you please," the Sea Queen said.

Ari stopped at the cave mouth, Bere halting beside her. The fresh air from the morning sea was invigorating but cold, the sun in the east barely warming them where they stood, the blood-red disk on the horizon a fat cold eye staring at them as though impatient for their departure.

No, it's I who's impatient to depart, Ari thought, unsettled by the stories told deep into the night. "Forgive me, Queen Coralreef, but I'm eager to go."

"Yes, I see that. Please pardon me an indulgence. If it's not too great an imposition, I would like to see your scroll."

"Eh?" Taken aback, Ari frowned. Letting an acquaintance see one's talisman was tantamount to exposing one's soul to a stranger.

"Forgive me, as I know that among Haveners this is a personal matter, but I beg you, as there may be more than you think is apparent."

Ari felt afraid. In a way she'd not felt throughout the excursion since leaving Scrollhaven. She couldn't have said why. The Queen Salina Coralreef had treated them with dignity and respect, had provided them with a sumptuous supper and soft mattresses to spend the night on, and had proved the perfect hostess.

Why Ari would feel inexplicably suspicious was a mystery she wanted to solve.

"Certainly," Aridisia said, and brief visions of calamity possessed her, then quickly faded.

"If it will allay your fears, there is a ledge where you may place your scroll," the Queen said. "My inspection will be purely visual, I promise."

Ari nodded, stepping from the cave mouth and into the cold northern sun. She saw the ledge and drew the scroll from her sleeve. The quill seemed to draw her hand as she laid the scroll upon the shelf, a lip of rock worn into the cliffside by a thousand years of surf, dry now these last few eons, the wind having added its wear ever since.

The Sea Queen stepped close. "If you'll pardon my appearance for a few minutes." The sheen of water that had clothed her from the crown to foot dried up.

She was magnificently beautiful with her sheen of water, that much more without.

Ari understood why the Sea Queen wore it, to prevent the distraction. She watched closely, keenly aware of the quill in her hand, while the merwoman examined Ari's scroll.

The pins though small were deep mahogany, knobbed on each end with bulbs the size of her thumb, their wood shiny with handling, the deep rich grain seeming to shimmer in the morning light. The vellum was a soft fuzzy sheepskin, the visible surface lightly marked with writing so faded, writing on top of writing, the canvas the recipient of so many of Ari's spells that no single sentence nor even word might be deciphered, as on any palimpsest.

"A well-loved scroll," the Sea Queen said.

"I've had it since I was young." Ari felt the warmth of the good queen's praise. How could I expect subterfuge from such a gentle creature? she wondered.

"Do you mind if I steal a reveal?"

Ari felt Salina's power, and although she felt reluctance, she also felt confident that Queen Coralreef meant no harm. She's as committed as I am to restoring balance to the world, Ari thought, nodding.

The merwoman's hands spread above the scroll, and her fingertips began to glisten. "Shroud conceal, mist congeal, with my vision, I do reveal."

A fine mist formed above the scroll and hung there, then evaporated quickly.

"Odd." The Sea Queen frowned at Ari. "Was that you?"

"Was what me?"

"That push I felt. Something nixed my magic, felt as if it came from you."

"No, Lady, or at least, I don't think so."

"What other talismans are you wearing?"

"Excuse me?"

"Though you've placed your scroll upon this ledge I feel the presence of more magical devices upon you. Where are they? That chain around your neck. What hangs between your breasts. Show me, I say!"

Air felt her hands lift of their own volition and draw out from under her tunic the mechanical clock she'd gleaned from the bandit Drupa Juni, who'd suddenly become obsessed with her, his intent protruding. She immediately likened her hands at work to the very same look upon his face as he'd lurched toward her, a hellbent gaze upon his face and flying a flagpole to signal his intent.

The Queen gasped upon seeing the clock. "You wear that which your creed decries. Upon your soul, do count your dole and reveal your role!"

The mist enveloped her face and Ari heard the words leap from her mouth unbidden by her. "It carries me hither and yon, but I don't own it. Nor does it own me, for I am not the object of its attentions." Ari wrenched herself out of the fog that Queen Coralreef had cast upon her.

Behind her, steel slid from scabbard.

"No, Bere," Ari pleaded. "Tis not she who plagues me. Sheath thy weapon, I beg you." Ari stared at her younger companion while she tried to catch her breath, the truth compulsion having emptied her lungs.

Ari watched Berenice carefully for a few minutes, knowing the younger woman would flay even the devil himself if she felt Ari were in danger. Recovering her breath, she turned to Queen Coralreef.

To her surprise, the Queen examined not the timepiece, but the scroll, where it lay placidly on the ledge.

"I thought for certain I saw in its place another scroll, one with gilded handles and gold-thread parchment." Queen Salina turned to look at Ari. "But only when you resisted my truth-spell."

Bewildered, Ari frowned. "But I didn't resist it."

Queen Salina raised her gaze from the scroll, looking deeply perturbed. "A foul force works its magic upon us, one whose fetor reminds me much of the warlock from the Halfmoon Sea, he who is known to us as Travert Crepitans Pictor, a Necromancer of highest order, rumored to resurrect from the dead those who've never been alive, known to dally in beings unknown to our existence. Whether this is his work, or perhaps a reverberation from a time disturbed by his interference, only the deep Sea Dragon knows, but beware in your dealings, for the thefts of the Sword, Scroll, and Stone from the Shire, Haven, and Vale does bespeak of similar machinations." Salina looked out the sea, turning away from the scroll laying on the stone shelf.

Quickly, Ari secured it, and also slipped the timepiece under her tunic. A great weight lifted from her when both were tucked away.

"Berenice Longblade, native of Swordshire," Queen Salina said. "Do bear witness these events, for the least bit indication that Lady Magux Aridisia Myric deviates from the rescue and return of the Sword, Scroll, and Stone, it may be incumbent upon you to intercept the evil which has taken possession of her soul and to extirpate the beast at its earliest moment of manifestation. That evil is extant upon us, recrudescent from a far more tumultuous time. Do you swear, Lady Sage Berenice Longblade, to extinguish that evil the moment it raises its head?"

Bere dropped to a knee. "Lady Sage Queen Salina Coralreef, I do so swear."

"Even if it possesses the body of your friend and companion, the Lady Magux Aridisia Myric?"

"Even so, Lady Sea Queen, I do so swear, though I beseech the stars to prevent its happening." Bere threw a nervous smile at Ari.

Ari smiled back. "If I'm possessed of evil, Bere, I'd want you to exterminate it by any means possible."

Bere heaved a sigh.

"Then rise, Lady Sage Longblade, and guard your friend and mine, the Lady Magux Aridisia Myric, from all evils." Queen Salina spread her hands above Bere's bowed head and emitted a dense fog from her fingers.

Dew lit up Bere's hair, the droplets catching the early morning sun and giving her a halo.

"Rise, child, and fare thee well, the both of you. Well met, Lady Myric, and Dragonspeed." She stepped back and water cascaded down her gentle curves once again.

Ari bowed and watched the Sea Queen retreat to her watery domain, the waves coursing gently around her as she walked deeper and deeper into the water. Soon, she sank from sight, and their last view of her was of a wide mammalian tail fin, which flicked into sight and disappeared beneath the surface without leaving a ripple.

"Magnificent," Bere said, looking longingly out to sea.

"Certainly very attractive," Ari replied. "Come on, before you walk into the water after her." She threw Bere a sly glance and turned to face the rising sun.

The susurrus of surf masked the soft sounds of their steps on the sand, the wind whistling around crevices and hardy bushes clinging to the cliff hanging precipitously above them. Ari was rapt and silent, just as Bere appeared to be, but probably for an altogether different reason.

The timepiece around her neck did seem a perilous piece of jewelry to carry around, its materials seeming to imply that she'd abandoned her scruples toward her scroll-spell craft. The multiple spells she'd cast with her scroll as a shield against other magic had not spared her the Sea Queen's truth-spell, as the scroll had been several feet away and not on Ari's person, where she usually kept it. The bandit Drupa Juni had separated her from her scroll by simply knocking her unconscious, a hazard she'd not expected, as physical assault within the kingdom of Scrollhaven was severely punished and almost unheard of.

Despite her having never used the talisman, the timepiece was dangerous to wear for its affront to the very social structure she sought to preserve. The founding of the Sword, Scroll, and Stone had occurred because of the chaos created by those who had mastered multiple fundaments, using their many magics to wreak havoc upon those around them.

Was it a relic of those chaotic times? Ari wondered, or perhaps a device of more recent manufacture meant to introduce instability?

And how had it found her?

And why?

Ari thought over the words that the Sea Queen had wrenched from her with the truth-spell. "It carries me hither and yon but I use it not. I do not own it, nor does it own me."

How odd, Ari thought, desiring to bring out the timepiece on its chain and stare at its burnished metal and glittering sapphire. Inside its mechanical workings, she knew, was secreted a scroll, one so small its inscription might barely be read with the naked eye, and the language so archaic that it probably resisted deciphering.

And what do I make of the Sea Queen's seeing a second, shadow scroll, one far more elaborate in materials and design, where my own scroll did sit? Ari wondered. What possibly could she have seen?

Though many spells might cause others to see what wasn't there, Ari doubted anyone might plant such deception for some redoubtable purpose. If magic were at work, as opposed to the Sea Queen feeling giddy for a moment, it would be to conceal something that was there. "A scroll with gilded handles and gold-thread parchment." How odd, Ari thought, trying to recall where she'd seen such before.

"I don't know if I could slay you, you know."

Ari grinned at Bere. "Well, thank the Almighty Scribe for that!" The two of them shared a laugh, and somehow their hands found each other. Bere's hard, calloused hand grasping her far softer one sent a thrill through Ari.

Last night, after a short bath, Ari had retired to the soft kelp beds that the Sea Queen had prepared for them, and Ari had lain awake, listening to Bere's even breathing, wanted to go to her and be held by her as she had that first night before entering the Wizened Forest. Not knowing the trials of the day ahead, Ari had resisted the temptation and had soon fallen asleep, only to awake that morning to Bere's arm around her, snoring softly in her ear.

The feeling of absolute perfection, of being held softly in the strong arms of the warrior princess, Sage Berenice Longblade, had been such a comfort that the feeling still quilted Ari in warmth as she and Bere walked hand in hand down a bench in morning sunlight.

We pray to the gods for an afterlife in paradise, never thinking we might find it here, Ari thought, smiling shyly at Bere.

"It's you who are fabulously beautiful," Bere said to her. "I'm afraid my father will wail and moan when I tell him it's a pampered scribe with hands softer than sheepskin whom I love."

The warm spread throughout Air, warmth so great she wanted to loosen her tunic.

If I do that, we'll stop on the bench and never reach our destination, she thought, knowing she was as enamored with Bere as Bere seemed to be with her.

Ari wanted to say she couldn't wait till they made camp but thought the better of it, knowing Bere would take her at her word and take her on the beach.

In full view of the Almighty Scribe and whoever else might be watching.

Ari scanned the cliffs as though in this remote a place someone might actually be espied.

A tiny figure atop the cliff waved side to side and jumped up and down.

Ari stopped, and a moment later the voice reached her.

"Ari!" said the voice. A second, taller figure, this of a man, joined the smaller, and Ari finally recognized who it was.

"Chiona!" she yelled. And her father, Zibeth Anthus.

* * *

Baron Marl Gneiss called a halt, their bedraggled and much reduced coterie looking almost pathetic, compared with the pomp and finery in which they'd left Castle Footsore.

They were barely half their number as well, some fifteen people buried in the last cave-in then seven more after that, six in Marl's aborted attempt to open the passageway and the Baron Footsore himself in his aborted attempt to kill the Baron Gneiss.

Marl hadn't wanted to become their leader, and if he'd had his druthers, he'd have buried himself under tons of rock.

Having been stopped by page Pavo, Marl doubted he'd have the courage to attempt a second time.

After Baron Footsore's blade had turned itself against him, Marl had just stared at the others. Folk not his kind, Shirees the lot of them, Pavo and Sagit included, and their fealty to Baron Footsore undiminished despite his death, his behavior having become remarkably bizarre since the Baron Gneiss's arrival, likely resentful that their master had died trying to kill him, his blade bending back awkwardly, magically bent in some unseen way by Marl himself, despite his having uttered no audible spell nor having visibly brandished his ruby but sure in their minds that Gneiss had somehow effected Footsore's demise.

None of them had said by hint of word or deed that they thought these things but Marl could see it in their eyes, the accusing glances, the resentful expressions, the half-hearted laughter at Marl's feeble jests.

No one objected to his calling a halt. The members of the spelunking party simply hurled themselves to the rough stone floor as though smited.

No one looked at him, not even his erstwhile companions, Sagit and Pavo.

"Tunnel seems endless," Marl said to no one, this stop onc of an uncounted number of stops since crossing the cooling lava bed, right after the Baron Footsore had died on his own sword.

Gone, Marl knew, was the routine of bedding down at night, as here there was no night. Gone was the routine of stopping for meals when mealtime came, as their rations were meager and all the more scarce were they to stop to consume any. Gone was the discipline of camp detail, for no longer did they camp but instead plodded between resting places, most of their camping supplies having been buried in that second disastrous cave-in.

"But at least we're climbing now," Pavo said.

"What does *that* mean?" And Marl winced the moment he'd said it, the words thick with spite and inferred innuendo.

Pavo turned his head away.

Marl looked among the others, their accusatory glances now imbued with contempt for his scorn of the boy. Marl wanted to apologize but he saw it was too late. It would be rebuffed and he would draw only further castigation.

And he still didn't know what the boy meant. Marl looked at the boy, whose gaze remained dolefully on the tunnel floor. Marl had noticed similar during the upward climb, but had attributed nothing to it.

Pavo looked pensive, as though he thought it meant something.

He scowled at them all and rose, and resumed the endless journey, the slight incline making the traverse all the more difficult.

The tunnel varied somewhat with width and height but only by a foot or two, and the floor remained the cobbled surface akin to that of a mountain stream, as though the pyroclastic flow had frozen in mid-motion. The footing was difficult but his ruby lit the way, alerting him to hazards before he stumbled upon them.

As before, the heat and exertion caused him to perspire profusely, and the ever-present aroma of sulfur was either exuded by the surround rock or by his leaky pores.

When the change occurred, Marl couldn't say. What he noted was that his sweat now dried so quickly that he felt an actual chill, and that his breath was starting to fog before his face. "When did it get cold?" he wondered aloud.

"Just in the past hour," Pavo said, his voice right behind him.

Surprised, Marl looked around, taken aback upon seeing the boy.

His tunic bunched up in front and drawn up over his mouth, Pavo shivered visibly, his cheeks drawn and thin. He looks emaciated, Marl thought, bringing his gaze back around to see where he was going.

A flicker of light a head caught his attention.

Ice? The cold! Of course! "I see something ahead!" he said over his shoulder. He hurried along the tunnel in spite of his fatigue, a tiny hope budding in his chest.

Glints of light reflected from frosty rock, reflections of reflections indicating a source farther along than he'd hoped. The others were right behind him, he saw.

He turned a bend in the tunnel, and ahead appeared a bizarre blue light. Right afterward, he realized it was a cavern.

Which widened as he approached.

And widened.

He stopped a few feet shy of the egress, feeling the others crowd up behind him.

The cavern yawned before him, like the gargantuan mouth of some Brobdingnagian beast, its ceiling festooned with multitudinous teeth, icicle stalactites of all shapes and sizes gnashing downward like scintillating scimitars, the floor covered with their broken remains, glinting white like the bones in an elephant graveyard bleached by the sun. High above them, Marl glimpsed a speck of sky through a vertical tunnel. A volcano spout? he wondered.

In the center, elevated above the jagged floor on a pillar-throne of clear blue ice was seated a blue-skinned figure who looked the picture of death, his fire-filled eyes boring holes through Marl, their pupils burning like midnight coal.

He wore a sword gilded in gold, and wielded a long feathered quill above a brilliant white parchment, and around his neck he sported a diamond the size of Marl's pinky.

Marl knew him instantly and couldn't have said the how of it. Nor could he articulate a name whose presence in his mind was primal and primordial.

"Come," a deep voice intoned, so deep it sounded as if it reverberated from the deepest mine.

An ice bridge formed from the tunnel mouth to the pillar where the figure sat, and Marl felt the compulsion to step out onto it. He resisted, his hand tight around his ruby, but the belt buckle pulled him relentlessly onto the thick bridge of ice, which hung suspended without visible means above a bed of sharp-edged shards, a bridge whose very friability was sure to give under a ponderous weight such as Marl's.

He stepped onto the slick, translucent surface, sweating despite the bone-chilling cold.

A stalactite wiggled loose and dropped from the ceiling, and its razor-sharp point clipped the edge and took out a chuck halfway to the column.

A deep laugh shook the cavern.

Marl looked at the ceiling to see if other stalactites threatened to fall.

"Farther," the deep voice intoned, and Marl couldn't resist the compelling command, stepping farther and farther along the brittle bridge.

At the midpoint, he hesitated, the ice below him cracked where the stalactite had removed a chunk.

The figure gestured with the quill-clad hand, and Marl walked past the cracked point as though without a fear. The bridge held somehow, Marl not knowing whether to be more afraid of the figure waving him onward or of the jagged death that awaited him below.

Twenty feet from the other, Marl stopped, not of his own accord, but simply because the compulsion lifted.

"Look at me, fat man," the figure said, his voice booming. "You know who I am, and you know what I want. Do you give it, or do I take it?"

And Marl realized he had a chance. "I would be happy to give it, but there's a condition."

The pause was pregnant. Marl didn't know whether the other man would burst into laughter or slaughter him on the spot. Not much difference except an "s" between laughter and slaughter, Marl thought inanely.

"You try my patience, fat man. There isn't any room for negotiation. Give it to me now or I'll take it along with your life."

"Kill me if you must, Ice Man, but let my companions go!" Marl drew himself erect and threw out his chest.

A deep chuckle greeted this display of bravado. "You don't know who I am, do you? Else you wouldn't feign defiance. I'll wager you don't know what you bring, either? Your fellow troglodytes have no doubt heard my name, their living like cavedwellers. You!" The blue-skinned figure pointed a long, crooked finger.

A rope of ice lassoed someone on the ledge behind Marl and reeled in the old man.

"You, itinerant woodwright, ancient beyond your years, traveler to hither and yon. You're Sagit Smoothgrain, and you'll tell his fat fool who I am, won't you?"

The frozen rope held Sagit above icy stilettos poking up from the floor. His teeth chattering, Sagit did not take his eyes off the blue-skinned figure. "Necromancer extraordinaire, Travert Crepitans Pictor, risen again from the dead and by his own hand, like as not. What foul plans are you hatching now, Lizard Wizard?" And Sagit nonchalantly opened his hand in his direction.

"Hurl your puny spells, Woodwright. Nothing is what they'll get you." And Pictor waved his hand to the side.

The frozen rope hurled Sagit and pulped him against the cavern wall.

Marl whispered, "Make me victor over Crepitans Pictor!" And with his hand he thrust the ruby to the end of his arm.

But it was larger than it had been, and heavier, and all the wrong color, Marl saw belatedly, not red at all but white and glittery like a diamond, its many facets reflecting and refracting the blue cavern light, and Marl realized as his arm reached its full extension that it wasn't his ruby with which he was casting a spell, but the fist-sized diamond which had served as scepter to the Lord High Adept for hundreds of generations, the One Stone Luxullian.

He realized concurrently that he'd borne the Stone all the way from Stonevale unknowingly and that his grip on the oversized rock was adequate for the much-smaller ruby but wholly inadequate for the largest diamond known throughout the four corners, and with an ease that sent his spirit plummeting to his toes, the One Stone Luxullian leapt from his hand and landed easily, almost daintily, in the palm of Travert Crepitans Pictor, as though Baron Marl Gneiss, he who had once aspired to accede to the position of High Adept, had casually tossed it to his nemesis.

The slap of Luxullian into the hand was the only sound.

And then Luxullian began to glow. Fire leaped from the coal black eyes of Pictor and swirled around Luxullian, and a hum pierced the air, the smell of sulfur became a stench. A column of fire leaped from the Earth behind Pictor and launched itself through the volcano mouth, and the ball of fire surrounding the Necromancer and talisman grew even larger, until it engulfed them, and Marl saw the ice bridge melting under him, and he turned, praying he'd somehow reach the ledge in time.

Something happened at his waist. The buckle worked itself free and spun like a top toward the Necromancer as Marl sprinted as fast as his fat body would take him, the ice under him splintering and the stalactites above him shaking loose, the hum increasing to a rumble, and each pounding step that Marl took sent fissures spreading through the ice bridge under him, the ledge tantalizingly close, but horrifically far, and the heat at his back felt as if it would bake him instantly, his shadow shrinking as the fire ball overtook him, but the force of the explosion caught his great girth and hurled him like a cannonball into the tunnel, and he tucked in his limbs and prayed to the Vault of Stones he landed just right.

And when he rolled to a stop, his backside warm to the touch but his body miraculously unhurt, the remaining members of their spelunking coterie surrounded him, laughing and crying by turns, congratulating him for saving their lives and patting him on the back.

"But … But … " he tried to protest.

"But what?" Pavo said, looking joyfully exasperated.

"But I handed him the diamond." Marl felt his pocket, wondering what had happened to his apricot-sized ruby.

"But nothing!" Pavo replied. "You saved us all. You stood up to him on our behalf and escaped with your life and saved our lives in turn. You're a hero. That was courageous!"

But Marl didn't feel like a hero. He located the ruby in his pocket, feeling oddly comforted by that.

"You distracted him with that silly stone," Pavo said, "and that's what allowed us all to escape."

"But Pavo," Marl protested, "It wasn't just some silly stone. It was Luxullian. I handed Travert Crepitans Pictor the sacred stone of Stonevale, Luxullian."

Chapter 11

"What did somebody do, hand him the One Stone, Luxullian?" Columba asked, gazing with the rest of them toward the south, where a deep, black cloud filled half the sky, the erupting volcano at Warlock's Mount a flickering orange point on the Halfmoon Sea.

"Pray to the Gods that *that* doesn't happen," Minette said, her hand working its way into her pocket, her heart-shaped diamond aglow through the cloth of her breeches.

"The Almighty Scribe will rend his scroll apart if Travert Crepitans Pictor gets a hold of Luxullian," Samshad Woodwright said, his axe blade glinting with its own internal fire. As a member of the Lumber Guild, he had been bestowed the magic of woodshaping and the axe to do it with. He looked to his two companions, as though to ask, "What now?"

Columba considered.

The three of them had journeyed two days from Stonevale to reach these environs. Though he'd been here but two weeks ago, Columba barely recognized the crossroads. Underneath this bridge, the bandit Skarn Arkose had attempted to abscond with all his possessions and leave him with not even his life. But he'd evaded her trap and now stood atop the bridge, although the world had changed dramatically in that short time.

Within an hour of their departure from the Vault of Stones, a shock wave had rippled through the earth beneath their feet, and in another hour a hot wind had struck, bringing with it the faint aroma of sulfur. Within four hours, the southern sky had begun to blacken to the south southwest.

Though nearly all the citizens of Stonevale were clustered close to the Vault, the roadways they traveled thickened with passersby heading the opposite direction, most of them mumbling to themselves and looking fearfully over their shoulders. The few who would give them the time of day simply advised, "I wouldn't go that way, if I were you," and threw another glance southwest before hurrying away the other direction.

On the second day, the snow began.

But instead of cold wet flakes that piled high in drifts or melted into puddles, the snow was dry, dusty, and warm, and left everything coated in gray dust, for it wasn't snow but ash. Soon their world was drab and gray, and their breathing became punctured with coughs as the dust from the falling ash coated everything, dulling their clothes and hair. They'd taken to wearing kerchiefs across their mouths, and to have a spare one nearby when that one clogged with ash.

And on the eve of the second day they reached the crossroads, where the four corners connected, and from here, due south as straight as the crow flew stood the Warlock's Mount, spewing into the sky its noxious, pernicious gasses, and raining down on the continent its gritty grimy dust.

Oddly, the trio had still encountered scallywags intent on relieving them of their riches. Twice they'd fought off marauding bands, and had nearly been attacked by a third band, Skarn's cortege of misfits, two of them looking badly scarred from burn. She'd called off the attack when she saw who it was.

But just those three in their two days of travel, Columba having expected more, the banditry in the outlands having spiked since the theft of the Sword, Scroll, and Stone.

He'd remarked as much to Minette Hornsfels, who'd thrown a haughty glance his way. "They see who guards you and shrink in dismay, but absent the knowledge that I'd be the first to throw you to the wolves."

Although he'd laughed, he'd heard the grain of truth and knew that, sans the oath he'd extracted, she'd soon as sacrifice him to save herself as to kill him out of simple joy.

"Just say the word," Shad had said later, fingering his axe blade.

"Not before we deliver the Sword, Scroll, and Stone from the pilferer. Not a moment before," Columba had warned him, knowing from the first bandit fight that Samshad Woodwright was as adept with his axe as Columba was with sword.

They climbed the last stretch of road to gain the summit, a saddleback from which both the lush valleys of Scrollhaven and the lush jungles around the Halfmoon Sea might be viewed.

From the summit only one point of light was visible, darkness having fallen it seemed prematurely.

That point of light was Warlock's Mount, a faint flickering orange torch whose occasional flair lit the roiling black clouds from underneath. Columba tried to comprehend the vast distance from where he stood to the volcano, and to divine from that, just how big the eruption was.

And failed.

It was too overwhelming to be understood by the human mind.

For what seemed hours, the three of them stood staring at the flickering orange light, its flickers so bright they were visible on each other's faces.

It was mesmerizing.

Columba knew intuitively that the eruption at Warlock's Mount had caused the earth to shake an hour after they'd left the Vault of Stones, had caused the hot sirocco not an hour later, and had spewed the ash that snowed down on them the next day.

"It's got to be Pictor," Minette said again.

"I'm betting it is," said a voice behind them.

Columba whirled, hand to hilt.

Skarn stood there alone, her hands at her sides.

"Meretrix," he hissed and unsheathed his sword.

"Wait," Minette said, "look at her, unarmed, defenseless."

"A scoundrel just as scurrilous, always armed and well-defended."

"But let me, please," Minette said, staring him down.

"Certainly." He relented, happy to let these two pit their wiles against each other. Columba lowered his sword but did not sheathe it.

Minette turned toward the bandit. "There's no place for you here, lawless one. We who uphold the laws laid down by our ancestors have no use for the likes of you, except perhaps to remind ourselves why we abide by them."

"You're in need of more than laws to deal with him." Skarn nodded to the sky south of them. "Travert Crepitans Pictor, the quintessential necromancer, he who necrophiliates Queen and Witch, he who raises from the dead that which never lived in the first place. You'll need me and a lot more like me, and you'll need that scallywag from Stonevale, the fat Baron Marl Gneiss, and the meretrix from Scrollhaven, the Magux Aridisia Myric. I'm here to help you, if you'll have it, and blast me if I know why, because your defeat will mean more low-hanging fruit ready for picking by me, but the Almighty Scribe with his raggedy palimpsest has sent me here for reasons I can't decipher, so help me."

Minette was silent a moment. "You'd swear on your skinny purse that you'll help us return the Sword, Scroll, and Stone to their rightful owners?"

Skarn Arkose nodded. "I do so swear."

"Why?" Columba asked. "To skewer me in my sleep, as you might have done last time, or to ambush our company after we've relaxed at a campfire, our bellies full with the evening repast?"

"Nowhere close," Skarn returned. "I've got bigger prey I'd like to skewer—about ten stone heavier, as a matter of fact—that whale, the fat Baron Marl Gneiss, the supposed thief of the One Stone Luxullian, who actually did steal my belt, and I'll stake his balls to the ground for it and reclaim my buckle." She cinched her tunic around her waist to indicate where she'd worn it.

Columba frowned. "Seems a minor item to be pursuing recompense for. Particularly since we're sure to venture into that fray." He gestured south, toward the flickering inferno, where he was sure, somehow, that they'd find the errant Baron.

"Never one to shy away from a scrape," Skarn replied with a shrug. "I like the challenge."

"What is it about the belt, Skarn? Out with it," he said, suspicious. "Tell me about the buckle."

She recoiled visibly, throwing a glance to the side, her jaw line rippling.

Got her, Columba thought, knowing now what motivated her. He wondered about the buckle he'd heard tell in legend that had properties beyond those of Sage, Magux, or Adept. "Metal on burnished steel perhaps? A ruby the size of your pinky on its face? A tiny scroll embedded inside, a catch on the edge to open the backside of the buckle, the writing on the scroll so small, it's indecipherable to the naked eye? Tell me, Bandit Skarn, why you desire its return so greatly that you'd risk your life with the likes of us?"

"Monofundament fool!" she hissed. "You've no idea the privation I've suffered at the wrath of that High Bitch Ravenna. You—" The woman's cheeks puffed out and her face turned red and she gasped for breath. "Take me with you or not, but pry no further into my affairs, bladesman. Which is it?"

Columba was at least satisfied she lacked any desire to harm him. "We'll need the Baron too, whatever your quarrel with him.

We restore the Sword, Scroll, and Stone, you retrain from harming the Baron until we've succeeded. Got it?"

She nodded glumly, seeming to deflate.

Columba glanced at Minette and Samshad to get their tacit agreement, then he looked at her. "Welcome, Skarn Arkose, and perhaps at the end of our journey, there's a pardon that awaits you."

"Well, thank you, although I dare say I've done nothing needs pardoning."

Columba nodded. "Let's camp beside the road here. We'll eat, sleep, and be up by dawn. We sleep in shifts, each of us to take a two hour shift at sentry. Minette, Shad, Skarn, and then me." He looked among them and smiled. "In the morning we descend to the Halfmoon Sea."

* * *

"We're still two days away from the Halfmoon Sea," Bere said, her eyes going to the blackened sky.

Ari shook her head, seeing the direction of Bere's glance and sharing the younger woman's concern.

But she also saw how winded Zibeth Anthus was, Chiona's father in his sixties and laboring to keep pace with them.

Reluctantly, Aridisia called a halt, the ground barely visible in the failing light, the terrain hilly here in southeast Scrollhaven, a range of sharp peaks to their left and the fertile valleys of south Scrollhaven to their right.

Ari hadn't dared to take their small contingent any closer to Scrollhaven proper than they already were. She doubted somehow she'd receive a hero's reception from the High Magux Ravenna Cithara.

When she'd spied the two figures atop the cliff in northern Scrollhaven, and had heard Chiona's voice tumbling down the cliffsides to her, Ari had rejoiced, having wondered what had befallen the precocious young woman.

She and Bere had climbed the cliff, where they'd joined Chiona and her father, Zibeth.

The seasoned man had thanked Ari profusely for giving Chiona the spell she needed to rescue her father from the mines of Swordshire, where he'd been sold by the slaver who'd bought him from the bandit Drupa Juni.

Though relieved to hear of the bandit's death, Zibeth Anthus had immediately expressed concern at the manner of it, and that Ari had taken—and kept—the odd mechanical time piece belonging to Juni. "Tisn't the piece itself as much as the manner of its taking, which bespeaks a violence to come when it parts from your possession. The piece is a curio and little resembles anything in my experience."

Ari had started to bring it out for his perusal when the earth had shaken beneath their feet, a rumbling that had sent rocks a-tumbling and had put a chop to the sea reminiscent of a storm. The motion enough to nauseate them, it hadn't thrown them from their feet, but just to be safe they'd moved inland, lest an aftershock collapse the cliff from beneath them.

They were still talking amiably two hours later when a hot sirocco buffeted them from the south.

"By the Almighty Scribe," the three Haveners had said, and Bere had blurted on epithet native to her shire, the four of them exchanging worried glances amidst their looks southward.

Deciding to camp there, pending further developments or additional augurs of depredation, Ari and the other three had settled in.

And in the morning had awakened to a blackened sky to the south. Its direction slightly west of due south, the cloud—if a single cloud it were—was ominous, and as she studied it, Ari felt a foreboding, as though impending doom were about to descend upon the four corners like some orthopteran pestilence.

The cloud might actually be that orthopteran pestilence, she had thought wryly at the time, but as the foursome had discussed it, they all reached the same conclusion through a variety of routes.

It had been Warlock's Mount, they'd decided.

And all of them knew they had no other choice but to go and see what was the matter.

"I pray the Almighty Scribe hasn't seen fit to allow that Necromancer to resurrect himself again," Zibeth had said. "T'would be just like him to blow the top off the Mount."

And they'd set off south, taking an arc that would route them to the east of central Scrollhaven.

Ari and Bere were hardened to travel, and Chiona had the resilience of youth, the three women having little trouble keeping up a grueling pace, but it was clear from the outset that Zibeth had neither the strength nor the stamina to keep up.

Ari might have sought someplace to leave him, except that she was reluctant to ask that of Chiona, who just recently reunited with him after he'd been passed from bandit to slaver to mine.

That, and her talent.

In the moments after the ground had shook, Chiona had glanced her direction, a deep worry etched into her face.

It struck Ari as odd that one so young should look so old. "What is it? China, you look worried."

"Warlock's Mount. It's … There's two magicians …" Her distant gaze refocused. "They've met, and it looked like some explosion."

"You saw it from this distance?"

"I saw you from halfway across Scrollhaven. How do you think I found you?" Chiona grinned at her.

"Who else can you see?"

"A magician leaving Stonevale, I can't tell you his name. Ravenna Cithara at the Crypt of Scrolls, Arcturyx Longblade at the Hall of Swords, Gabbro Scoria Hornsfels at the Vault of Stones. You, and those two at Warlock's Mount."

"Two?"

Chiona nodded. "I've been watching one of them, since we met him at the mines in Swordshire, the fat man—"

"Gneiss?!"

Chiona nodded.

"The supposed thief of Luxullian. What the Almighty Scribe is he doing at Warlock's Mount?"

Chiona stared back Ari, her gaze hollow.

Shaken, Aridisia and her companions had been left with only speculation.

When asked, Chiona had said, "I've been watching him since we encountered him at the mine, but I don't understand why I can see him—remember what I told you?—like the glowing point on a map, or the location of a tree on a valley floor when looked upon from a mountain ridge. What does it mean, Ari? Why am I able to see people's location?"

The slower travel caused by Zibeth's infirmity had allowed Ari the time to explore Chiona's skill, and bit by bit, through careful questioning, Aridisia had come to the conclusion that the girl could see prominent points or concentrations of magic, that she was receptive to ambient magic in general and perceived its relative distance and intensity. Aridisia also learned that prior to the thefts of Sword, Scroll, and Stone, Chiona had had no awareness of Columba Riverford, Aridisia Myric, or Baron Marl Gneiss, the reason a mystery.

The phenomenon bothered Ari, and she couldn't have said why.

During that second day of travel, as Ari explored with Chiona the nuances of her skill, the girl reported a dimmer, less prominent point moving slowly away from Warlock's Mount, the entity moving roughly north.

Chiona couldn't divine who or what it was. When the fine drift of ash had begun to descend, they quickly forgot the dim magical being moving north across the Halfmoon Sea. Bere, who'd never seen snow in the warmer climes of Swordshire, had initially delighted in the fine powdery flakes that fell from the sky.

But the other three from the cold climes of Scrollhaven had known instantly it wasn't the cold powdery stuff that melted on contact with skin and on really cold winter days piled high in drifts and made walking difficult and sometimes treacherous. No, this snow instead stuck to everything and left behind a fine gritty gray ash. Soon they were covered in it, as were the ground and the trees, and they had to cover their noses and mouths with wetted cloth to keep from breathing in the noxious particles.

"Volcano ash," Bere had said, shaking her head.

Aridisia had slowed their party even more, the hazards of breathing such foul dust likely to have unforeseen long-term consequences, she and her companions coughing and sneezing.

The dust continued to bother them so much in spite of wetted cloth that Ari finally decided to use a spell. "Breathing a must, dispel this dust." And their airways were clear and stayed that way.

By the evening of the second day, the volcanic ash had stopped falling, but Ari could tell by their pace that they wouldn't arrive at the edge of the Halfmoon Sea for two more days.

Chiona had approached her right after they stopped.

"Beg your leave, Lady Magux," the girl said.

"Call me Ari. I do so dislike the title."

A flash of amusement touched the girl's face. "You'd have to dress a lot better anyway."

Ari nodded, chuckling. "What is it, Chiona?"

She drew her away from the others. "I know my father's slowing us down."

Ari saw it would have been pointless to deny it. "You want us to leave you two behind, right? I won't have it."

"That was my thought, at least the morning, and then you did that spell to keep away the dust. I was thinking ... "

Ari heard her out and mulled it over. "I don't see why not. Come on."

Zibeth was sitting at the base of a tree, his breathing ragged, his face red and drenched with sweat. "I don't see why not," he said when asked. "That or I head for the Crypt of Scrolls. Wouldn't want my daughter to miss out on the adventure you're on." He winked at her.

So with his consent, Ari had brought out her scroll.

The mahogany rollers at each end seemed more lustrous than she remembered, and the finish finer as though with an under-coat of some silky smooth resin. Ridiculous, she thought, dis-missing the impression, her second look it confirming they were the same old beat up, dingy rollers she'd always had. After being unrolled, the vellum at first looked fine, white, and pure, like that of a scroll untainted with the stroke of a quill, the paper itself brushed and rebrushed to a clear, nearly brilliant white, but a trick of light perhaps caused by the odd haze of volcanic ash made her think it was something other than the wrinkled, stained, and oft-used palimpsest that she'd carried for years, where her thousands of spells lay written, each spell written across the top of the previous one, each so faded into the vellum that a person couldn't decipher any single spell, the scroll so dark with previous spells that she always doubted that the most recent spell would be visible on the fuscous surface.

Her quill poised, Aridisia pondered a moment. "Dilatory lungs abide my spell, lungs absorb and feet propel." Her quill danced with a flourish across the scroll, and the ink lit up then faded into the oft-scrawled vellum.

She looked at Zibeth.

He took a breath or two, seeming to have caught it for now. "A bit easier, at least. I guess we won't know until morning, eh Lady?"

Ari despaired of their ever calling her by name, the trappings of authority fitting her as well as an overcoat might a rabbit. "We'll see in the morning, Zibeth. And please call me Ari."

"Certainly, Lady." He snickered and gestured at the chain around her neck. "Been meaning to ask you, if I might see that piece you obtained from that ne'er do well."

Ari suddenly felt uncomfortable. This is Chiona's father, she reminded herself, and I trust her implicitly. Why wouldn't I trust him? She forced herself despite her discomfort to pull the time-piece from beneath her tunic.

The face was round and nocked at regular intervals around the edge, and the center turned with the sun and moon, its single arrow pointing straight right or left at dawn and dusk, straight up at noon and straight down at midnight, disconcerting how it knew. Sparkling like a noonday sun, a diamond the size of a kernel of corn twinkled at the center, and twice a day, at noon and midnight, the diamond flashed with the brilliance of the sun itself. The metal casing was burnished bronze and looked like blade metal manufactured in the great smithies at Swordshire. And on the back, although completely smooth and seamless, a small indentation invited a fingertip, and when pressed, the backing did open, showing inside a myriad of gears and springs, and to one side, held closed by a clip, was a rolled-up scroll, the writing so small it could not be deciphered by the naked eye.

Zibeth eyed the timepiece, asking that it be turned this way and that, peering at the diamond on the face, perusing the gears in back, scrutinizing the smooth seamless surface, all the while not daring to touch it. "This piece violates all convention."

Ari nodded, knowing it.

"You who aspire to Magux among the elite at the Crypt of Scrolls carry on your person a cipher whose possession would avail you instant ejection as apostate and blasphemer, the very antitheses that the hieratic proscribe amongst themselves. They would traduce you, if they knew. Why, praise the Almighty Scribe, do you bear it?"

Ari shook her head, for even under the weight of his scorn, she knew she would not abandon it. Somewhere deep inside, she knew it integral to the restoration of the Sword, Scroll, and Stone, but she could not have said how.

"Odd that a timepiece of such exquisite manufacture would find its way into the hands of such a miscreant as Drupa Juni," Zibeth said. "You say the large pointer turns with the sun, pointing left at sunrise and right at sunset, straight up at midday and straight down at midnight? To point at the sun of such times, one must be facing due south, yes? No coincidence, I'm sure, to the direction we're heading, now, is it?"

Ari agreed abashedly that it wasn't.

"And by the Almightily Scribe, what is that coincidence?"

"I don't know, Zibeth. I wish I could tell you."

He examined her face in the flickering flame from the firepit, the light having long since given way to the dark.

She felt small under his examination, but stood her ground, her gaze meeting his.

"I believe that you don't," he said a long time later. "I also find it odd that the infamous necromancer would build such a device only to track time."

"What are you saying?" She felt her hackles rising.

"Dear child, why would he restrict himself to tracking time, when his legendary powers might avail him the opportunity to stop time. Or even reverse time. And perhaps to advance time. If I were he and bent on the domination of the existing world, it's what I would certainly be tempted to do, wouldn't you?"

Ari met his stare again, and was certain with a conviction that left her nauseous that yes, they were powers that Travert Crepitans Pictor would certainly build into such a device. She also knew with the same force of conviction that she herself wouldn't want any of those powers.

Neither was she bent on world domination.

But a megalomaniac would certainly apply himself to discover how exactly to do those things, for to command time itself was one step shy of controlling everything. She examined the device in the flickering firelight, unable to see seam or nock or lever by which its mechanical parts might be moved.

Sighing, she put it away, adjusting her tunic to insure it was covered completely. "You seem to know a fair bit about these things, Zibeth," she said casually, stepping over the blaze.

Chiona attended to a stew coming to a boil over the fire. "Father won't acknowledge it, but he was once Guild Liaison for the High Magux Ravenna Cithara." It was clear she'd been following the conversation for a while.

Guild relations a frequent source of consternation for the Magux, Ari was thinking, his had to have been a difficult task.

Bere slipped into the firelight like a wraith. "We're being watched," she said, her voice low, her gaze boring into each of them by turn.

"Chiona, that spell …" Ari said.

The girl grinned, rolled backward from her crouch, and vanished.

Ari put her hand to the amulet beneath her tunic, the object warmer than usual between her breasts. Her other hand to her scroll, she muttered, "Spy to spy, surveil unveil."

Her mind's eye leaped above the forest canopy, and around them their positions lighted as though each carried a torch, their surveillers were revealed.

Surrounded.

* * *

Marl stopped kicking long enough to send his feet toward the bottom. He and Pavo had been paddling toward shore, buoyed by a piece of flotsam, all night long.

The whitecaps ahead glowed ghostly in the predawn light, the soft crash of small surf on gentle beach having grown closer across the last hour.

"I still can't touch," he told Pavo, his feet hitting nothing below them.

The dark line of land had grown gradually larger, and Marl knew they were making progress, but it seemed such insignificant progress that he despaired he'd never be dry again.

He and the ragged remains of Baron Footsore's retinue had found their way to the volcano surface a full day after the devil Pictor had smashed Sagit Smoothgrain against the cavern wall and had enchanted the One Stone Luxullian from Marl's possession.

It rankled him to know that he'd carried Luxullian to Pictor without knowing it. He was deeply perturbed he'd had been so cruelly used by the Necromancer. To find out he'd stolen Luxullian after all, and then had delivered it to the Necromancer like some errand boy, caused Marl Gneiss to feel as though everything he'd worked toward had been for naught.

It galled him to no end.

Upon emerging to the surface after their eight-day underground sojourn, the party had found themselves on the banks of the island volcano, the Warlock's Mount, the cindercone above them belching a boiling stew of gas, lava, ash, and rock into the sky in a constant stream of vomit. Down the sides of Warlock's Mount dribbled molten flows of rock, red-hot and burning, tongues of liquid fire licking at the roiling sea, sending gouts of steam exploding into the air.

Lava flows descending toward them, ashen rock raining down around them, the spelunkers had done the only thing available: jump into the sea.

Pavo and Marl had quickly found this log, buoyant enough to help them stay afloat. Other spelunkers had found similar flotsam, but some had not been so lucky and had drowned.

The sides of the Warlock's Mount had soon been overrun by pyroclastic flows. Had any retinue members remained ashore, they would have been crisped to a cinder instantly.

The roiling waters off the coast of the Warlock's Mount had dispersed the poor souls clinging desperately to their makeshift flotation devices, and soon Marl and Pavo had found themselves alone on the Halfmoon Sea, the night deep and dark and lit only by the fiery eruption of Warlock's Mount, which they sought quickly to put behind them.

Thus they had begun to paddle north.

All night they'd paddled, and then all day, then all night again, seeming to go nowhere, the black line visible ahead their only indication of a destination, the column of fire roaring into the sky behind them their only beacon. Had they gone the way the beacon beckoned, they'd have been lured to their doom.

As long as they kept it behind them, they couldn't be off course. The whitecaps of breaking surf visible, and its susurrus audible, Marl felt as though he could paddle no more, his arms like lead weights, his hands barely able to grasp the sodden wood any longer, his breathing so labored, such herculean energies did inhalation require that he might as well have expired as exhaled.

A wave slapped him from behind and nearly buried his head underwater.

Where did that come from? Marl wondered, spluttering for air.

"Tide's coming in," Pavo said, sounding excited. And the boy thrashed at the water with renewed paddling.

It will help carry us ashore, Marl thought, wondering if he were going to last that long, fatigue threatening to pull him into its warm comforting …

Hands grabbed him roughly. "Here, help me with the heavy one," a male voice said, and hands tugged on Marl's arms and clothing, dragging his feet across the sandy bottom. He wondered briefly why his feet wouldn't obey him.

The sand hitting his face like a right cross startled him, and he choked and gasped when weight on his back pushed his face further into sand but also pushed a great gout of water from his lungs.

Where'd that come from? he wondered dreamily, the pinkened sky replacing the rough sand. He drew a deep breath, coughed and spluttered once more then lay back, three faces occluding the pinkish roiling clouds.

"Pavo," he managed his voice hoarse and barely audible.

"He's fine," the big man said, his blond locks spilling down his shoulders.

Marl breathed a sigh and let his eyes close.

* * *

Marl breathed a gasp and snapped his eyes open.

"Easy, Lord Baron," Pavo said, his hands gentle on Marl's shoulder. "You'd have drowned within feet of the beach if Columba hadn't saved you."

"Who?" It was another gasp, as unintelligible as the first.

"Columba Riverford, the supposed thief of Genesyx, the One Sword."

A fit of palsy seized him then, his memories of Travert Crepitans Pictor flooding through him. He struggled to sit up, Pavo helping him.

The campsite was set back from the shore, a screen of palm and fern obscuring the sea but not its sound.

A towering column of fire to the south pumped billowing black smoke into an already impenetrable cloud that covered the sky from horizon to horizon.

Across the campsite, watching him intently, were two men and two women.

"What the gallstones is that meretrix doing here?"

"Thief!" Skarn shot back. "Careful who you call a whore, you lowlife social climber!"

The smaller of the two men rose from his crouch at the fire. "You can both stop or there'll be no more thieving, whoring, or social climbing for any of us."

Marl saw he wore a sword and knew this must be Columba, who'd been expelled from Swordshire on the accusation that he'd stolen the One Sword, Genesyx.

And Marl knew he'd done exactly that—without knowing it.

Marl groped the pockets of his breeches, then cursed, remembering that Pictor had taken back the belt buckle, which had always been his and his alone, made by his hand and fashioned, Marl now knew, to help the Necromancer obtain the One Stone Luxullian from the High Adept Gabbro Scoria Hornsfels through his erstwhile innocent servant the Baron Marl Gneiss.

But in his groping, Marl found his apricot-sized ruby, which he had thought was lost long ago. How had Pictor hidden the fist-size diamond Luxullian inside an apricot-size ruby? Marl wondered.

"He reaches for his stone," the other woman said.

Belatedly, Marl recognized Minette Hornsfels, Adept in her own right and next High Adept of Stonevale after her father—if there were a Vault of Stones to inherit. She would be at least as formidable as he, her mien minacious and mind sagacious.

"He'll not harm us," the one called Columba said. "Will you, Marl?"

Marl shook his head, knowing all but one of the present company. "Who's he?" He pointed to the burly man with an axe.

"Samshad Woodwright, sent to accompany us by the High Magux Ravenna Cithara in our quest to restore the Sword, Scroll, and Stone," Columba said.

"Woodwright?" Pavo said. "I'm apprentice Woodwright to Sagit Smoothgrain of Swordshire."

The burly man fingering the axe blade smiled. "Old Smoothgrain himself? I'd be honored to make his acquaintance, if you wouldn't ... uh, what's wrong?"

Marl and Pavo had glanced at each other before dropping their gazes to the ground.

"I mean," Pavo added, glancing to the south, toward the column of fire and ash, "I was. He didn't make it."

"What do you know of that?" Columba asked.

It seemed such an innocent question.

Marl seemed to have nothing short of a complicit answer. "I'm afraid that's my fault," he said, his shame and humiliation almost too much to bear.

"You gave him Luxullian, didn't you?!" Minette said.

Columba put his hand on her arm. "She'll not hurt you, Baron. And neither will the Bandit Arkose. They've both sworn upon the return of the Sword, Scroll, and Stone to leave you in peace. Minette, tell him."

The young woman stared through Marl like an arrow through its target. "I'll not harm a hair on your head until after the Sword, Scroll, and Stone have been restored, but I'll cut your throat the moment it happens."

Marl found no comfort in her vow.

"Skarn?" Columba said, gesturing toward the Baron.

"Where's my belt buckle?" the older woman said. In her forties, she had the weathered look of a person exposed to the elements for many years.

Marl wouldn't look at her.

"You gave that to Pictor too, didn't you?"

He didn't need to nod.

Skarn blew a hefty sigh. "What right do you have, stealing my property and giving it to that Necromancer, the one person with the least need for more magic talismans?"

"It was his all along," Marl said quietly.

"What the Almighty Scribe did you think—"

"What'd you say?" Columba said, interrupting Skarn.

"It was his, I said," Marl repeated, frustrated because they didn't understand. "He made it specifically for me, or whoever was going to steal Luxullian."

Give people gasped, including Pavo.

"You told me you didn't steal it," the boy said.

"I didn't know that I had, not then." Marl looked at the rest of them. "He concealed the One Stone Luxullian inside my ruby, somehow." He held up the apricot-sized stone, its facets scintillating in the mid-morning light. "None of us knew." He looked at Columba. "You didn't know."

The man looked bewildered. "None of us knew what? What didn't I know?"

"That we each did steal that which we swore to serve. That I stole Luxullian, that you stole Genesyx."

The man's three companions looked askance at him, and ever so subtly moved to each side.

"I stole Genesyx?" Columba threw his head back and laughed. "You're as daft as you are ambitious. I stole nothing of the sort."

"Ah, but you did," Marl said, his voice calm. "You have it on you now. On your person."

"I? Genesyx?" Columba sputtered. "Ludicrous. Where?" He spread his hands to invite Marl to indicate where he might be hiding it.

"Lay your sword on the ground between us," Marl said, hoping this worked.

"Eh? Disarm myself in your company? I hardly think so."

"And betray us all, as I have, by giving the dark Necromancer Travert Crepitans Pictor the second of three talismans? Look south, fool, and see the results of my foolery. I sought to use my very own ruby against him, not realizing I carried not my ruby, but Luxullian, the One Stone, which only revealed itself when I sought to use it on him. And of course my spell went awry and I cast toward him not any spell at all, but the One Stone itself, which he caught as casually as he might the toss of a fruit. Go on, fool Sage, deny me the opportunity to prove that you carry Genesyx and deliver it to him personally, as I did Luxullian.

"Deny me that and betray us all, fool Sage." Marl waved his hand dismissively and put away his ruby. He looked south, his shame and regret consuming him, wondering how by the grace of the Almighty Earth he might redeem himself after such a vile betrayal.

How could I have been so disingenuous? he wondered.

"Show me, Lord Baron." Columba said. "And forgive me my distrust." The sword lay on the sand between them.

"Tis a perilous time," Marl said. "Difficult enough to trust ourselves, let alone anyone else." He brought out his ruby again, holding it between thumb and forefinger and kneeling beside the sword. "I hope this works."

He extended it toward the sword until the ruby was mere inches from the blade, its reflection visible in several facets. "Reflect for me truly, ruby of mine, essence naturally, this sword so fine." And he shook the ruby above the sword along its length as though to sprinkle the spice of truth.

The sword lay there, unmoved, unchanged.

"Charlatan," Skarn said, "and liar."

Marl withdrew, pocketing his ruby. "Believe what you will. My not making a thing appear doesn't prove it isn't there." He looked at Columba. "Disbelieve me and take your folly there." He pointed south. "I for one will attempt to warn Aridisia Myric, the Magux who I know approaches these shores, bearing the One Scroll, Canodex. To you, I have done my duty to warn. My only proof is the reproof I have earned in not seeing the Necromancer's designs writ upon the winds of my fate.

"I may have failed to see, but I haven't failed to warn. Whether you heed my warning is writ upon the winds of your fate, now."

Marl frowned at the boy, Pavo. "Sagit was a good caretaker for you, wise in the ways of the world. Alas I cannot compare. Will you go with me to find this Aridisia? Or stay with this company, which is clearly determined to test its wiles against those of the Necromancer himself?"

Pavo looked between the two men. "I don't know, Lord Baron, not yet. I've a sense we're not finished here yet." He grinned at Columba.

"I'll say we're not. Lord Baron, you've much to share, I'm sure, and I'd be remiss not to take the time to listen. Stay with us here at least until tomorrow morn, and then be about to finding the Lady Magux Aridisia, if she hasn't appeared here by then."

"Eh? Appeared here? Why would she, except perchance being en route herself to a meeting with Pictor?"

"Just as I'm thinking, Lord Baron. As to this being Genesyx, well, I don't know. But perhaps Lady Adept Hornsfels can work her magic to reveal the true nature of my sword."

Marl looked at the Stonevale Princess. He found it odd that she accompanied the presumptor to Sage, among all those at the Hall of Swords, which if rumor were correct had banished him on pain of death for the theft of Genesyx, despite his denials of having carried out the deed. Marl knew that Columba was no more guilty of stealing Genesyx as he was of Luxullian, but it did not rescind his banishment. Only the High Sage Arcturyx Longblade could do that.

Why had Lord Adept Hornsfels sent his daughter with this lowly presumptor to the Hall of Swords. Had Stonevale no other representative it might send?

Marl watched the young woman prepare to cast her spell.

Minette crouched much as Marl had beside the blade where it lay on the sand, the nearly noonday sun barely penetrating the thick black cloud that hovered ominously above them, stretching horizon to horizon, only a slim glimpse of blue sky still visible to the north. The day was a normal day, but the pall cast by the black cloud gave the day the feel of a full-moon night.

She produced a diamond the size of an apple from under her tunic, its facets winking dully in the wan light. She held the stone between delicate, almost bony fingers of elegant length, fingers that had never seen a day of hard labor, the skin diaphanous and nearly translucent, the veins easily visible on the back of the hand.

She ran the diamond the length of the sword, her gaze on the stone itself, as though she were seeing the sword through the facets.

Then she wrapped the stone with both bands. "Reflect for me truly, diamond of mine," she said, her voice low and sultry, "the essence unduly of sword confine."

Marl felt as though she mocked him, but under her spell, the sword began to vibrate, setting the sand around it in motion, the granules jumping like droplets of water off a hot griddle.

The sword vibrated so rapidly that it began to blur with motion, its oscillation setting forth a dull ringing that grew in intensity.

Marl covered his ears against the humming, which seemed to pierce even his hands.

The sword appeared to float, having displaced the sand underneath, and in the trough beneath appeared a second sword below the first, this one gilded along haft and blade, the quality of its manufacture and materials far in advance of the simple blade that hovered about it.

"There!" Minette gasped, the diamond falling from her hands, and the sand trough collapsing around the sword.

Only the simple sword belonging to Columba remained.

"Yes, there," Marl said, looking looked at Columba. "Having seen, will you now launch an attack on Travert Crepitans Pictor and so eagerly deliver unto him the only sword he'll ever need again?"

Chapter 12

Columba stared at the Baron Marl Gneiss and didn't see him.

How could I have fallen dupe so easily to the Necromancer Pictor, Lord of the Black Arts and King of the Underworld, feaster upon dead flesh and fornicator of it too?

Sage Riverford stood and looked south, where beyond a thin veil of palm frond and fern branch, an inferno pumped ash and smoke and burning rock into an already blackened sky.

He turned to the Baron Marl Gneiss and bowed. "Forgive me my presumption and suspicion, Lord Baron. You have done me and Swordshire—indeed all three kingdoms—an inestimable service." Columba looked at both Skarn and Minette. "A service that invites forgiveness and redemption. Lord Baron, I for one will gladly petition the Lord High Adept Hornsfels to lift his edict and restore your lands, although I suspect the return of Luxullian will hold more sway than my humble plea." He looked among them all. "I suspect there is more to the Lord Baron than we know. Won't you linger for a time, Lord, and tell us of your adventures, and together we shall find our fellow thief the Magux Aridisia to warn her of her peril. What say you, Lord Baron?"

Columba let his hands fall to his sides to show he spoke plain, that no compulsion or coercion was forthcoming, that the Baron was being invited to stay on his own merits and not out of any obligation. Further, Columba wished only that Baron Gneiss aid them from within his sense of belonging.

"Well, I'd say," Samshad Woodwright interjected, "that you've been through just about as much as a person could stand, and that what you need this moment is rest and food, eh, Lord Baron?"

"I'm famished, now that you mention it," Gneiss said.

Appeal to a fat man's stomach, Columba thought. "And you as well, Pavo?"

The boy nodded, smiling at Marl.

While Shad began fixing them all a meal, Columba bent to pick up his sword. It looked no different and felt no different, its heft and balance unchanged.

What's changed is my perception, he thought. Now I know that it conceals Genesyx. Remembering the shadow sword he'd seen under the High Adept Hornsfel's inspection of it, Columba now knew what they'd both suspected.

Yes, unknowingly, Columba had stolen the One Sword, Genesyx.

And yes, he could return it to Swordshire and restore it to its proper place in the Hall of Swords.

"Presuming you could undo the spell that hides it," Skarn said.

He brought his gaze up to her face, not realizing she'd been watching him. Besides her stood the younger Minette Hornsfels. The weather in Skarn's face belied her age: she looked ten years older than she really was. The sheltered life that Minette had lived, child of privilege and luxury, cocooned in the wealth locked safely deep in the Vault of Stones, made her look years younger than she actually was.

Columba guessed that they were closer in age than anyone suspected, their differences as much a draw of curiosity, and their similarity of attitude toward him the source of their affiliation.

"Look, I know you'd both like me dead, but could you at least grant me the opportunity to put this back?" He gestured at the sword.

"Certainly," both women said at once, and then giggled at having done so.

"That'll be a tough spell to undo," Minette added.

"Tell me about Pictor," Columba said.

"There's so much to tell," Skarn said. "Where do we start?"

"The belt buckle," Columba said.

Skarn shuddered and shook her head. "I can't tell you about that."

She looks almost possessed, Columba thought. "If Pictor used the belt buckle to conceal Luxullian and draw it to him—"

"That's it!" Pavo said, tearing his gaze away from the food being prepared by Shad. "Baron Footsore looked obsessed with taking Baron Gneiss on a spelunk."

"He accused me later of mesmerizing him with a spell—long after it was too late to go back," Baron Gneiss said.

"Then what is he using to conceal the One Sword Genesyx from me?" Columba looked among the other; on one appeared to know.

"Why do you carry that knife?" Gneiss asked. "The one with the ruby."

"What knife?" Columba asked, even as he reached for Serpens.

"And what is he using to conceal Canodex from Aridisia?" Columba laid the knife on the ground in front of him, and looked at Minette. "Your father asked me why I carry a forbidden talisman."

"You said that it carries you." Minette stared at him.

"Eavesdropping?" Then Columba shrugged. "I'd do the same. Yes, that's what I told him. I'm not sure why. Baron, you recognized it because of the ruby, right?"

Gneiss nodded. "That, and I carried a buckle made of similar metal with a similar stone embedded in its face. A notch on the side opened the back, and inside was a small scroll, the writing on it indecipherable with the naked eye. As like to be written in a script so archaic, none of us save Pictor himself could read it anymore. I've heard tales about that one," Gneiss said, gesturing at the knife that now lay at Columba's feet.

He looked at the Baron.

"An old miner on our journey underground told tale of a battle between a Sea King and a serpent. The Sea King did win the battle, but was grievously wounded in the side with a knife that resisted all attempts to remove it. He washed up on the western shore of Swordshire with the knife still embedded in the festering wound and was never heard from again."

Columba nodded. "As deep and enduring his efforts to subvert the authority of the Sword, Scroll, and Stone, it'd behoove us to find out more about this knife, whose name is Serpens."

"A named weapon develops a life all its own," Shad said from across the fire, stirring the sizzling food in the pan.

Columba could see that both the Baron and the boy were ready to leap into the frying pan itself, they were so hungry. Although Pavo looked wan and thin from his two-day ordeal upon the Halfmoon Sea, the Baron looked as though five or six more days of deprivation wouldn't harm him terribly.

Mostly what they needed, Columba thought, was water. He said as much to Samshad.

"Aye, so right, Lord Sage, forgive me for not thinking of it before. Sitting in the ocean for two days is sure to have leeched the water right out of them." He separated the meal onto the plates and handed one to each. "You two eat slowly, lest you vomit what you just ate, eh?" Then he rose to get them water. "And drink plenty of this while you eat. No, Baron, chew your food, or by the Almighty Scribe, you'll make yourself sick."

Amused, Columba watched Shad minister to the boy and Baron.

"Lord Sage," Skarn said. "This Necromancer and all this talk of a knife with a life all its own . . . " She looked at him, her face apprehensive.

"Minette," Columba said, "any legends of objects being imbued with conscious thought, or with the spirits of the dead?"

"None to my knowledge, Columba," the Hornfels Princess said, "but this is Travert Crepitans Pictor we're talking about, who's rumored to have resurrected himself from the dead. Powers beyond the ken, as we say in Stonevale, and without a scruple against using them. As to actually doing it . . . " She shrugged and shook her head. "Seems as if the process would take as much from the magician doing it, perhaps resulting in severe impairment, or even death."

"Not a barrier for him," Skarn reminded them. "If that knife is all that, wouldn't it also have a scroll embedded somewhere on it?"

Columba exchanged glances with Shad and Minette, then looked down at the knife, which he'd carried across the continent, having acquired it mere hours after the disappearance of Genesyx and his subsequent expulsion from Swordshire.

The blade and haft looked full, hammered from metal oft used for swords. Had he compared the knife with his sword, he'd have seen no difference but for shape. The ruby at the base of the blade was small, no larger than a sunflower seed, and glimmered despite the dull smoky daylight.

The pommel—the butt of the knife—was also metal, but looked as if it might be a separate piece, as the seam between pommel and haft appeared to go all the way round.

Turning it slowly, Columba examined it carefully, the ruby casting dull rays from the sun off its tiny multitudinous facets. He wrapped the haft with his forefinger and held it tightly, then grasped the pommel with his other hand.

"You sure you want to do that?"

Columba whirled at the unfamiliar voice.

* * *

Aridisia lowered her right hand and, with it, the quill strapped to her fingers. "My name is Aridisia Myric, late of Scrollhaven, purported thief of the One Scroll Canodex, and you must be Columba Riverford, late of Swordshire and purported thief of the One Sword Genesyx. The hungry man yon must be the Baron himself, Marl Gneiss, late of Stonevale and purported thief of the One Stone Luxullian."

She smiled and bowed to them all. "An honor and privilege to make acquaintance with fellow thieves."

"Honored that you joined us," the Sage said.

"And an honor likewise for this thief to make your acquaintance," the Adept said, his fleshy jowls jiggling with a chuckle. "Suffice it to say we have established the adage to be at least a truism, if not completely true."

Ari smiled, looking over the camp. Telltale signs indicated they had not been there long, perhaps just since morning, and certainly not overnight. She turned to introduce her companions, seeing instantly the enmity between Berenice Longblade and Columba Riverford.

He, she noted, concealed it well, but Bere looked as though she might lop his head off in a heartbeat, her hand strangling the haft of her sword.

"Bere!" Ari said sharply.

The younger woman seemed to snap from a trance.

"We are here to restore the Sword, Scroll, and Stone."

Bere's gaze dropped to the ground. "Yes, Lady. As commanded by my father, Lord High Adept Arcturyx Longblade."

"And whatever animosities you bear are subordinate to that goal, as your father commanded."

"Yes, Lady," Bere said, dropping to a knee. "Forgive me my forgetting that."

"Of course, you're forgiven, my friend. You've served me well and will continue to do so, I'm sure. But I do need to know, Bere, whether you'll continue to obey my command even if my command is that you obey that man." Ari pointed at the Lord Sage Columba Riverford.

The silence thick, broken only by the soft sounds of surf and the waft of breeze through palm fronds, the young woman struggled visibly with herself, her expression changing from despair to fury and finally to resignation. She sighed and glanced over at Columba, then looked directly at Ari. "In the name of Sword, Scroll, and Stone, Lady, yes, I can and will obey."

"Thank you, Bere, on behalf of all the people between the four corners, thank you for that commitment." Ari turned and looked at the other group, nodding to Samshad Woodwright, for whom she had crafted a spell, in that short time when she had been a Magux at the Crypt of Scrolls, if only a pretend one.

"Lady Myric," Columba said. "There is one barrier yet to securing the Lady Longblade's loyalty, a barrier that I myself have just learned of in these last few hours from the Lord Baron Gneiss." He glanced over at the Baron.

Deep into his meal, Marl Gneiss shrugged as though helpless.

Ari looked at Columba.

Who sighed. "Much to my dismay, I do have the One Sword Genesyx."

Bere was quick, but Ari was quicker and tripped her before she got past her. Ari leaped upon her and grabbed her by the collar. "Did I give you permission to assault anyone? Did I order you to attack anyone?"

The younger woman struggled for a moment but Ari's grip was firm. "We should have gutted him on the spot!"

"If that's what your father had wanted, he'd have done it. Are you ready to listen?!"

"But—"

Ari caught the cheek with a right cross, and pulled her arm back for a second blow. "Well?"

Bere burst into tears and covered her face with her hands and wrapped her in her arms.

Ari got off the younger woman and helped her to her feet. "I need you with us on this journey, but I need you to follow orders. Look at me, Bere. I don't want to send you back to your father as incorrigible or insubordinate. I don't think you're either one, but I have to know I can count on you. Are you ready to listen?"

Bere nodded, her tears mixed with blood.

"No one here is your enemy. No one. We have only one enemy, this Travert Crepitans Pictor. If Sage Riverford has Genesyx, it's because Pictor intended it. It wouldn't surprise me to find out that I have Canodex on my person at this moment—"

"Uh, Lady—" Marl began.

"Don't interrupt me!" She turned back to Bere. "We have to work together, and that means setting aside all our animosities. Are you able to do that?"

"Yes, Lady Magux Myric." Bere's face was ashen but she met Ari's gaze.

"And will you follow my orders?"

"To the death, Lady Magux Myric."

"And his orders, if I told you to follow them?"

The hesitation was slight. "To the death, Lady Magux Myric."

Ari turned to the rest of them. "Does anyone here doubt another so severely that it cripples your ability to work with them, fight alongside them, and if necessary to die for the sake of restoring the Sword, Scroll, and Stone? If so, say it now and be quit of this company immediately!"

No one spoke.

Ari looked at each one directly.

Every single one of them met her gaze.

243

"I for one am proud to be a member of such an august group." Ari said. "Thank you, all of you, for your commitment." She turned to Bere and kissed her. "Sorry I had to hit you." she said, her voice soft.

"Guess I deserved it," Bere replied, shrugging.

Ari smiled and stepped toward the Baron. "Any more of that stew? I'm famished."

Shad rose. "Let me put something together for all of us."

We'll need it," Ari said, looking among the others. "The Necromancer will send against us a host the likes of which this world has never seen. We battled some of them in the southeastern woods of Scrollhaven.

* * *

On the forest ridge southeast of the Crypt of Scrolls, our company tired for having travelled most of two days, we found ourselves surrounded. Three of us against thirty, maybe forty.

But who were they?

After Chiona fled using her invisibility spell, Bere, Zibeth, and I backed ourselves up to a tree, armed with our magics.

"Who goes there?" I said, directing my voice out into the forest. Were they bandits, gathering to feast on these few vulnerable travelers unescorted by an armed contingent through lands where the High Magux no longer held sway, now deprived of the One Scroll, the law of the land, Canodex? Or were they warriors allied with this same High Magux Ravenna Cithara, sent to carry out the sentence that she had decreed some three weeks ago, when she declared that I, Aridisia Myric, was banished from Scrollhaven on pain of death, and yet here through Scrollhaven I traveled in stark disobedience to her edict, therefore deserving of the full penalty of law? Or were they a loose knit group of local denizens, concerned about the anarchy that raged unchecked elsewhere, combining their might in arms for mutual self protection and alarmed by the recent shaking of the earth, overcast daytime skies, and thick coating of ash that had descended from heaven, so alarmed that they had elected to venture this direction in their search for meaning from these cataclysmic events?

As like as any, was my thought at the time, not wanting to entertain my deeper, darker fears, not knowing what we faced here, the conjuration of the evil Necromancer Travert Crepitans Pictor likely to exceed the most horrific creation of my imagination by leaps and bounds.

Of course, I received no reply to my query, as I thought I would not, for any necromanced interlocutors as my imagination could produce who might be surrounding us would betray neither their position nor identity by responding.

Our hearts beating like rabbits' in our throats, we waited, crouched at the base of a tree, grateful for its protection, the waiting game all to our advantage.

The stirrings here and there in such a nighttime forest—the fall of a dried twig, the rustle of breeze through a floor of leaves, the burrowing of a ground squirrel in its nest—all held ominous portent of impending attack, each sound in our minds the initial motion of the launch, each the harbinger of flashing blades and blood-curdling screams. These stirrings were all the more ominous under a sky so thick with volcanic ash that nary a star nor glimmer of moon did pierce the dark. My heart stopped at each sound, my breath catching in my throat, my palms so slick with sweat that I'm sure my scroll still bears imprint of my grasp, and my hair must have surely turned a frightful gray.

The fetor of decay was so rank that I might have retched if I hadn't been so frightened. Every step on the thick bed of forest floor leaves caused a fresh spray of decay-laden stench to erupt from around our feet.

Bere and Zibeth spoke not a word as we awaited our fate, their fear palpable as I'm sure mine was too. The skin crawled up the back of my neck like some necrophiliating beetle, and I regretted having called out earlier, sure that my terror had set my voice a-quaver.

"Quick, light from above," Zibeth said.

"Spite the harkness, light the darkness," Bere said, her sword singing through air. The trees above us lit the darkness.

Bodies five thick crowded round us, and we attacked.

Bodies they were, shells without souls, agglomerations of vegetative rot necromanced from the forest floor, their parts as putrid as the decay from which they'd been made. But those parts held weapons—clubs, rocks, staves—and in the dance of death we found it wasn't enough to dismember them limb to limb, but to deprive their trunks of legs and arms and heads.

Bere was a dervish, and Zibeth no slouch with spell, but we three were nearly overwhelmed anyway, the thick waves of putrefaction pooling at our feet. Knee deep in sludge, we could barely move, and in fact, found the sludge surging higher upon our legs.

"We're trapped," Bere said, her sword useless against the recrudescent rot.

"Bere, grab the rope," Chiona said, appearing between two trees and well beyond the reach of the rot. She slung up a rope with a couplet, "Rope, please, bear my friends from these." The rope wrapped a branch with one end, then snaked itself around Bere under her arms, and lifted. The slime slurped and sucked in protest but could not hold onto her.

Chiona then threw a rope for me.

"No, help your father," I protested, seeing that her father was sunk nearly to the waist. "Forest floor," I spelt on scroll, "reclaim your muck and cease to suck." And the decay fell away from me. As I stepped out of the morass, I saw that Zibeth too was being pulled free.

We took a moment to survey our damage. The muck had consumed our campsite entire, leaving us with just the possessions we wore, and we consulted amongst ourselves. Rather than trying to set up another camp and sleep in uneasy fear of another attack, we decided it better to set out even in the darkness toward the shores of the Halfmoon Sea.

* * *

Ari looked at Baron Marl Gneiss. "So I'm carrying Canodex, eh? Have the whole time, I suppose?"

Marl nodded. "Indeed, Lady. Thieves, every one of us, in spite of our vehement denials. What prestidigitation do you suppose the Necromancer used to filch the Sword, Scroll, and Stone and then conceal each upon our persons?"

Ari shook her head. "And now he's got Luxullian."

The Baron dropped his gaze to his empty plate.

"None of us could have known, Lord Adept," Ari said. "You just happened to meet him first."

"Lady Magux, at some level I knew," the Baron said. "And I did nothing about it. The Baron Caelum Footsore showed me what I carried, right before he tried to kill me. He knew, and he tried to stop me from delivering it."

Ari nodded and looked over her shoulder. "Chiona!"

The girl approached, having just finished dressing the cut on Bere's cheek. "Yes, Lady?"

"You said you saw someone faint of magic leaving Warlock's Mount right after it erupted. Was that the Baron?"

Chiona nodded. "Yes, Lady."

Columba stepped up beside her. "You can see people from a distance?"

"Well, their magic, Lord. I can see their magic. It's like a point of light in the sky, some brighter, some dimmer. Yours and Lady Myric's are very bright. Lord Gneiss's magic was very bright, but dimmed moments before the eruption. Of course, Pictor's magic right now is brightest of all."

Ari exchanged glances with Columba and Marl.

"Pictor also took his belt buckle back from me."

The story of Cincinatus Ripplebark came to mind. "Of burnished steel," she said, "a small ruby in its center, and visible through the back a scroll so tiny the writing could not be read."

She saw the two men exchange a glance. "I saw you at the mines of Swordshire," she told Marl. "You were wearing it then, weren't you? A forbidden talisman, one for each of us, to conceal from us what we carry, to protect us from harm and to drive us relentlessly toward him who created these forbidden talismans. For Marl a belt buckle, for Columba a knife, and for me a timepiece."

She drew out the timepiece by its chain from beneath her tunic. "Zibeth Anthus, formerly Guild Liaison for her grace the Lady High Magux Ravena Cithara, questions why a magician so powerful as the Necromancer Travert Crepitans would create a timepiece of forbidden manufacture with the ability to track time but without the ability to stop time, advance time, or reverse time. What I don't see, if indeed this talisman can do these things, is by what mechanism."

"It has a scroll, yes?" Marl asked.

"It must," Columba said, pulling the knife from his belt. "Just as this knife must have a scroll embedded somewhere in it."

They compared the two objects. The steel used in their manufacture was identical, bearing patterns of hammer impacts that were indistinguishable.

"The same forge and steelsmith," Columba said.

The rubies were identical in size and cut, the number of facets no different. "The same rubycutter," Marl said, "and perhaps cut from the same motherstone. Plus, identical to the stone embedded in the face of the belt buckle, I'm sure of it."

"Made at the same time, do you suppose?" Ari asked.

They conferred on the respective tales they had heard regarding their creation. It didn't appear that they had been created contemporaneously, the belt buckle having originated first, and the knife Serpens last.

"So the chances of their being linked is small," Ari said.

"What would that avail us?" Columba asked.

"Two against one—knife and timepiece against buckle," Ari said, smiling. "If they *were* linked, that is."

"How do we know they aren't?" Marl asked.

"How do we find out?" Columba asked.

"We've compared steel and stone, but not scroll," Ari said. She turned over the timepiece and fitted her finger to the slight indentation. The spring-loaded backing popped open. There, nestled between gears and springs, was a thumbnail-size scroll, faint lines of script visible but indecipherable to the naked eye. "Based on the way it's wedged in there, I don't think the timepiece will work if I remove it," Ari said.

Columba held up the knife. "I was about to open this up when you appeared, Aridisia."

"Call me Ari."

"Certainly, Ari. Was there a reason you stopped me?"

"I've heard tales of the havoc it's caused, the knife," Ari said. "I didn't want something to happen to you."

He seemed amused by that, giving her wry smile. "Serpens it's called, although how I came across its name, I couldn't say. Let's see what's under this pommel."

The knob looked to Ari as though it were separate, the seam between pommel and haft going all the way around. "Twist off."

Columba frowned at her but shrugged. He placed one hand on the haft and put his palm over the pommel.

Ari noticed how calloused his hands were, and heavy-pored with the experience of hard work. Not the soft-palmed, scholarly type, this one, she thought, remembering the oft-times narrow-minded bureaucrats at the Crypt of Scrolls, their minds occupied with the current text they were deciphering, and little concerned with real world events, sheltered inside the Crypt like the necromancified zombies of some long dead civilization.

Did I ever really want to become a Magux and spend my remaining days crouched over a palimpsest? Ari wondered.

Columba twisted the pommel off the haft.

Rolled tightly inside the haft was a scroll, the writing of similar size and equally indecipherable as that in the timepiece.

Ari held the timepiece close to the knife.

Accidentally, the rim touched the haft.

The heat of a pyroclastic column of rock, ash and fire roaring behind her, Ari looked to the north, the shores of the Halfmoon Sea visible in a neat semicircle around her, the junglescape green visible through the ashy haze that had settled upon the four corners since the eruption began over two days before. In front of her, circling the tunnel of her vision, wraiths flocked like wolves to the slaughter, their black, diaphanous, sheet-like bodies flying in tight circles outward from the line of her sight.

Her attention focused on the base of the north-south road where it ended at the Halfmoon beach, where once the boundary of a kingdom had lain, where before it had sunk below the waves. Travert Crepitans Pictor had once ruled his kingdom, his domains extending to that boundary now known as the Halfmoon shoreline, his kingdom having sunk below the waves in the horrific eruption of the volcano that had been known even then as Warlock's Mount.

Ari snapped back into her body and looked at Columba.

The horror in his eyes told her he'd seen the same as she.

"He sends his wraiths as we speak," they both said.

"Huh?" Marl said. "Why'd you say that at the same time? You both look like you've seen the devil himself."

"Something like that," Ari said. "Everyone," she called out, turning her attention to their small group. "We only have a few minutes to prepare. The Necromancer sends the undead against us."

Marl rolled his ruby between his fingers and looked south.

The ten members of their company stood in a phalanx, Bere and Minette at the head, Columba and Ari at the tail, the latter two somewhat dismayed at their rearguard position, the majority having overruled their taking lead positions.

"These wraith are coming after *you*," Marl had finally told them. "If you get captured, what chance have the rest of us against Pictor with all the talismans?"

To the south, rocketing toward them over roiling waves, was a knot of black menace. The ball of dark vapor might have been launched from a precision cannon, and it might not have been noticeable had Ari and Columa not accidently touched time-piece and knife.

Now at least they knew that these three devices, though manufactured by Pictor at long intervals in between, were not only connected but provided a glimpse into their creator's thinking.

"My one concern is that it may also give him glimpse into ours," Marl had told them.

Now, between their group and the rapidly approached wraiths was miles of empty ocean surface. The wake of their passage spread a thick black taint, the sea behind the wraiths oily as a tarpit and seeming as dead, even the wind reluctant to set the still, black water a-ripple.

The time to prepare had been wanting, the attack imminent. What they were facing was as unknown to them as the necrotic rot arisen from the forest floor had been to Ari and her company the night before. All they knew was that Travert Crepitans Pictor had necromanced them into being.

And launched them at the group.

Skarn, standing opposite Marl on the other phalanx, grinned at him. "Let's make ghosts of these wraiths," she said, her magical cloak in hand.

Isn't that what they already are? he wondered idly, as the black blot over the sea directly south of them grew larger by the moment.

And that's what gave Marl the idea.

He brought his ruby to his mouth and breathed on it. "Fire, wind, earth, and water, do my bidding and undead slaughter." And he hurled the spell south at the approaching wraiths.

A spinning swirl of the four elements hurled from his hand and met the wraiths head on about a mile offshore.

A maelstrom erupted, wraith and elemental twirling in the air just above the water, a circular dance that caught first air and then water with it, a funnel cloud leaping to the murk-filled sky.

The funnel fed on water and smoke and soon grew fat, draining the sea for a half mile round, then just as suddenly it collapsed, leaving its contents suspended in a column which dropped like a waterfall in midair. Surrounding sea and collapsing funnel both rushed to fill a space too small for both.

The water retreated from the beach as Marl searched for the least sign of wraith.

Their company cheered as it became plain Marl's spell had worked. He received their gratulations with grace and aplomb and happened to glance out to sea. Where funnel spout had been was now piled high a great wall of water.

"Uh, one small drawback," he said, pointing out to sea.

Columba stepped up beside him, his sword out of its sheath and gleaming despite the thick, black clouds occluding the sun. "I beg you, Lady, Queen of the Seas, suspend your wave and calm your surface. I call upon you, Octans Tala Chert, to reign in your seas."

At the base of the giant wave, which was now moving inexorably toward them, appeared a mermaid, suspending herself above the surface by the force of her tailfins. "You, Lord Sage Columba Riverford, would have me hold back consequence? And for what do I exchange this favor? Why should I choose your side when the Necromancer Travert Crepitans Pictor himself beseeches my help to drown you with this very wave you created?"

"You and your sister, Queen Coralreef of the Northern Seas, have resisted his blandishments and suasions for centuries," Ari said. "And you consider giving in to the mongrel now? He will pollute your seas, kill your fish, blast apart your reefs, and soil your pristine beaches. His taint will infect your domains with his pernicious evil for the rest of time."

"The wave must be allowed to restore equilibrium," the Queen declared, and it washed over her and thundered toward them.

Bere thrust with her sword. "Wave abide and divide."

And the wave split apart as it crashed over them, the water going to each side, the force of its crash vibrating the ground beneath Marl's feet, and the water swept into the jungle, taking with it most of the vegetation, only a few pliable palms resisting the initial surge.

The backwash was difficult and might have been worse if they hadn't been prepared for it. Muddy water clotted with debris surged seaward past them, taking with it what the initial wave had uprooted.

They made their way inland through the morass, despite their happy chatter at winning this first battle, cognizant what it had cost the land around them.

Marl was thinking that this—the flooded-out remains of the jungle floor—was why their ancestors had invested their energies in creating the Sword, Scroll, and Stone. In the constant wars, the greater long-term costs had been ignored for short-term gains.

Yes, a Sage might conquer a valley and rule it for the rest of his or her life and perhaps even pass it on to progeny, but the war to conquer those lands often laid waste the land itself and certainly decimated the local populace, leaving both traumatized—

so severely that a return to full productivity often took longer than the lives of those who ruled it.

If they kept it. If they weren't in turn attacked by some interloper, seeing that the cost of victory had so weakened the victors as to make them now vulnerable to incursion.

Marl followed the discussion of his comrades, feeling grateful to have fought off Pictor's first attack but dismayed at the devastation that that had precipitated.

"It's not as though we launched the attack," Minette was saying.

"So how do we protect ourselves without harming the lands and people around us?" Chiona asked, using her staff to pick her way through the knee-deep muck.

No one really had an answer for Chiona.

The north-south road which eventually led to the Crypt of Scrolls had become a river, carrying much of the effluent dislodged by the initial wave. Flotsam and jetsam made the road non-navigable, and the group made their way generally northward within sight of it.

Marl slogged through a break between two clumps of palm, their trunks wet high above his head and slathered with debris. He himself was soaked to the waist.

"The first thing we do," Columba said, "is restore the Sword, Scroll, and Stone, the quicker the better."

"To do that, we need to defeat the Necromancer," Skarn said, holding her cloak high to prevent its getting wet.

"More difficult than it appears on its face," Zibeth said, pushing aside a bough with his cane. "He's raised himself from the dead before and it's a sure bet he'll do it again."

"We'll need to do both—defeat him and nullify his ability to resurrect himself." Pavo swung his miter at some flotsam.

"Let's talk about how to defeat him first." Ari said, "And once we've a plan for that, then how to contain his magic."

"Perhaps we do both," Bere said. "Defeating him doesn't mean we have to kill him. What we do need is a way to contain or nullify his magic, some geis to turn his spells awry, so they never do what he intends they do."

"I say we cut his body apart and pickle the pieces," Samshad said, thumbing the shiny edge of his axe and grinning.

Even Marl laughed at the picture that came to mind: a cellar full of pickled Pictor.

"One thing is sure," Columba said. "He prepares his next attack even as we speak, and if all we do is defend ourselves from his attacks, then we may win every battle, even as we lose the war. We must take the battle to him."

Chapter 13

Columba looked sharply between Marl and Ari, then brought his gaze back to Marl. "Are you sure that's the way you want to do this, Baron?"

"I am," Marl said. "It's the only way to be certain we've defeated him."

Moved, Columba sighed and glanced at Ari. "What about you, Lady? Any questions or concerns?"

She looked as stunned as Columba felt. "That's an incredible sacrifice, Lord Baron. I'd object, except that I know you're right. It's the *only* way."

The three of them stood atop a knoll to one side of their campsite. They'd traveled inland nearly five miles before finding dry ground, where they'd set up camp.

Everything south of them was awash from the tidal wave.

As they had begun to set up camp, Marl had pulled Columba aside. "I need to talk with you. It's confidential."

Sensing that the Baron had been cogitating deeply throughout their retreat from the sea-drenched shore of the Halfmoon Sea, Columba had wondered what the Baron was brewing. Far in excess of what Columba had expected, the idea was equally attractive and repulsive. "You know what I'd like to tell you, Lord Baron?"

"Absolutely under no circumstances will you allow me to do any such thing," Marl said with a shrug. "To which I'd reply that nothing you can say or do will stop me. It's my decision and mine alone, and if you try to stop me, I'll accomplish it another way, with or without your permission, with or without your help. Alone, my chances of success are far more slim. With your help, they're much greater, if still daunting. The probability that we'll have to endure this devil spawn for all eternity is higher than any of us want to think, anyway."

Columba nodded and frowned. "What about the knife and the timepiece?"

"I take those with me," the Baron replied.

Columba threw a glance at Ari.

"It would be fitting to do so, Lord Sage," the Magux said.

He brought his gaze back to the Baron. "If all of us are right behind you, serving to distract him, your chances rise by half."

"I know it," Marl said, "and all the more with such experienced folk." He gestured at the group in the dell below them.

Columba had watched the interaction between the Baron and his page. "What about Pavo?"

Marl didn't hesitate. "I'll see that he gets the care he needs, Lord Sage."

He saw that there was nothing he could do or say to dissuade the Baron Marl Gneiss. Columba nodded and sighed. "All right. Now, how do we get there? Our getting there unscathed and undetected are vital to this plan. We have to get there quickly, as well."

"I have an idea," Ari said. "Queen of the Northern Seas, Salina Coralreef, departed upon the back of a whale so huge that it might have transported a hundred people in comfort. Could the Queen of the Southern Seas help us find such a beast?"

"We can find out. On its back, we'd be vulnerable, though."

Ari nodded, deep in thought. "I wonder how big its stomach is."

Columba chuckled and shook his head. "And what do we tell them?" He gestured toward their companions.

"Our plan is to blast the Necromancer with the combined force of our talents and blow him backward into the erupting volcano to incinerate him completely," Marl said, smiling.

Columba nodded, admiring the facile mind of the cunning Baron. "Ari, can you let them know? I'll need to get the water's edge to summon Queen Octans Tala Chert."

"All right. How is Samshad's cooking?"

"Better than most." He grinned at her. "But none of us is a gastronome to speak of. Anyone in your group?"

She shook her head. "See you when you get back." She took the Baron's arm companionably and led him back to the camp.

Columba watched them go, despairing but hopeful, the Baron's dedication instilling awe. To his mind, they faced a formidable foe, whose minacity even through legend and fable was intimidating.

Who has the power to send minions across hundreds of miles, from Warlock's Mount to the shore of the Halfmoon Sea and indeed all the way to the southern forests of Scrollhaven!

Columba emerged onto the north-south road.

Far to the south, the erupting volcano at Warlock's Mount spewed its column of fire and ash relentlessly.

If it isn't stopped, our whole world will be coated in ash and its skies completely blackened, Columba thought.

The water had mostly retreated to its former shores, the aftermath of the inundation plain all around him: trees skewed at all angles, many of them uprooted, slit thick on everything, as though some baker had slathered everything with a thick coat of dull, brown icing, and even the road under his feet nearly impassable with sludge. Darkness was full before he arrived at the shore.

He navigated as close to the ocean as he could, the beach strewn with detritus, and he summoned the Queen of the Southern Seas, Octans Tala Chert.

She slipped up from the surf like a siren, her tail morphing into legs. She wore not even the coating of waves as she stepped toward him and stopped but inches away. "You have come far since that first day we met," she said. "I am uncloaked this time by my choice."

As tempting as she was, Columba wouldn't be distracted. "We have a request, Lady Queen, a whale large enough to transport all ten of us to the slopes of Warlock's Mount."

Her eyes went wide. "He'll blast you off the back of any whale I send, no matter what its size."

"One large enough to swallow us whole."

"And excrete you onto the slopes when it's done?" She threw her head back and laughed. "Silly mortal. Not necessary. You can all ride in comfort in its mouth." Then she smiled.

Columba guessed what was coming next.

"I can't give you anything without demanding something in return, you know," Queen Chert said. "Pictor would decry it as favoritism and demand something ridiculous of me. There *was* something I wanted."

And Columba was swept off his feet and out to sea before he knew it.

* * *

Aridisia yawned and looked around the fire.

Natural affinity had paired them off, and five pairs of people chatted amiably around the hearth. The night crickets chirped, if subdued by the thick mud, and a few nocturnal birds venturing to sing. A thick stench of swamp pervaded everything, which their noses had long since acclimated to.

Bere sat beside her, of course, and Ari was leaning into her embrace.

Beside them were Chiona and her father Zibeth.

Columba and Minette sat beside each other, amused wonderment on his face and open adoration on hers.

Samshad and Skarn leaned against each other, looking comfortable.

And Baron Marl Gneiss doted over the page Pavo, the small boy leaning back against the man's great bulk. His collar was turned up on the left side of his neck, an oddity for a man so fastidious as he.

None of them spoke much, a condition equal parts the apprehension at what they would face on the morrow and the reluctance to let go of feeling good today.

They had battled the Necromancer Travert Crepitans Pictor today and had won.

Columba had returned to their campsite not an hour before and had announced to the group, "In the morning before daylight, we board a gray whale and ride in its mouth across the Halfmoon Sea to the shores of the Warlock's Mount—and hopefully arrive undetected. Then we mount our assault on the Necromancer." Then he'd held up his hands. "No questions tonight. All of them can wait until tomorrow, when we're inside the great beast and traveling southward. Tonight we rest, meditate, and pray. Because tomorrow, we fight."

The group grew somber under the facade of conviviality, their surface joy floating happily on a deeper river of doubt.

For tonight, anyway, Ari and Bere had secured the place at the base of a knoll between a log and a tree, where they would be shielded from view.

Ari looked around the fire, saw the desire that she felt building inside her reflected in many faces.

She found it comforting and awe-inspiring that people of such diverse background might find each other in the wilderness and share a brief instance of intimacy even as they faced the possible loss of limb or life, or perhaps the loss of the person with whom each had shared that intimacy.

And in the face of possible loss, to take the risk to become intimate anyway.

Courage, she decided.

It took courage to live life to the fullest in spite of its possibly ending the very next day.

But isn't that true whether there's a battle to be fought, or not? Ari wondered. The fate that might befall any of them always included the chance of imminent death. Somehow, everyday, we push that possibility aside and live as though we're going to live forever, pray like we're going to die tomorrow, and love as though we haven't a moment to lose.

Her head tucked into Bere's shoulder and her hands between Bere's knees, Ari didn't notice until long after they'd gone that Marl and Pavo had retreated to their own private place.

Chiona and Zibeth grinned at everyone else and volunteered to clean up after the meal, which Samshad and Skarn had prepared.

Columba and Minette excused themselves separately but neither returned.

Then Samshad and Skarn did the same, although less discretely.

"Come on," Bere said. "I can tell you you're falling asleep."

Ari giggled and let herself be led.

Afterward, the stars appeared to be visible through the overcast haze, as Bere snored softly against her, the soft lassitude of post-coital bliss rarely inducing sleep and more often giving Ari a sweet sensual awareness of everything around her.

She awakened preternaturally, her senses tuned—but by what? she wondered. Aridisia looked around, making no sound, all senses on high alert, the hair on the back of her neck crawling, as though covered with ants.

Sensing nothing untoward in the darkness, she checked Bere's soft breathing beside her. The memory of her paroxysms tempted her to wake Bere for another episode. Instead, Aridisia rose and slipped into her tunic and trousers.

The ground cooperated and did not give away her approach.

Beside the fire was the great bulk of Baron Marl Gneiss, his back to her.

She wondered at his being up so early, not a hint of the next day anywhere. She estimated it was still the dead of night, perhaps four to five hours after midnight.

"Awake as well?" rumbled his quiet voice.

Surprised, as she'd given no indication of her approach, Ari sighed. "Anxious. You too?"

He nodded.

She knelt beside him on his left, the gray ashes in the fire pit still emitting warmth.

Half-hidden by the upturned collar, he threw her a glance.

He looks as if he hasn't slept, she thought, seeing deep fatigue in his face. "How long since you saw home?"

The big Baron turned his big head toward her. "Too long, and while I miss the Barony for some of its finer comforts, what I really miss is my old home in East Stonevale, which I've not seen in near a year." His voice was a murmur, his eyes wistful.

"Before you inherited your uncle's estates?" She saw him nod. "A simpler time it must've been."

He grunted. "You?"

"Six weeks, two months," she replied, southwest Scrollhaven having somehow been too far for her to detour, even for a visit. "The whole town pitched in to send me to the Crypt of Scrolls. 'Become a Magux and do us proud,' they all told me. Little did I know."

"Or any of us," the Baron said.

Ari nodded, saw him suppress a yawn, and realized he probably hadn't slept, wondering that she had been able to catch even a wink. Her rest, despite Bere's attention, hadn't been very restful.

A twig cracked to the left.

There stood Columba, rubbing his face. He joined them, silently knelt at the spent hearth, his anxiety plain.

Like her, he didn't look rested.

"Didn't sleep much either?" he mumbled as he crouched on the other side of the Baron.

Ari shook her head, Marl replying similarly.

"Fine looking lot, aren't we?" the Baron muttered.

"Not likely to win a beauty contest, are we?" Ari said.

The three of them shared a companionable chuckle.

"I've been wondering what he looks like, being so old," Columba said.

"Wrinkled, bald, and toothless," Ari quipped.

Marl shook his head. "If only," he said. "Comely, sveldt, and coiffed to the nape, dressed immaculately as though going to a royal ball, patrician lines to his face and athletic lines to his body. He looks all of twenty-five years old."

"Rejuvenates as well as resurrects," Columba said, looking between them. "Listen, we need to be prepared. Any of our company might have been suborned. Between us three, I have no worries, as we've each been cruelly used in his designs to achieve ultimate power. I'll be asking each of the others to play a critical part, but we each need to step into the breach, if someone doesn't follow through.

"And both of you, guard your persons. A moment of inattention or betrayal might tip the balance. The advantage is ours at two talismans to one. Genesyx and Canodex against Luxullian, but we're at a disadvantage because we can't use them fully. These other two devices, Serpens and the timepiece, we can't rely on; they'll betray us in battle, being of his handiwork.

"Which is why we have to rely on our own craftiness and that of our allies." Columba sighed and glanced between them.

"Baron, I like your plan, but if you need to abandon it, let us know sooner than later, eh? And I've got a back-up plan that I'd like you to hear." He turned to Ari. "Bring out the timepiece."

She did as he bade her.

He stepped around the cold firepit and knelt beside her. "You haven't tried to use this, have you?"

She shook her head. "I've been afraid to since Zibeth alerted me to its properties."

"Mastery of time itself." Columba shook his head. "There's no time to experiment now, but I'm guessing you can operate it with a hand of either side—one front and one back—and twist them against each other."

"Like this?" And Ari placed the timepiece face down in one palm, then placed her other palm atop it, and moved her two palms in opposite directions. Nothing happened.

"Mastery of time itself," Columba repeated, shaking his head. "There's no time to experiment now, but I'm guessing you can operate it with a hand on either side—one front and one back—and twist them against each other."

"Like this?" And Ari placed the timepiece face down in one palm, then placed her other palm atop the timepiece. A surreal disbelief suddenly struck deep fear inside her. She did not move her hands, fearing she might be caught in some endless loop, her hair to turn gray, her skin to shrivel and her flesh to desiccate right off her bones in this very spot, were she to continue.

"Something like that," Columba added. "I'm guess you'll have to turn the clockface to achieve any effect."

"Yeah, probably," she said, her excitement difficult to contain as she realized it had worked. "We should be going soon," she said, quickly tucking the timepiece into her tunic.

Oddly, no trace of her fatigue remained.

"Yes," Columba said. "We should be going."

* * *

264

The Baron Marl Gneiss greeted the Wizard Necromancer Travert Crepitans Pictor on the beach, the slopes of Warlock's Mount rising steeply behind the other man, the volcano eerily quiescent.

The great white shark that Marl had ridden from the shore of the Halfmoon Sea slipped back into the water, seeming to grin at Marl as if to say he'd be waiting to dine on Marl's flesh when the Necromancer had finished with the Baron.

The Necromancer stood on a promontory, a master of condescension, glancing down at the beach where Marl stood, deigning to notice Marl as an elephant might a flea, as likely to crush him by accident as by whim, the Necromancer's posture declaring to all how terribly he suffered to have such a lowly being as Marl enter into his presence. "What."

It wasn't a question.

It was a demand to know by what right did the Baron dare disturb his majesty the Necromancer from a beauty sleep, without which he might endure some minor imperfection in his immaculate and fastidious appearance.

"Bless you, Lord Necromancer," Marl said, "for entertaining my untimely request for audience."

"I don't find it at all entertaining, Gneiss," Pictor hissed. "Out with it, or begone."

"Yes, Lord, of course, Lord." And Marl couldn't help bob his head in obeisance, although he owed no allegiance. "I propose a bargain, Lord Pictor."

The Necromancer threw his head back and laughed, and the volcano behind him belched a fireball, which arched into the sky and splashed with a fiery hiss not far offshore.

Sweat broke on Marl's brow.

"Bargain? You'd do better to beg. What could you possibly offer me, Wretch?"

"Four talismans for one, Lord Necromancer!" Marl stood tall and proud. "You give me Luxullian to rule Stonevale as I please, and I'll get you the other two precious relics and those little toys you invented, that knife and that timepiece."

The volcano behind Pictor abruptly erupted. "Fool!" he screamed. "What makes you think I need your pitiable help?"

Marl wondered how he'd heard the man over the roar of the volcano behind him, and he realized that Pictor's voice was inside his head. He decided to think his thoughts at Pictor. "You face daunting odds without my help," he thought.

"Nothing insurmountable, I assure you," Pictor's voice rang in his mind.

"But so much easier if you have my help, Lord Necromancer. And you'll have my allegiance, as I'll be forever indebted to you. All I've ever wanted was to rule Stonevale, all for myself."

"Just as your friends on the shores of the Halfmoon Sea now have your allegiance? Once a traitor, always a traitor, Gneiss. You sicken me to no end." And Pictor waved his hand as though brushing off a fly.

Hurling Marl heels over head backward far out to sea, his scream audible for miles.

* * *

Four hours later, Marl climbed out of the giant beast's mouth, carefully avoiding the delicate baleen, and sloshed through the knee-deep water to the shore, his companions following him.

This beach was empty this time.

The Baron shook off the memory of Pictor's hurling him out to sea from this very same beach, wondering if they'd find the Necromancer where he and the Baron Footsore's spelunking party had—in the ice-coated cavern deep beneath Warlock's Mount.

Marl had inferred that Pictor had accepted the Baron's terms. If he hadn't, Marl thought, he'd have exterminated me on the spot. And Pictor had even sent the great white shark back to return him to the shores of the Halfmoon Sea, where he'd been able to slink back into camp with no one the wiser.

Ari's finding him at the extinguished fire, wearing the same clothes he'd worn the day before, had nearly sent him into a panic. But he'd been able to dissimulate and dissemble as though he hadn't slept well, and she seemed to have accepted his prevarication on its face. Soon they'd embarked upon Marl's fifth traverse across the Halfmoon Sea.

Sloshing his way to shore, relieved that the beach was empty, Marl saw that the volcano was quiescent again. He wondered what linked the Necromancer with the volcano, a seeming symbiosis between the multiple-lived man and the unliving if lively Warlock's Mount.

The rocky, jumbled shore was difficult to navigate, its surface a jigsaw of sharp, tinkly pyroclastic rock, busted apart by its cooling, the stench of sulfur mixed with boiled brine. The rock chattered with Marl's every step, his nine companions having no better luck across the brittle surface.

Initially unable to find in the changeable landscape the gaping maw in the mountainside that led downward to the chambers of Travert Crepitans Pictor, Marl began to panic.

There! he saw, behind the promontory from which Pictor had mocked him but hours ago, the one place not slathered with a fresh coat of basaltic rock.

He led the way over, the wind buffeting him from across a shore of newly-cooled rock. He stopped at the cavern mouth to wait for the others to catch up.

"Down here, Lord Sage," Marl said, indicating the yawning mouth, the stench of sulfur particularly strong here, as though below brewed the sickening stew of some foul miasma.

Columba paused. "Everyone knows their part, right? We each will be as gnats to an elephant, but enough gnats will distract any elephant."

Columba then Ari then Marl entered the tunnel, the remainder right on their tail. They all knew that only the first three had the means to defend themselves from what was likely to be a relentless fusillade of magic spells.

"If Pictor is smart, he'll have armies of foul creatures defending his lair," Columba said over his shoulder.

"That Necrophiliating Romancer can assemble transmogrified mongrels from the most inert of materials," Anthus said from behind, "Beings our company isn't prepared to fight."

The demons of forest-floor detritus that had attacked Ari's company and the writhing wraiths that had hurtled out of the night from across the Halfmoon Sea were just two examples of the unimaginable, ineffable, phantasmagoric creatures at his disposal.

The tunnel led them inexorably downward, the stench thickening with every step, the heat and humidity increasing as they closed the distance between themselves and the Necromancer.

"Is that his breath or his flatulence?" Ari asked, trying to cover her nose with her sleeve.

"Their aroma," Marl quipped, "is the same."

The tunnel walls fell away and they all stood exposed on a high shelf at the top of a cavern that initially looked bottomless. The brilliant refulgence that shimmered off the Cavern walls was nearly blinding.

Marl blinked and squinted until his eyes adjusted, his breath condensing in front of him.

Gone was the sweltering tunnel with its cloying sulfur stench.

Gone was the suffocating dark.

Far below sat a figure whose jet black hair stood stark against a glittering ice cathedral. Behind the Necromancer boiled a vat of lava, seeming unaffected by the blistering cold in the cavern.

Marl traced the path leading to the Necromancer backward, and realized that it doubled back up the cavern walls twenty, thirty times, and would leave them exposed throughout their descent.

The Necromancer, Travert Crepitans Pictor, appeared to be looking their way but was motionless, giving no indication he'd seen them enter.

"There must be another entrance," Ari said.

"I don't remember this long winding path down the cavern side," Marl said. "I do remember that it seemed days before we reached the surface. Perhaps we wandered these bowels before accidently finding a way up." The instant he said it, he knew it wasn't true, as nothing happened on Warlock's Mount that wasn't of Pictor's design.

"No," Columba said, "he wants us here. He wants to wear us down with an exhaustive, difficult hike."

"It'll be just as exhausting to climb straight down," Ari said.

"If, as you said," Marl added, "he wants us here, why are we concerned? Let's go. He won't attack."

Columba and Ari exchanged a bewildered look.

Marl shrugged and set out. "Come on," and he waved them to follow, his sweat freezing on his brow, afraid that Pictor would blast him off the path like a fish in a barrel.

And just as certain that his companions would somehow know he had visited Warlock's Mount the night before and would blast him off the path for his perfidy.

As the path dropped him below them in its first switchback, Marl glanced back.

Guardedly, his companions followed him, strung out on the ledge and easy pickings for anyone with a little magic to spare.

And yet Pictor remained motionless.

The further Marl descended, the more confident he became.

As he descended, Marl noticed how Pictor's eyes followed him—and not his companions. Good! He thought, the more I draw his attention the better.

In his descent, Marl also examined the escarpment at the base of their descent, the bridge of ice that linked the twisty path with the pillar where Pictor sat enthroned.

Bridge of ice.

Marl remembered his previous battle with the Necromancer, in which the magician had used frozen ropes and a thin ledge of suspended ice.

If my companions step out on that, he'll surely melt it from beneath them.

Below the bridge of ice lay glowing rivers of lava.

Marl was trying to connect how the Necromancer kept the icebridge frozen above a boiling cauldron of pyroclastic bubbling lava fresh from the bowels of the earth.

He reached the bottom of the twisted path, which ended in a ledge just large enough for all ten of their company to stand. His eyes now level with Pictor's, Marl held his hands out behind him to bade his companions to go no further.

"Columba," he said softy, not removing his gaze from Pictor.

"Yes, Marl?"

"The knife, Serpens, please."

The metal felt odd in his hand, as though it sought to repel his touch.

"Ari," he said softly.

"Yes, Marl?"

"The timepiece, please."

The palm-size device felt heavier than he'd thought it looked, as though reluctant to lay at peace in his grasp.

"Now, everyone, do not step onto the ice for any reason. And do not launch an attack on our adversary until he attacks me. Understood?"

Marl waited while Columba swore them all to abide by the request.

"That's suicide," Pavo said.

"Hush, Pavo," Marl said, not removing his gaze from Pictor. "We must be done with this devil forever."

Marl waited while Columba distributed their eight other companions at various points along the last two switchbacks on the trail, so they weren't vulnerable to a single spell from the Necromancer.

"Have you quite finished preparing?" Pictor said, his voice a murmur from across the cavern, the cold seeming to carry the sound in crisp, clear tones. Pictor's nonchalance was the eidolon of arrogance. His utter unconcern with these interlopers galled Marl.

Unless he really believes, the Baron thought.

The lack of defense also attested to the Necromancer's supreme confidence. Pictor had sent not one of his resurrected monstrosities after them, nor did a single one guard him now.

Marl set out across the icebridge, the escarpment wide enough for ten men abreast.

His feet chunked into the ice, the roadway as solid to his girth with the heft as any rock. The chill of its absolute cold crept into his feet through the thin layers of his shoes, ones meant for a much warmer clime.

"Stop there," Pictor said.

Marl stopped. He was three quarters of the way across. During his last episode on such an insignificant surface, he had almost plummeted into the roiling lava below.

He held out the timepiece and knife.

"Did you tell your friends you were going to betray them?"

"Of course not." Marl scowled, his voice low. "Do you think I'm a fool! Give me Luxullian and let's be done with them!" He threw a thumb over his shoulder. "Quickly, before they suspect."

"Slide them both across the ice toward me." Pictor produced Luxullian from underneath his long black cape.

"The knife first," Marl insisted, "and then you give me Luxullian, so I can rule Stonevale with an iron fist!"

"Both first, Baron, or no deal."

"Do you really think I'm that much of a fool?" He held up a fist. From it trailed the chain with the timepiece. "They attack on my signal. Do it my way or suffer an onslaught."

Pictor threw his head back and laughed, his voice booming off the cavern walls. "As you wish, Baron. Slide me the knife."

Still holding the timepiece aloft, Marl tossed the knife underhand.

It skittered across the ice and Pictor stopped it with his foot. He then sent the One Stone Luxullian rolling toward the Baron.

Marl picked it up. His, finally. He grinned at Pictor.

Now the tricky part.

He turned his back to Pictor and rolled Luxullian toward Columba, hiding his motion from Pictor with his bulk, then grasped the timepiece between two hands as he'd seen Ari do a few hours earlier. And turned his palms opposite each other.

Turning around, he charged toward Pictor.

The volcano erupted just feet behind Pictor, a column of roaring lava.

Three Marls appeared between him and Pictor.

Startled, Marl thought, No! Don't let it distract you!

On his face a burgeoning panic, Pictor flicked his robe aside.

Marl turned his palms opposite each other.

The volcano erupted just feet behind Pictor. Two Marls appeared in front of him. Still charging, Marl watched Pictor.

On his face a burgeoning panic, Pictor flicked his robe aside.

And Marl turned his palms.

The volcano erupted just feet behind Pictor. One Marl appeared ahead of him. Still charging, Marl watched. On his face a burgeoning panic, Pictor flicked his robe aside. Marl turned his palms.

The volcano erupted just feet behind Pictor, and still charging, Marl muttered under his breath, "Can't stop me now, Necromancer!"

The robe flicked aside but before Pictor could launch a spell, Marl's great bulk barreled into him, and a blast of magic from behind launched them into the column of lava, delivering the Necromancer into death, the knife, timepiece and belt buckle with him.

And the sweet relief of death consumed the Baron Marl Gneiss.

Epilogue

Columba slowed to a stop on the approach to the gates at the Vault of Stones, Ari beside him and Minette just behind him.

The throng around them was deafening, their cheering so loud that Columba could hardly think.

They cheer for someone who can't be here, he thought, recalling again those last few moments, which he'd watched in disbelief.

The fiery lava column had swallowed the pair, and Columba had gotten only a brief glimpse of a darker knot as the erupting lava had launched the incinerated remains skyward through the vent. And as the volcano subsided, the only sound had been that of the weeping boy, Pavo.

Afterward, their company, minus its most famous member, had traveled the length of the continent, going first to the Hall of Swords, where the High Sage Lord Arcturyx Longblade had received them with all the pomp and ceremony at his disposal. The One Sword Genesyx restored to its rightful wielder, Arcturyx had feted them all with a banquet so lavish that its like hadn't been seen in a hundred years.

And in an equally elaborate ceremony, the High Sage had awarded Columba Riverford full sageship in the Hall of Swords, bypassing the usual apprenticeship.

Replete with honors and the repast served him, Columba had then led their company to the Crypt of Scrolls, where they had been similarly received, the One Scroll Canodex restored to its rightful scribe, the High Magux Ravenna Cithara awarding Aridisia Myric the title of Magux, promoting her to full membership past the obligatory novitiate term.

At each stop, they told the tale set forth in these pages, the feats of their lost companion, the Baron Adept Marl Gneiss, posthumously restored to his lands and awarded in absentia the coveted title of Adept, his exploits growing a little each time in the telling, the nobility of his actions evident despite the humility of his origins, a nobility amplified by the ultimate sacrifice that he'd made.

And none of their company contested the embellishments, none of them minding that a deed of theirs was ascribed to him who had lost his life in saving them all.

For what purpose was there in creating a hero if not to make him or her larger than life?

About the Author

Scott Michael Decker, MSW, is an author by avocation and a social worker by trade. He is the author of twenty-plus novels in the Science Fiction and Fantasy genres, dabbling among the sub-genres of space opera, biopunk, spy-fi, and sword and sorcery. His biggest fantasy is wishing he were published. His fifteen years of experience working with high-risk populations is relieved only by his incisive humor. Formerly interested in engineering, he's now tilting at the windmills he once aspired to build. Asked about the MSW after his name, the author is adamant it stands for Masters in Social Work, and not "Municipal Solid Waste," which he spreads pretty thick as well. His favorite quote goes, "Scott is a social work novelist, who never had time for a life" (apologies to Billy Joel). He lives and dreams happily with his wife near Sacramento, California.

How to Contact/Where to Find the Author

Websites:
http://scotts-writings.site40.net/
https://www.smashwords.com/profile/view/smdmsw
http://www.linkedin.com/pub/scott-michael-decker/5b/b68/437